"You Starfleet folks have any luck today tracking down those Xindi and their superweapon?"

The muscles in Travis Mayweather's neck tightened involuntarily. "Captain Archer and the whole senior staff are doing everything they can," he said quietly.

"If you can't find 'em, Ensign, we can't kill 'em," Chang said. In a single smooth motion he rose from the bed and stood at parade rest, still regarding Mayweather with that raptor's stare.

"If *we* can't find the Xindi, Corporal, then *nobody* can," Mayweather finally said. "And aren't you late for your duty shift?" After all, the whole point of the current so-called "hot-cotting" living arrangements was to ensure that those who rotated in and out of *Enterprise*'s overcrowded crew living quarters barely saw one another, let alone had much time to get into one another's way.

"Major Hayes gave me some extra liberty time. Well, I'm off to the gym," Chang said before heading for the door at full march.

The door hissed closed, leaving Mayweather alone in the quarters that were no longer his island of privacy.

Other *Star Trek: Enterprise*™ books:

What Price Honor?

Surak's Soul

Shockwave

Daedalus

Daedalus's Children

The Expanse

Rosetta

STAR TREK
ENTERPRISE™

LAST FULL MEASURE

MICHAEL A. MARTIN
and ANDY MANGELS

Based on *Star Trek®*
created by Gene Roddenberry
and
Star Trek: Enterprise
created by Rick Berman & Brannon Braga

POCKET BOOKS
New York London Toronto Sydney

An *Original* Publication of POCKET BOOKS

POCKET BOOKS, a division of Simon & Schuster, Inc.
1230 Avenue of the Americas, New York, NY 10020

This book is a work of fiction. Names, characters, places and incidents are products of the author's imagination or are used fictitiously. Any resemblance to actual events or locales or persons living or dead is entirely coincidental.

ISBN-13: 978-1-4165-0358-3
ISBN-10: 1-4165-0358-7

This Pocket Books paperback edition May 2006

10 9 8 7 6 5 4 3 2 1

Manufactured in the United States of America

For information regarding special discounts for bulk purchases, please contact Simon & Schuster Special Sales at 1-800-456-6798 or business@simonandschuster.com.

For James Montgomery Doohan (1920–2005),
whose passing has made this planet a much sadder
place; for Robert Sheckley (1928–2005), who
provided inspiration and convival times;
for Army Specialist Casey Sheehan, (1981–2005),
who gave his own last full measure of devotion
in Iraq; and for Cindy Sheehan, a bereaved
mother possessed of the courage to stand
against the unjust, illegal, immoral, and wholly
unjustifiable war of aggression and occupation
that took Casey's life and has killed, crippled,
and orphaned more than 100,000 others.
Semper Invictus, Cindy.

—M.A.M.

To my father, Walter Gilbert Mangels,
founder and curator of the
Miracle of America Museum in Polson, Montana.
May the history you keep continue on well into
the twenty-second century and beyond!

—A.M.

ACKNOWLEDGMENTS

Thanks are due to Rick Berman and Brannon Braga for creating *Star Trek: Enterprise,* to Gene Roddenberry for originating the universe that the crew of the NX-01 heralded for its four brief, shining seasons, and to Arthur C. Clarke and the late Stanley Kubrick for bringing the reality of space to the silver screen decades ahead of schedule (and, eventually, to a fateful movie night aboard NX-01). The authors also owe a nod of the environmental suit helmet to J. M. Dillard, whose novelization of Berman and Braga's *Star Trek: Enterprise* episode "The Xindi" informs the story between these covers, and award special commendations to Deborah Stevenson and the fine folks at Memory Alpha for their perspicacious data gathering on such subjects as Starfleet and MACO supernumeraries and the Xindi. Lastly, though certainly not leastly, we owe shuttlepods full of gratitude and appreciation to our editor, Margaret Clark, whose suggestions never failed to make the work better—and who was the very soul of patience while this tome was being written.

HISTORIAN'S NOTE

The main events in this book take place during the summer of 2153, between the *Enterprise*'s discovery of a Xindi who was working in a mining complex ("The Xindi") and before the ship is stopped cold by a spatial anomaly and is boarded by pirates ("Anomaly").

. . . from these honored dead we take
increased devotion to that cause for which
they gave the last full measure of devotion . . .

—From President Abraham Lincoln's
Gettysburg Address, November 19, 1863

PROLOGUE

Sunday, August 12, 2238,
San Francisco

THE OLD MAN DREW strength from the scent of freshly mowed grass, which smelled like home. In spite of that, the duffel bag he carried across his shoulders seemed to be growing heavier with each step forward. Under a glowering, cantaloupe-colored sky that seemed barely able to hold back its tears, he slowly ascended the hill until he stood in the monument's soft, mercurial shadow.

"I wish you'd let me carry that," said the much younger, sandy-haired man who was walking alongside him.

"I'm old, Larry," drawled the silver-maned man with the duffel as he smiled and squinted into the scattered, fog-obscured morning light. "But I'm not an invalid. At least not yet."

"I just worry sometimes that you're going to sprain something."

The old man looked the brilliant young engineer up and down and chuckled tolerantly, shaking his head. Laurence Marvick couldn't have weighed much more than sixty-five kilograms soaking wet, so he wasn't exactly credible when he held forth on the subject of hauling freight.

"If I'd gotten into the habit of letting other people do everything for me," the old man said at last, "then I never would have made it past my hundredth birthday." The old man didn't like to consider that the date in question had come and gone twenty—no, make that twenty-one—years ago.

Turning away from Marvick, the old man stared mutely at the monolith before him, which had been erected nearly eighty years earlier to commemorate the thousands of casualties Starfleet had suffered, despite its sincere efforts to extend humanity's olive branch across the galaxy, stretching back to a time before that very first Federation Day back in '61.

All the way back to the Xindi attack, the old man thought. The intervening decades might have washed away much of the bitterness he'd felt back then, but the pain the Xindi had inflicted on him remained in fairly close to mint condition. Since then he'd observed on a number of occasions that war was a ravenous, unappeasable beast. More friends and loved ones than he cared to count had been snatched up in its jaws. Somebody usually prevailed in a war, but nobody really won.

He wondered how many more of his family, friends, and enemies had succumbed to the far slower, but no less insatiable, ravages of time—especially during the past few years. Sooner or later, time would come for him as well, even if war and conflict hadn't.

"It's hard to believe it's been seventy-six years since they signed the Federation Charter," the old man said at length.

"Seventy-*seven* years," Marvick said quietly, sounding almost embarrassed to be correcting the man who had taught him so much over the years. The ink was barely dry on Laurence Marvick's doctorate, so the old man was willing to overlook the kid's tendency toward pedantry. *He might be a bit overprecise,* he thought, *but at least he's proved he can stop himself from saying too much when it counts.* The lad had already proved his ability to keep a secret on any number of occasions.

"Seventy-seven years," the old man repeated. "Right."

The old man allowed his gaze to drift past the monument. Perhaps a hundred meters away, a stand of tall sycamores shifted in the summer breeze like fidgety children. A young family—a red-haired man dressed in a red Starfleet uniform, accompanied by two energetic-looking little boys and a woman attired in a lightweight summer dress—approached from nearby, just out of earshot on the hillside adjacent to the monument. Thankful that the place wasn't more crowded, the old man craned his neck upward to take in the full height of the great memorial spire before him. Its proud, tapering length seemed to spear the heavens, reminding him of the brute-force chemical rockets built by the space pioneers of a bygone age.

Taking in the harsh, granite reality of the monument conjured painful memories, just as he had expected; his gaze kept sliding past the stone spire into the fog-shrouded distance, where the Golden Gate Bridge seemed to be holding a silent, early-morning vigil. San Francisco seemed preternaturally still, even for a foggy summer Sunday; for the moment, at least, all ground-vehicle and hover-car traffic had ceased along the bridge's span. Except for the occasional reverberating cries of gulls and the barks of sea lions, silence had engulfed the nearby parklike grounds of Starfleet Academy. The lull transported the old man backward nearly eight decades to the days immediately preceding that very first Federation Day, when the city had often seemed to hold its collective breath in much the same manner, as though pausing in anticipation of its unknowable and unavoidable future.

Like many of Earth's major cities at that time, San Francisco had still been healing from the fear and violence of the recently concluded Romulan-Earth War, not to mention the homegrown terrorism wrought by the xenophobic Terra Prime movement only a few short years before that. Ahead, a new alliance beckoned, this still untried, untested United Federation of Planets—and whatever unforeseeable mix of benefits, liabilities, and complications that might accompany it.

And a whole hell of a lot has happened since then, the old man thought, visualizing the powerful, graceful new starship whose keel was now being laid in the spacedock that hung invisibly overhead, far beyond San Francisco's omnipresent ceiling of fog. He remained as determined as ever to do more than merely make anonymous marginal notations in Marvick's *Constitution*-class construction blueprints.

Though he had no doubt that he was approaching the end of his days, he knew he was living nowhere near the end of history. *The adventure's really only getting started,* he thought, and experienced a momentary surge of envy toward young Marvick and his contemporaries. He knew he needed to linger in the material world at least long enough to see the first new ship of the line leave spacedock, if only to prove to himself that a sustained cruising speed of warp six was actually possible.

"You look like you've never been here before," Marvick said, interrupting the old man's reverie.

He cast a quizzical look at the young engineer. "San Francisco? I've been here hundreds of times, when I served in Starfleet. You know that."

Marvick shook his head and pointed to the stone spire that loomed overhead. "I was talking about the Starfleet War Memorial."

The old man felt his deeply lined face slacken as a wave of sadness swept over him. "Guess there's got to be a first time for everything, Larry."

He noticed the expression of concern on the younger man's face, and it reminded him of the lad's great-grandmother, whom he'd gotten to know years before the signing of the Federation Charter, way back during the time of the Xindi hunt. Not for the first time, Marvick prompted the old man to reflect on the whims of fate; had things gone only a little differently back then, Marvick would not be here—and, perhaps, neither would the great vessel that was being assembled now in the skies over San Francisco.

"I was only wondering why you'd never visited the memorial before," Marvick said, looking troubled. "Are you all right?"

"Relax, kid. I'm not planning on dying anytime soon, if that's what you're worried about."

Marvick's eyes grew huge and he held up his hands as though trying to ward off an evil spirit. "Whoa. Who said anything about dying? I was just wondering why you stayed away from this place all these years—until now."

It was only at that moment that the old man realized that he had no idea how to answer that question. A single fat raindrop landed behind his collar, startling him with its coolness. His chest tightened, and his gaze was drawn back to the obelisk.

Leaving Marvick to watch in silence, the old man ascended the three stone steps that fronted the monument, then knelt before the spire, close enough to touch its eternal stone face. He released the duffel bag from across his shoulder, then gently set it down before the granite base.

He studied the flawless duranium-silver plaque that was bolted to the obelisk's solid rectangular base. He read the inscriptions that commemorated various red-letter days in Starfleet's annals of warfare, until his eyes stopped on March 22, 2153—a day that was graven indelibly into his memory. But most of the text that followed the date escaped him; his vision had begun to smear and blur behind a sudden onslaught of unshed tears.

"All that death has got to mean something," he whispered. "It's got to mean *something.*"

Marvick's question haunted him as well. The old man asked himself why, in the eighty-five long years that had passed since the twenty-second of March, 2153—a quiet Thursday when a powerful Xindi test weapon had come to Earth and vaporized seven million people—he had never made the time to come to this place. . . .

LAST FULL MEASURE

ONE

Tuesday, July 24, 2153,
Xindi Council Inner Sanctum

WHENEVER DEGRA CONSIDERED the end product of the Weapon Project he had spent the last several moon-turns supervising, he saw the smiling face of Naara in his mind's eye. When he pictured his wife, she was always standing with their children, Piral and Jaina, both of whom were frozen in time as young-sters, as if posing for a portrait. Though the chil-dren were grown now, Degra believed he would probably always see them that way.

Particularly when he thought of the implacable Terran enemies who would stop at nothing to destroy them and the rest of the Xindi humanoid race, as well as every member of the other four sen-tient Xindi species, three of which had representa-tives sitting with him today around the Inner Sanctum's wide, circular Council table.

One of Shresht's chitinous, exoskeletal appendages

slammed across the black tabletop hard enough to rattle it. *"The human vessel continues encroaching upon our territories, undeterred even by the Orassin distortion fields!"* the Xindi insectoid shouted in his species' prevailing language, his mandibles chittering and clicking in near-hysterical fashion. With Shresht in such an exercised emotional state, Degra found that mentally translating the percussive sounds of his mouthparts into intelligible language was an even tougher chore than usual. *"And yet we continue to do nothing!"*

Is that why the Council has been called back into session so soon after our last meeting? Degra thought. It had been barely four rotations since the last time they had all gathered here, and Degra knew that his science and engineering teams had little real news to report as yet. Everyone else here had to know that as well. Degra wondered how the Weapon Project was ever to reach fruition if the paranoia of the insectoids and the reptilians continually interrupted his work with still more meetings.

"There is little to fear, Shresht," said Mallora, shaking his head in the direction of the insectoid and his aide, both of whom possessed enormous compound eyes that shone like iridescent rainbows beneath the subdued ceiling lights. "The Earth ship's destruction within the Orassin distortion fields is all but certain, thanks to the space-time anomalies endemic to the region. Besides, the vessel's movements still appear to be random and nondirected."

Although Mallora, a member of Degra's Xindi primate species, fairly exuded confidence, Degra found himself having difficulty sharing in it entirely; images of Naara and the children once again implored him, quietly arguing in favor of Shresht's surfeit of caution.

"And we've hardly been doing nothing, Shresht," Degra added. "Work continues on the Weapon, per the agreed-upon schedule. In less than six turnings of the outermoon, it will be deployed. Then Earth will be reduced to rubble, along with the threat it poses to our respective races."

Shresht's mandibles clacked with unconcealed impatience. *"Six turnings. A great deal can happen during that span of time."*

"However resourceful these humans may be, they would need far longer than that for their purely random search to lead them to our world," Mallora said. "We mustn't allow their continued presence in the vicinity to panic us. Remember, they have but a single ship—and a primitive one at that."

"I find I must agree with Degra and Mallora," Narsanyala Jannar said slowly, leaning forward very deliberately in his chair as he scratched at the thick mane of white fur that ringed his prognathic face. One of the Xindi homeworld's arboreal/marsupial sentients, Narsanyala displayed languorous mannerisms that concealed an intense and astonishingly quick intellect. "If the humans really did have the slightest inkling of the location of either our homeworld or the primary Weapon Project facility, would they not now be heading directly toward one or the other of those locations?"

"That the humans have *at least* an 'inkling' as to our homeworld's whereabouts is abundantly clear," Commander Guruk Dolim said, speaking in a scorn-tinged rumble that always reminded Degra of the unpredictably shifting crustal plates of the homeworld's primary volcanic zone. The hulking Xindi military leader belonged to the highly aggressive Xindi reptilian species, a fact now even more in evidence than usual because of the raised posture of the scales around his leathery, muscular neck.

"Why does that worry you so?" Narsanyala said. "Because a single human vessel continues blindly searching amid the Orassin distortion fields?"

"Of *course!*" Guruk said, growling. His aide, an equally fearsome green-skinned reptilian seated at his side, muttered in guttural agreement.

The chamber suddenly reverberated with a mournful, keening sound that was equal parts song and speech. All eyes, single and compound, turned at once toward the clear aquarium wall that occupied one entire side of the Xindi Inner Sanctum.

"The sector containing the Orassin fields contains many thousands of star systems," sang Qoh Kiaphet Amman'Sor, whose long, gray, streamlined body swam slowly and sinuously toward the table, stopping at the limits of the vast, seawater-filled tank. Degra silently congratulated himself that his ability to tell the two nearly identical-looking Xindi aquatics apart seemed to be improving.

Qoh's companion, Qam, descended from the top of the tank, body inverted; belonging to a species that had adapted millions of cycles ago to an aquatic environment, both Qam and Qoh were essentially heedless of the gravity that ruled the Xindi homeworld's large landmasses. *"The human vessel might search for hundreds of cycles before happening upon either our homeworld or the Weapon,"*

Qam said, warbling a mournful undersea aria in the process.

"These humans are devious creatures," Guruk said, addressing the Xindi aquatics. "If we leave any avenue of attack unblocked, they will find it."

Though he often found himself at odds with Guruk—reptilians tended to settle most problems with violence even when circumstances called for finesse—Degra could not disagree with the commander's assessment of the severity of the very real and looming human threat. The humans could be permitted to find neither the homeworld nor the Weapon that was being built to protect it; the results would be catastrophic. Though the humans' chances of success on both fronts were already small, the odds could never be remote enough to satisfy the entire Council, particularly the reptilians and the insectoids. And Degra knew that if he was honest with himself, he had to admit that Naara, Piral, and Jaina could never be safe enough to suit him either.

Perhaps the time has finally come to expend some of the assets Mallora and I have been holding in reserve, Degra thought. He knew all too well that doing so might delay the final deployment of the Weapon by one or two moonturns; but if the tactic also increased the chance of ultimate success until it became a virtual certainty, the trade-off might well be seen by the whole of the Council as worthwhile.

Degra fixed his gaze first upon Shresht, then upon the hard, amber-eyed predator's glare of Guruk. "Very well. I have a contingency plan that just might allay your concerns."

Shresht clacked his mandibles loudly. Guruk nodded curtly in Degra's direction, baring rows of needle-sharp teeth. "Tell us."

Degra cleared his throat. "All right. I propose that we let the Earth vessel find what it seeks—"

Degra was interrupted by roars and chitters and mournful wails. Both Shresht and Guruk appeared ready to draw and quarter him right here on the Council table. Narsanyala seemed to have narrowly avoided falling out of his chair, and even Mallora looked surprised.

Degra raised his hands and patiently waited for the tumultuous reaction to die down. Then, very slowly and patiently, he began laying out his plan, explaining precisely what he had in mind. . . .

TWO

From Ensign Travis Mayweather's Personal Correspondence File:

Dear Mom,

Tell Paul his big brother is having a ball at summer camp.

Just kidding. It's been eighty-four days since we entered the Delphic Expanse. There's nothing new to report, unfortunately; we've still found neither hide nor hair (nor scales) of the Xindi, or the large-scale particle-beam weapon they're preparing to deploy against Earth. Everyone aboard *Enterprise* is getting good and cranky about the lack of results so far in our search.

If we succeed, you and Paul will eventually get to read all of these entries in order. (But I'll certainly understand if you're tempted to skip forward to the end, where we finally catch up to the alien killers we've been chasing.)

If we fail, you'll find that out when the *Horizon* receives word that the entire planet Earth has been blown to rubble by a hidden weapon built by those very same aliens.

As always, I am hoping for the best while preparing for the worst.

Your loving son,
Travis

Friday, September 7, 2153,
Enterprise NX-01

Yet another alpha shift passed uneventfully, almost like a milk run aboard the freighter where he was born and raised.

But that's not a good thing, Ensign Travis Mayweather thought as he left his post following the shift change and headed for the bridge turbolift. Boredom always exhausted him far more than vigorous activity did.

And he knew that boredom was the last thing the crew of *Enterprise* needed right now. It was the last thing *humanity* needed at the moment.

Because it meant that the search for the aggressive aliens known as the Xindi, the mysterious race whose unprovoked attack on Earth had killed more than seven million human beings, was very quickly going nowhere.

Mayweather stopped the turbolift on E deck, then trudged from the turboshaft toward the port-side rim, where his quarters awaited him.

He hesitated for a moment outside the door, not exactly afraid to go inside, but not quite eager to do so either. *I could go to the gym instead,* he thought. *Work off some of this energy.*

But he'd need his workout clothes. And to get them, he'd have to go into his quarters. Chang might be there, and Mayweather simply wasn't in the mood to deal with his MACO roommate at the moment.

Dammit, these are my *quarters,* he thought as he slammed his palm against the reader mounted on the bulkhead beside the door. *Chang is only a guest here.*

The door slid open obediently and Mayweather entered the cramped room. He eyed with suspicion the alien presence that had taken it over these past few hectic months.

Corporal Chang sat cross-legged on the bed—My *bed!* Mayweather thought indignantly—dressed in the khaki fatigues that many of the Military Assault Command Operations personnel wore when they weren't on duty. His eyes were closed as though he were lost in meditation. The corporal's relaxed yet formal posture reminded Mayweather of the stoic Sub-Commander T'Pol.

Only Chang made the fastidious T'Pol look almost slovenly by comparison. Although he was wearing what amounted to casual exercise clothing, it was neatly pressed and pleated, all spit and polish, as though a MACO general might conduct a surprise inspection at any moment.

Mayweather cleared his throat.

Chang opened his eyes. "Hello, Ensign."

Mayweather nodded. "Corporal." He dispatched yet another silent prayer of thanks that he was not required to address the corporal as "sir."

"You Starfleet folks have any luck today tracking down those Xindi and their superweapon?"

The muscles in Mayweather's neck tightened involuntarily. Why did Chang feel obliged to sound so dismissive and patronizing whenever he mentioned the crew's ongoing effort to find the Xindi?

"Captain Archer and the whole senior staff are doing everything they can," he said quietly, meeting Chang's steely, accusatory gaze without flinching. *You'd just* love *to think you made me look away, wouldn't you?*

"If you can't find 'em, Ensign, we can't kill 'em," Chang said. In a single smooth motion he rose from the bed and stood at parade rest, and regarded Mayweather with that raptor's stare.

He's only staying here until we find the Xindi, Mayweather reminded himself yet again.

He was tempted to tell Chang about some of the new leads that Commander Tucker and Lieutenant Reed were busy pursuing this very moment. But he knew that Captain Archer wouldn't be pleased with any news being released outside official channels, especially when so many of the leads the crew had chased over the past few weeks had come to nothing. Besides, he didn't feel very highly motivated to please Chang.

"If *we* can't find the Xindi, Corporal, then *nobody* can," Mayweather finally said. "And aren't you late for your duty shift?" After all, the whole point of the current so-called "hot-cotting" living arrangements was to ensure that those who rotated in and out of *Enterprise*'s overcrowded crew living quarters barely saw one another, let alone had much time to get into one another's way.

"Major Hayes gave me some extra liberty time," Chang said. "I'm working a short shift today."

Hayes probably thinks you need to take up a hobby, Mayweather thought. "Oh. Good for you," he said aloud. The gym suddenly beckoned; it seemed to be his best refuge against any further chance encounters with Chang until the corporal's truncated duty shift began. He moved toward the shelf where he kept his gym bag.

It wasn't where he had left it. Chang must have been cleaning the place. Again.

"Well, I'm off to the gym," Chang said before heading for the door at full march.

The door hissed closed, leaving Mayweather alone in the quarters that were no longer his island of privacy. He gave up searching for the gym bag, since the gym was now the last place on the ship he wanted to go anywhere near.

He glanced at the top of the bureau beside the narrow bed. Several mottled gray, camouflage-pattern MACO duty uniforms and at least one pristine set of dress uniforms, their triangular, two-striped corporal's rank insignia clearly visible on the sleeves, lay in impossibly neat stacks on the top shelf. An optimist at heart, Mayweather allowed himself to hope that

Chang had put them there to avoid crowding him out of the bureau drawers below.

Or did he leave the MACO uniforms prominently visible to send Mayweather yet another subtle message about whose contribution to the mission to find and punish the Xindi he considered the most indispensable?

He scowled as he noticed something else. *Where the hell did he put my model of the* Horizon *this time?*

Monday, September 10, 2153

"We'd better find the Xindi soon, Hoshi. Otherwise I just might have to kill my roommate," Mayweather said very quietly. He tried to punctuate his words with an easy smile, but he suspected it looked more like the grimace of a man passing a kidney stone.

"Oh, come on, Travis," Ensign Hoshi Sato said, grinning around the last few bites of a Reuben sandwich. She leaned forward conspiratorially across the narrow mess-hall table as she scooped up some of the sandwich's remaining innards, which had plopped unceremoniously onto her plate. "You've had to live in close quarters with other people before."

Mayweather took another sip of his still too-hot coffee. The burning pain felt perversely good as it spread and slowly faded. "Sure I have. But aboard the *Horizon,* I was mostly among family. *This* situation is different. Corporal Chang is a MACO, and I'm Starfleet. That's about as far from family as you can get. It's more like enforced confinement with some hostile alien."

Hoshi snickered. "Don't you think you might be exaggerating just a *tiny* bit?"

"Maybe. But not by much. Come on, Hoshi, you can't tell me you that you and Corporal Guitierrez have exactly become sorority sisters."

Mayweather saw Hoshi's expression darken slightly; the recent cramped living conditions aboard *Enterprise* had to be taxing the patience of even the most pleasantly disposed crew members. "Not exactly," she said at length. "But I'm not quite ready to do her bodily harm yet either."

"Then maybe you're just more patient than I am," he said, wondering if anyone who could make a career out of parsing unknown languages might possess patience of an entirely different order than his own. "Give it time."

She shrugged, as though conceding his point, but only somewhat. "You must have learned a thing or two about patience during those long freight runs aboard the *Horizon,* lumbering along at warp three from Draylax to Vega."

"Try warp one point eight," he said, grinning.

"You're making my point for me, Travis. You're a space boomer. You learned more patience working on that freighter than most people develop over a whole lifetime."

"But I also *lost* my patience for that sort of life, remember? Which is a big part of the reason I ended up here."

She sighed. "Still, things can't possibly be that bad between you and Corporal Chang."

He shook his head. "Oh, you bet they can. I swear, one or the other of us is going to leave feet-first in shirtsleeves through one of the airlocks."

"This isn't like you, Travis. What's he done that's so awful you'd fantasize about making him walk the plank?"

Mayweather opened his mouth, then closed it again. He realized all at once that there wasn't any single incident he could point to. Rather, his irritation stemmed from a seemingly endless series of tiny slights and indignities; it came from the relentless accumulation of Chang's presumptuousness and arrogance.

"For one thing, he's a neat freak," he said at length.

There was pity evident in Hoshi's eyes, but she also looked perplexed. "A 'neat freak.'"

He nodded. "It must be pathological. My quarters are so spotless they make Doctor Phlox's sickbay look like a Tandaran labor camp. You could eat off the deck plates!"

Impatience began to displace Hoshi's expression of baffled sympathy. "And that's a bad thing?"

"It is when you can't find your own stuff half the time because of it. The copy of *Chicago Mobs of the Twenties* my brother gave me went missing for two days until I found out Chang had stuck it in the bottom of one of the footlockers. I asked him if he suffers from clutterphobia, or some sort of obsessive-compulsive disorder. He said it was just standard MACO discipline and suggested that I try a little of it sometime."

As though anybody could grow up on a freighter as busy as the Horizon *and not learn a thing or two about discipline along the way,* he thought.

Hoshi suppressed a laugh, which came out as an abbreviated snort. "I don't think the compulsive neatness is necessarily a MACO thing. Selma Guitierrez is a complete slob. Having to clean up after her probably bugs me almost as much as Chang's habits bother you."

Mayweather grinned. "Maybe we ought to consider swapping roommates."

"Very funny. But maybe you've put your finger on a partial solution to your own problem. Why don't you ask D.O. to give you a different room assignment?"

"And admit defeat in front of Lieutenant O'Neill?" *Enterprise*'s third-watch commander, Donna "D.O." O'Neill, had earned her reputation as a no-nonsense officer; the last thing Mayweather wanted was for either O'Neill or Sub-Commander T'Pol, both of whom were working hard to oversee the present difficult crew living arrangements, to start thinking of him as a whiner.

"Okay, then ask T'Pol," Hoshi said with a shrug.

"No, thanks," he added. "Those are *my* quarters. Remember, I'm not the interloper here; Chang is. Besides, shuffling the room reassignments around won't solve the underlying problem: we're serving aboard a fully-crewed Starfleet vessel designed for a complement of eighty-three—and we have to accommodate a cadre of thirty-six MACOs on top of that."

"Only until we resolve the Xindi problem, Travis."

But there was no telling how long that might take. "Let's just hope we get a few Xindi in our sights before Chang and I get into a shooting war of our own."

"Shhh! He might come in here any minute." Hoshi looked surreptitiously around the room. A handful of off-duty personnel—including a pair of fatigue-clad MACOs—sat quietly, absorbed in their meals and conversations.

"Not a chance. We're 'hot-cotting' these days, remember? I'm sure Chang's off doing combat drills right now, preparing to defend the human race from the Xindi while we lowly Starfleet types handle all the scutwork involved in getting them to their appointed place of battle."

"You sound almost jealous, Travis. That's also not like you. Remember, 'They also serve who only sit and drive.'"

Mayweather was surprised at how her comment wounded him, though he could see from her bantering expression that there was no malice whatsoever behind her words. "You sound just like Chang," he said. "He seems to think I'm some sort of interstellar bus driver." He realized only belatedly that he had spoken a bit too loudly.

Hoshi held up her hands in a placating gesture. "Easy, Travis. You know that's not what I meant."

Mayweather noticed then that two of the Starfleet people present and one of the MACOs was staring at him silently. He tendered an awkward smile, which the other officers returned before turning their attention back to food and talk.

He felt stupid for having blown up at Hoshi. In a much gentler—and quieter—tone, he said, "Look, however good these MACOs may be in close combat, fighting the Xindi is going to take a lot more than just three dozen gung-ho, egotistical ground-pounders."

"True enough, Travis. But the MACOs are definitely going to give us an edge when the shooting starts. They certainly earned their rep when they went up against those pirates in the Janus Loop. '*Semper Invictus.*'"

"'Ever Invincible,'" Mayweather said, translating the MACO force's famous official Latin motto into English. "I heard they've picked up a few other choice labels over the past few months as well."

Hoshi nodded, smiling an ironic smile. "One of them is even in Latin. *'Semper Invisus'*: 'Ever Hateful.'"

Mayweather couldn't help snickering. "Chang wasn't very happy last week when he overheard Ensign Marcel using that one. He accused Starfleet of being *'Semper Invitus.'*"

"Ouch. 'Ever Unwilling.' I had no idea your roommate was such an accomplished linguist."

"Haven't you heard? MACOs are great at everything."

Hoshi made a gentle "tsk" sound. "You sound like you've adopted one of the other new Latin mottoes a few of the MACOs have tried to pin on us: *'Semper Invideo.'*"

Mayweather favored her with a shrug and a blank stare. "What's that mean? 'Ever Movie Night'?"

"No. 'Ever Envious.'"

Mayweather had to will his back teeth not to grind together at that, but without complete success. "Listen, Hoshi, I don't doubt the skills of the MACOs for a minute, and I really don't think I'm jealous of them. I just resent the fact that they don't seem to appreciate *our* abilities. Lieutenant Reed has a whole brace of variable-yield antimatter torpedoes with 'Xindi' written all over them, and he'll need me on top of my game running the helm to help get 'em to their targets. Chang's not giving us nearly enough credit for knowing what the hell we're doing on this mission. His whole attitude seems to be 'We're the fearsome sharks and you're just lowly squids.'"

"That's not surprising, at least from a linguistic perspective," Hoshi said.

He frowned, unable to see just where she was heading with this. "What does linguistics have to do with this? Apart from the silly Latin slogans, I mean."

"Well, the acronym for Military Assault Command Operations sounds quite a bit like *mako,* the Maori word for shark." She pronounced the word "mahko," rather than the "may-co" that the MACO troopers used.

Mayweather's eyebrows lofted of their own accord at this revelation; *now* he understood why the MACO contingent attached to *Enterprise* wore the image of a voracious great white shark on their uniform insignia.

"And Chang's not the only MACO I've talked with who seems to feel this way," he said. "It's like they're privileged members of a special warrior caste."

A pained expression crossed Hoshi's usually smooth, unlined face then. "Guitierrez has a bit of an arrogant side as well. I chalk a lot of it up to boredom and impatience. After all, the MACOs have been locked and loaded and combat-ready for months, and we still haven't found a single enemy they can put in their crosshairs. I think it goes all the way to the top; even Major Hayes has been sort of snippy lately."

Come to think of it, Mayweather thought, *Captain Archer hasn't exactly been Mister Congeniality lately either.*

"They're impatient?" he said. "I'm just as eager as Chang is to teach those Xindi bastards a lesson."

Hoshi nodded, looking grave. "Me, too. But I'm willing to cut Corporal Guitierrez some slack on that score."

"Why?"

"For starters, her academic specialty was languages and communications," Hoshi said. She paused as a melancholy expression crossed her smooth features. "And she had some cousins and an uncle living in the same part of Florida that Commander Tucker did. The Xindi attack completely vaporized their hometown."

Mayweather suddenly felt very small and petty. A protracted silence stretched between them, until he said, "Let's just hope we find the Xindi before things get any worse."

Not for the first time, he considered the notion that patience might well turn out to be at least as precious a commodity as antimatter, food, or water.

THREE

COMMANDER CHARLES "TRIP" TUCKER III exited the shuttlepod, ducking to avoid the open hatch as he pulled himself up through the outer airlock door on his way down to the gangway of Launch Bay 1. Captain Jonathan Archer was standing outside the craft in the landing bay, with Sub-Commander T'Pol alongside him. Two engineers, Ensigns Nguyen and Camacho, were already checking the outside of the just-returned shuttlepod for repair needs and refueling.

"That's what you wore?" Archer asked, gesturing toward Trip, a grim look of bemusement on his face.

Trip looked down at his clothes, a mixture of a kimono and a pair of jodhpur-like breeches, covered in pastel floral designs. "It's what we needed to wear to fit in," Trip said, his Southern North American drawl creeping in even as he fought back a more defensive answer. "It's considered a very *manly* look on Haket's Moon."

"Especially when worn with these pointed shoes," a smirking Lieutenant Malcolm Reed said, exiting the shuttlepod just behind Trip. He carried the lime-green shoes that Trip had earlier doffed, holding them aloft like a cobbler proudly displaying his wares.

"Yes, especially with the shoes," Trip said, snatching them out of Reed's hands.

Archer nodded, his amused expression sliding away until only grimness remained in his countenance. "Trip, those coordinates you sent us: Are you pretty certain we'll find information there that'll lead us to the Xindi?"

Trip put a hand up. "That isn't quite what we said, Captain. We have a lead on a place that's frequented by the Xindi—"

"Supposedly," Reed added quickly, interrupting Trip.

"Supposedly," Trip echoed. "Those coordinates are for a planet that houses a number of spaceports. Freighters and smugglers and traders, many of whom apparently do a bit of business with the Xindi. At least, so say the contacts we've developed."

Archer nodded. "We're en route there already. I hope this turns out better than our trip to Tulaw. I've had enough of trellium mines to last for a lifetime." He began to turn away. "Let's do a full briefing in the command center on B deck at fourteen hundred, with Major Hayes and his staff. Meanwhile, get changed and try to enjoy some downtime."

Enjoy, Trip thought. *Now that's not something I've been doing very much of these days.* Ever since the attack on Earth and the death of his sister, nearly six months earlier, he'd enjoyed very little. Although he was doing his best to hide the rage that still blazed within him, he discovered that it was finding other ways to manifest itself, most notably via the nightmares that recurred on a nearly nightly basis even now. Only the Vulcan neuropressure treatments he had recently begun receiving from T'Pol had allowed him to sleep peacefully without having to resort to Phlox's drugs, or some of the Denobulan doctor's even scarier, many-legged remedies.

After T'Pol's last neuropressure session with him, however, Trip found that his dreams had begun to take an entirely different direction.

As T'Pol turned to leave as well, Trip reached out toward her, though he took care not to touch her. "T'Pol, would you want to get lunch with me, before the briefing?"

She tilted her head slightly, and he saw the delicate line of her brow shift subtly. "To discuss this mission, or your neuropressure treatments?"

"Maybe a bit of both." Trip could feel his ears beginning to burn slightly. He was keenly aware that Reed was still standing very close to him, and had probably heard the exchange. "Probably more of the former."

T'Pol nodded curtly. "Very well, Commander. I shall meet you at thirteen hundred hours in the crew mess."

As soon as the captain and the Vulcan had exited the docking bay, Reed spoke up. "What was that about neuropressure treatments?"

"Nothing," Trip said quickly. Too quickly, he realized.

"Then why are you suddenly as red as a hothouse tomato?" Reed asked, his tone gently chiding.

Trip turned and squinted at him. "T'Pol's just teaching me some Vulcan relaxation techniques to help me sleep better, okay? That's *all.*"

"Ummm-hmmm," Reed said, his smile betraying a hint of incredulity.

Trip spun on his heel and stepped away. "I'm getting out of these clothes. See you at the briefing."

He imagined that he could feel Reed's eyes on his back, even as he replayed the last few minutes in his mind. Whatever Reed wanted to think, there was nothing between him and T'Pol except the neuropressure treatments. *Strictly professional.*

Except in his dream last night.

There hadn't been much between them *at all* then.

T'Pol stared across the mess-hall table at Tucker, observing both the sincerity and the slight hint of fear in his eyes.

"I have never heard of the neuropressure treatments affecting other parts of the psyche," she said after taking another small sip of her *plomeek* soup. "But they have also never before been used on humans to my knowledge, so perhaps they are exposing or opening new pathways within your body."

"Emotional pathways?" Tucker asked. He quickly took a bite of his grilled-cheese sandwich, apparently avoiding her gaze.

"Not for Vulcans, of course," T'Pol said. "Generally speaking, the treatments open pathways of energy and memory. Are you experiencing heightened emotions, or memories?"

Tucker's face flushed the color of the ShiKahr desert. "Not memories. Definitely emotions."

T'Pol pressed him. "Emotions you haven't experienced before?"

"Well, not with—" He paused abruptly, shaking his

head, clearly discomfited about something. "Not *this* way. I've felt these emotions before, just not quite like this."

T'Pol put her spoon down into the soup bowl. She found herself wearying of the hide-and-seek nature of the conversation. *How strange that humans criticize us Vulcans for being emotionally reticent,* she thought, her keen sense of irony suddenly fully engaged. *And yet they never seem able to simply say what they mean.*

Aloud, she said, "Perhaps it would be best if you just explained to me specifically *which* emotions you are experiencing, so that I can better help you analyze them."

Tucker dipped his head and whispered loudly at her. "Could you be a little quieter, please? I'd really prefer not to broadcast that we're treating each oth—" He suddenly stopped himself again, apparently struggling to regain what little emotional composure he possessed. "The whole ship doesn't need to know that you're helping me with this."

Leaning forward, T'Pol lowered her voice and said, "Fine. What are the emotions you're facing? Or would you rather discuss it in private?"

Tucker opened his mouth to speak, but a loud crash behind T'Pol interrupted him. T'Pol turned to see Ensign Kranz standing nearby, his tray of food scattered across the deck. Kranz was vibrating, his hands and body rigid as if in the throes of a seizure.

"Call Doctor Phlox," T'Pol said to Tucker, even as she began to rise from her chair.

Then she saw that Tucker was vibrating as well, his teeth chattering and his hands moving spasmodically on the tabletop. Before she could react, he, too had knocked his food onto the deck.

In an instant, as she surveyed the crew mess, she saw that *everyone* in the room, nearly a dozen crew members in all, appeared to be in a state of full seizure.

Everyone except for *her.*

"What are we looking at here, Doctor?" Archer asked.

Phlox looked up from his scanning instruments, the data scrolling on them fresh in his mind. "It's clearly a central nervous system disorder of some kind, Captain, though the precise neurochemical mechanism has eluded me so far."

Archer frowned. "So you can't even tell whether or not it's some sort of disease?"

"At the moment all I can tell you is that it's a highly unusual pathology. Only one of the affected crew members is prone to seizures, and he is on medication for the condition. Moreover, the effect seems only to have caused problems for the *humans* who were either inside the crew mess hall, or within about a seven-meter radius of the room." He gestured toward T'Pol. "Our Vulcan officer was not affected at all."

Archer turned to face Reed, who was standing nearby, his countenance taut with anxiety. "Malcolm, do you think this was caused by some kind of Delphic Expanse spatial anomaly?"

"If it was, Captain, it came and went very quickly," Reed said, holding up a padd that displayed the results of his after-the-fact scans of the crew mess. "It was almost like a wave that passed through that section of the ship. We're still taking readings from the crew mess now, but they've all been fairly inconclusive so far. Until we know more, I've ordered the affected sections quarantined, which amounts to most of the starboard side of E deck."

Archer sighed. "E deck starboard. Talk about hitting a man right where he lives."

Literally, Phlox thought. The captain's quarters and personal mess were both located just down the corridor from the crew mess, along E deck's starboard rim.

Phlox could see that Reed understood Archer's meaning completely. "We checked your quarters as well, sir. Porthos is just fine."

Archer looked greatly relieved to hear that his beloved beagle was safe, though he also seemed to be doing his best not to let his feelings show. Phlox took great comfort in the fact that the man in charge of the ship possessed such powerful, yet controlled, emotions.

"I suppose that's more evidence that whatever hit us only affects humans," the captain said.

Reed nodded. "I agree. And I'd feel better if you bunked elsewhere for a while. At least until my people can confirm that E deck is completely safe."

Archer favored his tactical officer with a bitter smile. "We're in the Delphic Expanse, Malcolm. According to Ambassador Soval, this place turned the bodies of a Vulcan crew completely inside out. So 'completely safe' probably isn't an option for us as long as we're here."

Before Reed could reply, Archer gestured toward Trip and Hoshi, both of whom lay unconscious in sickbay beds, as did several other crew members.

"So, meantime I've lost my chief engineer, my communications officer, and fourteen other members of my crew." He turned to Phlox. "Are the effects of this thing reversible?"

Phlox nodded. "I believe so, Captain. I'm keeping them all sedated for the moment for their own safety, but they're all showing signs that their current aberrant brainwave patterns are beginning to slowly level out toward normal."

"How slowly?" Reed wanted to know.

"It may be a matter of days, but they should all pull through this ordeal with minimal wear and tear." Phlox hoped he sounded confident enough; he couldn't be absolutely certain that his patients would suffer no permanent ill effects, though the scant data he had gathered thus far was consistent with a hopeful diagnosis.

Unless we hit some other new Delphic Expanse anomaly in the meantime, he thought.

Phlox did his best to banish those dark thoughts. In his time among humans, he had learned that they fundamentally *needed* to hear good news, even if it meant clinging irrationally to even the most slender shreds of hope. While this was certainly *not* one of those situations—at least not yet—he still felt it was better not to classify the fate of Tucker and the rest as an imponderable.

Archer sighed heavily and put his fingers to the bridge of his nose, looking as if the weight of the world was pressing down on him—which, Phlox knew, was fundamentally the case; Archer clearly felt personally responsible for ending the mortal threat that the Xindi posed to the entire population of the planet Earth.

"Malcolm, do you have all the information that Trip was going to present at the briefing?" the captain finally asked.

"Yes, sir," Reed said, his body subtly shifting to a more formal stance.

"Then let's go meet with Major Hayes," Archer said.

As the command trio exited sickbay, Phlox heard a subtle clacking sound. Grabbing a rubberized grip, he quickly went over to Ensign Sato's side. Gingerly, he pulled her clacking teeth apart and inserted the grip between them.

"Can't have our communications officer unable to speak because she's chipped her teeth, now, can we?" he said to Sato. He smoothed a lock of black, perspiration-slicked hair away from her forehead.

Enterprise had been searching the Delphic Expanse for the Xindi for just over twelve weeks, and this new seizure-inducing phenomenon was the seventeenth anomaly that had affected the ship in some manner. It was the first, however, that had affected the crew directly. Given the horror stories that had circulated for months aboard ship about the Expanse, Phlox sincerely hoped that the captain could find a way to protect *Enterprise* from these anomalies, and soon. If not, he feared that *Enterprise* and everyone aboard her might *become* yet another one of those horror stories.

Assuming, of course, that anyone aboard remained alive to tell the tale.

Corporal Selma Guitierrez wasn't exactly glad that Sato was absent from their shared quarters right now, especially given what she knew about Sato's sudden and mysterious medical condition. But as she stared at the scanner's small readout screen, she was certainly more than content to be alone *now*.

The test had come up positive. Again.

Seven weeks.

She was pregnant.

With a growl of inchoate anger, Guitierrez threw the scanner at the room's single narrow bed, ignoring it as it bounced off, struck the nearby bulkhead, and landed in a heap beside the two others. She paced for perhaps a minute in the cluttered, darkened living quarters, then lashed out and hit the wall with her fist. Pain flared brightly in her knuckles and up her forearm, but her ingrained MACO discipline overrode most of it, even as it failed to govern the roiling emotions that had goaded her into lashing out in the first place.

How?

Her mind raced to answer the question. She had engaged in a brief affair with Sergeant Nelson Kemper a week into the mission into the Expanse. They were both originally from Minnesota, so they had some things in common to discuss during their mutual down hours, and she had always been a sucker for guys with chiseled, cleft chins.

She had been bold enough to make the first move, as she usually did, since most men seemed to find her intimidating; during a training drill, she had gotten a bit friendly while following him up into one of the artificial gravity system's power junctions. Two days later, they'd made love for the first time, but hadn't used any contraception; after all, she'd been assured years earlier by several doctors that she would never be able to conceive.

Although relationships between MACOs of the same platoon—or even of the same company—were officially frowned upon, Guitierrez and Kemper were hardly the only couple that had formed within the small MACO company serving aboard *Enterprise.* And they weren't even really a couple in the traditional sense; she had thought of the relationship as "friendship with benefits," and felt confident that Kemper felt the same way. Of greater concern was the matter of their respective ranks and their position relative to one another in the MACO chain of command; Kemper was not only senior to her, but was also part of the same squad. But they had always kept their public displays of affection down to a minimum, and no repercussions had come down from Major Hayes. Yet.

And now this. *That's it for me. If I keep the baby—if I even* can *keep the baby—that takes me right off the career fast track.* And getting back onto that track, especially within an elite military organization like the MACOs—and with a blotch on her conduct record, no less—would be next to impossible.

Shit!

She decided that the first order of business was to see Phlox, even though the Denobulan doctor made her shiver whenever he displayed his unnaturally wide grin. She always felt as if he were either going to try to eat her or assault her; it was the same look her childhood cat had evinced whenever it spotted a wayward beetle crawling through the grass.

But Phlox was the ship's chief medical officer, and would therefore be better able than anyone else aboard *Enterprise* to tell her if this pregnancy was real, rather than some sort of scanner glitch. *Right,* she thought. *As if three different scanners could come down with the exact same glitch.*

More importantly, Phlox would be able to tell her whether or not she was capable of carrying the child to term.

And depending on the answer to that question, she would have some very hard decisions to make. Years ago, she'd made peace with the thought that she'd never experience motherhood, and she hadn't given the matter much thought since. She also had to face another reality honestly: Kemper was hardly father material, and she simply didn't feel strongly enough about him to even want him in her life for more than an hour or two at a time. It was a cold realization, but she knew that it was the truth.

On the other hand, the idea of establishing a new family held a certain fascination for her; she was an only child, after all, and both her parents had died during her teens. So she was the last member of her family—the *only* member of her family—unless she brought this child into the world.

Guitierrez clambered onto the bed and reached for the scanner again, grudgingly glad to see that it was still working despite her tantrum. She tucked her dark hair behind her ear.

Run the scan again, Selma. *Maybe it was wrong. Maybe.*

As the door to the command center slid open, Captain Archer was relieved to see everyone already assembled for the briefing. T'Pol, Reed, and O'Neill were conferring over data that scrolled on a wall-mounted monitor, while a spit-and-polish Major Hayes and a group of five camo-clad MACOs stood at attention nearby.

"Let's get started," Archer said perfunctorily as Reed and the others turned to acknowledge him.

Reed cleared his throat, and gestured toward one of the side monitors. "Our informant told us that the Xindi and their associates have been known to frequent the spaceports at Kaletoo. Extreme-long-range scans have shown that the atmosphere of the planet is nonconducive to further scanning, but the informant told us that the spaceports are this region's main hub of economic activity, of both the respectable and the illicit variety."

Archer found none of this terribly surprising so far; in the absence of some central governing authority in this region of space, any number of nearby worlds might serve as havens for all sorts of nasty goings-on. Unpleasant memories of the trellium mine on Tulaw, where he and Trip had very nearly been enslaved and murdered, sprang to mind unbidden.

"Judging from the debris and ionic trails we've found as we get closer to Kaletoo's solar system," Reed continued, "I'd say that there is definitely a significant amount of traffic going toward—or away from—this planet. Probably both."

"Do we have any way to find out where the Xindi might be before we establish orbit around Kaletoo?" Archer asked.

"Not until we get much closer," T'Pol said. "Though the planet is Minshara-class, there are sufficient traces of ionized oxides of nitrogen, sulfur, and kraylon present in its upper atmosphere to obscure long-range sensor scans. We will have essentially no chance of pinpointing Xindi-specific biometric signatures on the ground until we get within several kilometers of the planet's surface."

"Captain, I'm not sure that bringing *Enterprise* directly into orbit around Kaletoo is such a good idea," Hayes said. "With all the questions we've been asking throughout the sector over the past few weeks, the Xindi *have* to be aware that we're here and that we're looking for them—even if we haven't made much real progress so far in tracking them down. It might be better to use a shuttlepod to conduct our search of the planet."

"I concur," T'Pol said. "In any case, you would need a shuttlepod to get sufficiently close to the planet's surface to begin running detailed bioscans."

Archer suppressed a wince at Hayes's comment about the lack of success thus far in the ongoing hunt for the Xindi and their homeworld. While his crew hadn't managed to find much concrete data about the Xindi, or even a trail that might lead to them, it wasn't for lack of trying. Between the mysterious nature of their quarry and the dangerous, unexpected anomalies the ship kept encountering within the vast, unknown reaches of the Delphic Expanse, the mission was proving to be extraordinarily difficult.

But Archer doubted that Hayes and his people could have found the Xindi homeworld any more quickly than *Enterprise*'s crew could have, even had the increasingly impatient MACOs been placed in charge of the mission.

Archer nodded in his first officer's direction. "A

shuttlepod was already part of my plan. I'll lead a landing party down to Kaletoo. O'Neill, you and Reed will come along. Major Hayes, choose three of your best people and get them geared up, just in case we find ourselves in a combat situation down there."

"Captain, given what happened in the trellium mines on Tulaw, do you think it prudent that you lead the landing party?" Hayes asked.

Archer couldn't read his face, and Hayes's affect was flat, but he nevertheless felt challenged by the MACO leader.

"Major, on this ship, *everybody* gets his hands dirty, including the captain. I suspect that over the last two years, *Enterprise* and her crew have weathered threats that you and your people haven't seen in your wildest training simulations. Exploring uncharted space hasn't exactly been a cakewalk."

He paused, noticing that while the other MACOs present had stiffened in their stance, Hayes was still appraising him coolly. "We may not have all the combat training that you go through, but we've been through the fire dozens of times. Sometime soon, to quote Lincoln, we are going to be 'met on a great battlefield of that war' against the Xindi. And not only will I be a part of that fight, I intend to make certain that we win it together."

Even within his righteous anger, Archer felt a stir of embarrassment at his own hyperbole. Still, he had been feeling tension and impatience from the MACOs toward his crew for quite some time now, and perhaps this briefing was as good a place as any to begin, at last, resolving those festering conflicts.

"Any questions, Major?"

Hayes shook his head, then spoke in an extremely formal tone. "No, sir."

Archer turned toward his other crew members, and saw that T'Pol's eyebrow was slightly raised. He couldn't guess what she was thinking—and wasn't sure he wanted to do so at the moment.

"T'Pol, you'll have command of *Enterprise.* Keep whatever crew you need to on-shift to replace those who've been . . . temporarily incapacitated by our mess-hall anomaly. Put some of O'Neill's third-watchers on double duty if need be."

Archer swept the room with his gaze, a grim smile on his lips. "Shuttlepod One leaves in seventy minutes. Everybody lock and load."

Major Joss Hayes felt heat creeping up the back of his collar as he exited the command center, his quintet of MACO officers following close behind him for the brief turbolift ride down to the armory on F deck. Archer's little dressing-down had been humiliating. *What kind of idiot ship's captain puts himself directly into harm's way at every opportunity?*

And then there was Archer's implication that the *Enterprise* crew was as capable of dealing with danger as were the MACOs. *Absurd.* If the squids were so capable, then why had General Casey assigned Hayes's MACO company to the NX-01? Clearly, Starfleet had misgivings about Archer and his crew's ability to deal effectively with the Xindi threat.

It galled Hayes too that, despite his rank, he was equal only to the top lieutenants in *Enterprise*'s command structure. He half-expected the prissy Lieutenant Reed to pull rank on him soon, and the scene that would surely follow immediately afterward would *not* be pretty.

Still, a part of him grudgingly respected Archer for wanting to jump into the fray. Hayes was the same way himself, always leading from the front rather than from the rear. He was seventh-generation military, and his father and grandfathers had experienced armed conflicts going as far back as Earth's Second World War. And all of them had been decorated after battlefield engagements. "A Hayes doesn't run from the enemy," his father had told him often while he was still a teenager, back when he was still preparing for his first MACO candidate entrance exams. As he'd run his son through drills and calisthenics, the elder Hayes would offer many such adages in what sometimes seemed to be an endlessly repeating loop. Pushing him, reminding him never to quit, no matter how tired or dispirited he might become. *Semper Invictus,* Hayes thought, just as he had done repeatedly as a teen whenever he had questioned whether he really was MACO material. *Ever Invincible*.

Just after the group emerged from the turbolift near the armory, a voice jolted Hayes out of his momentary reverie. "Sir, I'd like to lead the squad going to Kaletoo," Corporal Fiona McKenzie said. She walked briskly at his right side, her pace even with his own.

He shook his head. "No. I'm going with Archer, to make certain he isn't taken prisoner again by any more slavers." He regretted for a moment that he had made this sarcastic comment out loud, but a quick glance to the rear told him that none of the other MACOs present appeared to have heard his words.

He stopped and faced the petite brunette woman, and the rest of the group stopped behind her, standing at attention. "You can have dibs on the next suspicious aliens that *Enterprise* encounters, McKenzie." He pointed to one of the other MACOs. "Kemper, get your gear. Notify Peruzzi and Money that they'll need to suit up as well."

The ruddy-faced Kemper gave Hayes an inquisitive look. "Money, sir?"

"Yes," Hayes said, nodding with a slight grin. "I think our youngest shark needs a bit more time in the tank. Besides, her scores on the firing range beat yours to hell and gone."

He remembered another of his father's proverbs: "You're never too young to shoot a gun."

Private Money might be a bit of a greenhorn, but Hayes knew she would do just fine.

FOUR

KEMPER TRIPLE-CHECKED HIS WEAPONS as he stalked down the corridor on E deck's port side. He had a phase pistol holstered to his right hip, a phase rifle over his back, a grapple gun secured snugly to his heavy Sam Browne belt, knives strapped to each calf, and a whipcord suitable for garroting circling his waist.

"Nelson."

Hearing the familiar voice call his name, he stopped and turned. In his intense concentration, he hadn't even realized that he had just passed the quarters that Selma shared with Ensign Sato. Guitierrez was standing in the open doorway.

"Hey, Selma," he said simply to the dark-haired woman standing in the entry. "I'm headed out for my mission."

Guitierrez nodded and looked down at the floor, but as she did so, he saw that her eyes were puffy and red. *Why's she been crying?*

"I know," she said, her voice plain. "The major just posted a communiqué to the company."

He put a hand up to her shoulder, but she seemed almost to shrink away from his touch. "Are you okay?"

"Yeah," she said, nodding. "Just not feeling well. I'll get over it."

"Go see Phlox. He could probably use a break from dealing with the anomaly victims."

She nodded again several times, rhythmically, and made a noncommittal noise.

What is up with her? Kemper wanted to care—he *did* care, even though their relationship was supposed to be casual—but he was also aware that he was going to be late if he lingered here.

"Selma, I've got to join my team. We're briefing in just a couple of minutes."

She looked up at him then, seemingly *through* him, her dark eyes wide with some emotion he couldn't quite identify. Then she offered him a wan smile. "It can wait. Go. Be careful."

After glancing quickly down the corridor in both directions, Kemper leaned in and gave Guitierrez a quick kiss on the lips.

"I'll be careful. See you soon."

She retreated behind her door, and he sprinted along a curving corridor, then turned left at one of the several straight, radial passageways that honeycombed E deck. Kemper arrived at the doorway to Launch Bay 1 with mere seconds to spare. He tapped the entrance pad, and the door slid open. The others were already inside, and he saw that they were dressed in drab brownish woolen cloaks that mostly covered their gray camo MACO assault uniforms. Kemper watched as members of the strike team made some final checks on their gear. Private Sascha Money was fidgeting and hopping slightly; her adrenaline was clearly up.

Corporal Meredith Peruzzi brought a cloak over to Kemper. "According to Reed's intel, the people on Kaletoo tend to bundle up to protect themselves from sandstorms. I suspect we'll be hotter than hell, though."

"As long as I can get to my weapons when I need them," Kemper said, swirling the cloak over his shoulders and fastening it.

As he moved to join the others, he noticed that Lieutenant Reed and another *Enterprise* crew member were loading a few small canisters onto the shuttlepod. "What are those?" he asked, gesturing.

"After the trading fiasco on Tulaw with the manager of that trellium mine," Peruzzi said, "Captain Archer thought it might be a good idea to bring some platinum and other trade items *with* us, to avoid having to run back to the ship."

So we can buy *information about the Xindi instead of negotiating with our phase rifles,* Kemper thought, feeling somewhat ambivalent about the idea. *Only a squid could have thought of that.*

Kemper caught Hayes's eyes for a moment then, just long enough to see that something about the mission still seemed to be bothering the major.

He didn't know if the problem was Archer, Reed, the mission, or any of a myriad of other factors. Hayes always seemed to be uptight about *something.* In the two years he had served under the major, Kemper had learned that the best way to deal with his CO's sometimes mercurial moods was to be ruthlessly efficient—and to stay out of the man's way.

As he boarded the shuttlepod, Kemper resolved to do exactly that.

Kaletoo

Lieutenant "D.O." O'Neill sat at the controls of the shuttlepod, with Lieutenant Reed seated beside her. Archer was on the adjacent com station, giving orders to Sub-Commander T'Pol aboard *Enterprise.*

This was O'Neill's first away mission with the captain, and she had privately wondered why he had chosen to place her on the strike team. She suspected that with several of the senior first-watch bridge staff either currently down in sickbay or else busy running the ship, Archer needed someone who could handle piloting the shuttle. And—perhaps most importantly—he needed someone who was rested.

Like Mayweather, O'Neill was a space baby, "born on a freighter and raised in microgravity," as she liked to say. She had learned to run flight-control consoles while sitting on her father's knee, unaware until years later that her brilliant flying maneuvers at age five were really the result of preprogrammed auto-astrogation subroutines.

As she grew, O'Neill knew that she wanted something different for her life, and eventually she found that calling with Starfleet. She attended flight school in San Francisco, graduating just three years after Captain Archer. Following postings on the *Essex* and the *Archon,* two of Starfleet's *Daedalus*-class starships, she had joined the crew of *Enterprise* near the end of '52, shortly before Archer had been captured by the

Klingons. *That* had certainly been a mission to remember.

Although O'Neill had expected to be given a job as a flight controller, for some reason, Archer had made her a watch commander. She didn't mind the assignment, though she sometimes wished she could have a more hands-on role in piloting the ship, even if the job of pilot was considered "below" her rank.

Guess I'm finally getting my wish, she thought, checking coordinates and headings on the shuttlepod's navigational computer. Through the wide forward window, she watched the desiccated, dust-shrouded, tan-and-orange lump of a world that was Kaletoo as it grew ever larger. According to the data being received by the small auxiliary craft's sensors, numerous vessels were currently arriving at and departing from Kaletoo; other than the occasional streak of light caused by some ship's fiery passage through the planet's soupy atmosphere, however, she couldn't spot any of this traffic visually.

"We'll be entering the planet's exosphere in about three minutes, Captain," she said, glancing over her shoulder at Archer.

"Thanks, Donna," said the captain, who had just signed off with T'Pol. He edged forward, half-crouching between O'Neill and Reed. "We're on com silence from here on in. Ensign Marcel is pulling *Enterprise* back to the periphery of the system."

"Good idea," Reed said. "There's no point in announcing our presence to any long-range Xindi sensors that might be present down there."

O'Neill nodded. "Or to ships departing from the surface, or arriving from off Kaletoo."

Reed cast a slightly worried glance at Archer. "Just how far into the 'periphery' does T'Pol intend to withdraw?"

"The safety of the ship is the most important consideration," Archer said. "So I've given T'Pol a lot of discretion. I doubt she'll want to get *Enterprise* so far from Kaletoo that she can't maintain contact with the deep-space probes we launched into this system."

"But I suppose *Enterprise* will probably be too far away to give us a quick rescue should the need arise," Reed said with a resigned chuckle.

Archer gestured with his thumb toward the silently attentive MACO team, strapped into their seats in the aft compartment and armed to the teeth. "Let's hope we brought all the rescue we're going to need here with us."

"Understood, sir," Reed said, nodding.

O'Neill could no longer suppress what one of her flight-school colleagues had called her "fatalistic grin."

"Cheer up, Lieutenant," she said as she slightly leveled out the shuttlepod's approach vector. "Like the captain said, we've got Earth's finest fighting force watching our back. What could happen?"

"There's nothing quite like swimming in the shark tank, is there?" Reed muttered, so that only O'Neill and Archer could hear.

Archer smiled grimly as he patted both O'Neill and Reed on the shoulder. "Take her in."

A minute or so later, the shuttlepod passed the rarefied topmost layer of Kaletoo's atmosphere, and swiftly descended toward the planet's far more substantial thermosphere and mesosphere bands.

O'Neill fought the controls for a moment as sudden and extreme turbulence buffeted the ship.

Reed looked from his data screens to the forward window. O'Neill was about to give up on the latter, since nothing was visible other than brown, swirling air masses and great, cyclonic earth-tone clouds. "I haven't seen an atmospheric layer so thick this side of Venus," Reed said. "It's like trying to pilot through a sandstorm."

That's because it is *a sandstorm,* O'Neill thought as she struggled simultaneously with the shuttlepod's pitch, yaw, and trim. "I've been through worse," she said, though she hoped Reed wouldn't ask her anything specific about the circumstances. "I'd better keep our approach on manual."

"The computer can react faster if we end up crossing contrails with another ship inside this mess, Lieutenant," Reed said.

O'Neill grinned. "The computer can't 'feel' its way out of a storm. Besides, if any other ships come too close to us, we should get enough warning from the sensors to avoid them. We only have to miss them by the width of a paint job, and this is a big planet."

Reed looked at her with mock surprise. "Oh, you think you're *that* good? We've only got maybe a forty-meter sensor range inside this mess."

She grinned at him. "I'm that good."

Almost as if on cue, three shapes smashed into the forward window, their fist-sized feathered bodies splatting messily. O'Neill and Reed jumped, startled.

"The sensors certainly didn't see *those* coming," Reed said, nervousness coloring his voice. O'Neill couldn't help but wonder how much faster those birds would have had to be moving in order to crack the front window; after all, not even transparent aluminum was completely indestructible.

"I don't think the birds saw us coming either, if it's any consolation," she said. "Now quit bothering the driver."

Reed lapsed into an unhappy silence. As the heavy winds scrubbed the carcasses of the fowl from the window, O'Neill quietly hoped that this little incident hadn't been an augury of worse to come.

Ensign Ravi Chandra stared out the forward window at the panorama below them as the shuttlepod sped over the landscape. The surface of the planet was mostly desert, though there appeared to be some kind of hardy scrub vegetation that grew in patches. They were still too far from the surface to see any of the local fauna, though he could make out a number of tiny settlements dotting the mostly flat, cinnamon-colored topography. Studying the terrain that steadily unfurled below, Chandra began to suspect that Archer had chosen him for this mission based on the geography of the region on Earth that he called home.

He had grown up in Patna, the capital city of Bihar, in northeastern India's Gangetic Plains, and was used to a much more lush and fertile climate than Kaletoo's. But India's Thar Desert contained dry, desolate vistas that closely resembled those that now rolled past below the descending shuttlepod. He recalled visiting the dunes just west of the Aravalli hills, before his family had made their way to Barmer and Jaisalmer on business.

Chandra's father, Kamal, was a senior vice-president of Patna Air and Space, the company that owned the lion's share of continental and extra-planetary shuttle facility contracts on the Indian subcontinent. It was through him that young Chandra had gained an appreciation for the stars, and from him that he had inherited the determination to one day reach them; after all, Kamal's great-grandmother Abhirati Indrani had been one of the patient thousands whose steadfast exercise of passive resistance had eventually driven the tyrant Khan Noonien Singh from power at the end of the Eugenics Wars of the 1990s. Grandmother Abhirati's actions had bestowed upon each subsequent generation of the family a sense of forward-looking resolve. Strangely, Kamal Chandra himself had never traveled beyond Earth's atmosphere, telling his son instead, "You will be the first from our family to travel the heavens."

Chandra realized with a start that it was almost Dussehra, the Hindu holiday celebrating the victory of Rama over the evil Asura king Ravana. Five years ago, the festival had marked his departure from home to join Earth's burgeoning Starfleet; now he would be observing the tradition in another solar system, in another sector of the galaxy entirely. From the time he'd placed his exoanthropology degree into the service of *Enterprise*'s mission of exploration the previous year, he had faithfully kept a log of his voyages, intending to share it with his family after his return to Earth—and to share it eventually with the wife and children with whom he hoped someday to share his life and experiences.

Lieutenant Malcolm Reed's lilting voice pulled Chandra out of his reverie. "Sensor readings show extremely faint ion trails that resemble the fuel residue found in the wreckage of the Xindi probe." Reed pointed toward a viewscreen located just beneath the forward window; the screen displayed an aerial image of a desert settlement, overlaid with the lines of a tactical grid. "About five kilometers ahead, at that large settlement."

"Any hails or challenges from the surface?" Archer asked.

"None, sir," Reed said.

"Then start looking for a place to set us down," the captain said to Lieutenant O'Neill, who dutifully set about entering final approach instructions into her flight control console.

Chandra surreptitiously studied Archer's grim, distracted expression. These days, he rarely saw the captain smile—the captain's demeanor had significantly changed since the Xindi attack on Earth—except for once when he had passed by Archer's quarters as the captain had exited, and Archer's dog had barked playfully at him as he'd passed.

As the shuttlepod descended further, it became apparent that the settlement was more like a sprawling city. Few of the buildings were over three or four stories high, while dozens of ships, some of them quite large, were in view at various landing sites and hangar facilities.

"Coming up on the site where the Xindi ion traces are strongest," O'Neill said from the pilot's seat. "Should we land here, or pick a spot a little bit farther away?"

Chandra was still amazed that they had the freedom to simply land without having to obtain any official clearances. How did this place manage to operate with no legal authorities in evidence? The thought filled him with foreboding, making him wonder what other, more insidious means the locals might use to maintain order—or to assert control over offworld visitors.

"Let's take the bull by the horns," Archer said. "Set us down here."

Minutes later, as the shuttlepod touched down, swirls of gray-tan dust eddied about the ship, once again obscuring the view from the forward window. Chandra noticed several figures near other ships parked nearby, but they seemed to be paying little attention to the new arrival.

Chandra saw the MACOs triple-checking that their weapons were set under their cloaks, and he made certain that his own phase pistol was in place as well. Then, surprisingly, Archer handed him a translator padd. "You run the program, Ensign Chandra. O'Neill and Reed will have backups running as well."

"Yes, sir," Chandra said, tapping a few keys on the padd.

After Chandra made a final confirmation that the atmosphere outside was safe, Peruzzi and Kemper opened the shuttlepod's starboard-side hatchway, leaving both the port-side hatch and the dorsal airlock closed and latched. As soon as the gull-wing hatch began swinging upward, a small swirl of dust blew deeply into the vessel's interior, riding one of Kaletoo's unpleasantly hot breezes. The pair of MACOs exited first, and although they weren't brandishing their weapons, Chandra could see that they were completely alert and combat-ready.

Major Hayes signaled for everyone else to exit, and the group immediately began to do so, starting with the captain and Lieutenant O'Neill. Exiting last, Chandra put his hand up to his eyes as he came out into the bright sun, shielding himself from its merciless glare.

A corpulent, sluglike creature approached them. It was as tall as a human, but its body was gray-green and wrinkled. Its hide was covered in a viscous liquid, which, in turn, was matted with sand and other windblown debris. It had two pudgy arms and three-fingered hands, and its mouth had to be nearly a meter wide. The being began speaking in unintelligible gutturals, perhaps offering a greeting, and its long tongue twitched from side to side as though seeking to escape from the loathsome body to which it was attached. Chandra silently chastened himself for appraising this being with such provincial eyes.

"Would you repeat yourself, please?" he said, holding the translator padd before him as though it were a shield. Though he hadn't understood the slug's speech, he gathered that the creature was presenting itself as someone in authority.

The being chattered again for a moment, saying, *"fieoh hugek sm'por-por reskit ao huirt."* Then an approximation of its voice echoed out of the translator in standardized but stilted English. ". . . per day, although it is cheaper if you wish to pay by the six-turn."

"One more time, please," Chandra asked, wondering whether a "sixturn" might be the local equivalent of a Terran week.

"Gods of *Jerotkixl!* Have you never been to Kaletoo before?" The creature seemed to be growing annoyed.

"No, we haven't," Archer said, stepping forward. "In fact, this is our first visit to your fine planet."

The creature snorted, and a wet, viscous splotch of something scarcely identifiable flew out of what Chandra supposed was one of its nostrils and spattered messily onto the sand-swept landing field. "Fine planet? It's a *peldmes*-hole!"

"I'm Captain Jonathan Archer, and I'm hoping you can help me."

"Help you how? Find a bigger ship? Your crew must be cramped in that little *sbnuite,* 'Captain.'"

Archer ignored what seemed to be something of a verbal jab. "As a matter of fact, we do need to find a ship, though not for us. We also need information. What did you say your rate was for docking here for a week—a sixturn?"

"It's negotiable. Are you paying with platinum, gold-pressed latinum, kildrats, or mercury?"

"Platinum or mercury, your choice."

The creature smiled, showing the stumps of rotted teeth in his gelatinous gums. "Mercury. Three liters."

Archer stepped forward and put his arm around the bulky creature, then spoke to him in almost conspiratorial tones. "We won't be staying here for more than, oh, a turn or two, but if you get us the information you need, you'll still get an entire sixturn's payment."

"What are you looking for?" the creature said. "Or who?"

Reed stepped forward. "The Xindi. We traced one of their ships to this spaceport."

The creature nodded quietly, as if thinking. "Xindi. They don't come around my facilities very often. I think we last had a Xindi vessel here five daycycles ago, maybe six."

"What were they doing here?" Archer asked.

"They had business with one of the couriers who works here. La'an Trahve. He's a pilot who doesn't ask questions when he shouldn't."

"And how do we find this La'an Trahve?" Reed asked.

"He's usually parked on the other side of town. Drinks a lot at the cantina near the Bresian whorehouse." The creature looked up at Archer, slime from atop his head sluicing onto the captain's arm. "I'll give you directions, but if you want to have a look at him first, it'll cost you extra."

"What do you mean, 'Have a look at him'?" Reed asked, sounding suspicious.

The creature pointed a pudgy finger up toward the top of a building nearby, then swept over to point at another nearby rooftop. Chandra and the others turned and saw the wall-mounted recording devices that had been placed at strategic intervals around the rooflines. *Security cameras. Very smart, for a man in this business.* In a flash, he realized that Hayes and the MACOs—even Reed—might have already noticed the cameras; since Chandra had been assigned to diplomatic duty, he hoped his failure to notice the alien surveillance equipment would be considered forgivable.

"I'm sure I have archive images of Trahve meeting

with the Xindi," the creature said. "But it'll cost you triple your docking fees if you want to see them."

"We'll give you double up front," Archer said, his voice steely. "Triple after we actually speak with this Trahve."

The creature turned its back. Chandra thought it had rejected Archer's offer, until it motioned with one of its fat-marbled arms for the others to follow him toward one of the nearby outbuildings. Moments later, Archer, Reed, Hayes, and Chandra followed the sluglike landing-pad owner into a foul-smelling control room. Chandra marveled at the bizarre, motley mixture of technology he saw haphazardly piled everywhere; he wondered how much of it actually worked, and how much of it might have been stolen from those parked at the pad.

The creature stopped at a dusty viewscreen and began tapping data into a wall-mounted pad equipped with huge keys that had obviously been designed to accommodate his wide, blunt fingers. A visual of the landing pad as seen from about a hundred or so meters above immediately appeared on the screen; the picture wavered as the operator scrolled quickly through it, making ships appear and vanish with frenetic randomness as long periods of time—months on the terrestrial calendar, Chandra assumed—spooled swiftly backward. Finally, the frantic spooling stopped, and the camera angle changed to a viewpoint matching that of a person standing on the ground. A bird flying over the landing field confirmed that time was now moving forward at its customary rate.

"Whatever they wanted, they got," the creature

said. "These Xindi always acted as though they owned the whole *kreffing* planet."

Chandra's blood froze as he saw a pair of reptilian though vaguely humanoid creatures walk into frame, pulling behind them an antigrav cart on which a variety of containers were stacked. It was the first time that Chandra had seen a "live" Xindi, though everyone serving aboard *Enterprise* was by now very familiar with the images taken of the corpse of the one found in the wreckage of the Xindi superweapon that had slain all those millions back on Earth.

Pushing the cart from behind was a humanoid male, who did not appear to be Xindi; his pale, bland features in no way resembled those of the late Xindi humanoid Kessick, whose image Chandra had also become familiar with following the Tulaw trellium mine affair.

The slug pointed at the humanoid displayed on the screen. "La'an Trahve. And before you ask, I don't keep audio. That's just asking for trouble. I don't know what they discussed, and I don't know what Trahve couriered for the Xindi lizards."

Chandra watched Reed raise his padd, clearly intent on capturing the images. The slug glared at him dangerously.

"Trying to steal my images, are you?" the creature's translated voice rumbled. "That is most impolite, my friend. Must I add that device to my collection?" He waved a stubby arm toward the stacks of mismatched equipment strewn about the cramped chamber.

Reed looked intensely frustrated, but obediently lowered the device. Seeing that the lieutenant had not activated the device's scanning functions, Chandra surreptitiously flicked a toggle on his own padd. To Chandra's great relief the slug, still intent on Reed, did not appear to notice.

"How often did you say the Xindi came here?" Archer asked, apparently eager to divert their host's attention from Lieutenant Reed. The captain's brows furrowed together as he studied the image on the monitor.

"Only rarely did they visit my landing field, and they won't be welcome here again," the slug said. "One of them emptied his cloaca in the southeast corner. Disgusting creatures! Couldn't even be bothered to use the plumbing fixtures the way any other sentient would have. Stank up the whole pad for turns before I discovered the cause."

"Can you get us a better shot of Trahve?" Hayes asked. "From one of your other cameras?"

The slug toggled another switch, but the next image that appeared wasn't much better than the previous one. "Best I've got," he said. "Study it now, and I'll give you directions to Trahve as soon as you've paid me."

"Let's go back out to the shuttlepod and bring the man his pay," Archer said. He cast a final glance at the monitor, and Chandra saw his jaw clench so tightly that he feared the captain might break his teeth. Then, Archer turned and stalked out of the office.

As the slug followed several meters behind, Chandra, Reed, and Hayes flanked Archer.

Archer caught Chandra's gaze and whispered, "Malcolm, were you able to scan those images of Trahve?"

Reed's face was beet red, and apparently not from

the heat. "I'm afraid not, sir. The . . . gentleman caught me in the act of trying."

"Damn," Archer muttered.

Still nervous about being found out by the slug, Chandra spoke up, though quietly. "Sir, I believe I captured Trahve's picture on my padd."

Archer grinned momentarily before composing himself for the slug's benefit. "Well done, Mister Chandra."

"That was almost too easy," Reed said very quietly.

"I'm aware of that," Archer replied, equally *sotto voce*. "But we've finally got our first solid lead. We *know* Trahve is working either with or for the Xindi. For once we have more than just rumors."

Chandra felt a question gnawing at him. "How do we know that the proprietor won't just turn *us* over to the Xindi?" he said.

"I have a feeling that he was telling the truth about having no love for them." Archer said. "And before we leave this planet, not only will he have his payment in full, but Major Hayes will make certain that the Xindi will never find any evidence that we were ever here."

Hayes nodded. "A focused EMP burst should disable our friend's recording devices and erase his drives." He paused, then added, "Or are you saying we should make certain that he won't even be able to *tell* anyone we were here?"

Archer stopped and glared at Hayes. "I'm not authorizing anything of the sort, Major. He's played ball with us so far. I think he's greedy, but not stupid."

They resumed walking and neared the shuttlepod, beside which O'Neill, Kemper, Money, and Peruzzi were standing at attention.

"Measure out two liters of mercury for Mister . . ." Archer turned back toward the slug, who was slowly bringing up the rear. "I'm afraid I didn't quite catch your name earlier."

"Grakka," the creature said. "My full name is too complex to repeat, and not important to our business anyhow."

Archer turned back toward the MACOs. "Measure out two liters of mercury for Mister Grakka." Then he raised his voice a little louder. "And make certain to set the explosive shields on the shuttle for when we leave. I'm certain our host has *excellent* security measures, but to be safe, we'd best ensure that *anyone* who tries to enter our ship without authorization will be dead within moments."

Chandra suppressed a grin at the captain's hyperbole, and sneaked a quick glance at Grakka. The creature's eyes bulged slightly and its tongue disappeared between its meaty lips. Had the creature intended to add to his mismatched hoard of alien technology by burglarizing the shuttlepod?

Let's hope our host won't want to risk mounting any surprise shuttlepod inspections while we're out testing the reliability of his information, Chandra thought.

But he had little doubt that Grakka had told the truth about La'an Trahve and the Xindi. The chilling visual images of the Xindi reptiles—living, breathing representatives of the very same species that had already slaughtered millions of humans, and even now worked toward the goal of exterminating all the rest—were all the confirmation Chandra really needed that they were following the right trail.

FIVE

"IF YOU ASK ME, CAPTAIN, it sounds a little too good to be true," Reed said, turning sideways to let a group of dark-cloaked natives pass him on the narrow, dusty street.

Walking alongside Reed, O'Neill, and Chandra on the ancient, teeming roadway, the captain squinted under the sun's merciless glare. "Maybe it is, Malcolm. But it's a lead. And we've had damned few of those these past couple of months."

Reed certainly couldn't argue with that. He shared the captain's eagerness to ferret out the Xindi. But he also knew all too well that erring on the side of caution was a big part of a tactical officer's job. "We might be walking right into a trap, Captain," he said.

"Then our MACO complement just might come in handy on this mission," O'Neill said.

Reed suppressed a smile at this backhanded compliment. Sergeant Kemper, taking the point, kept his eyes focused straight ahead as he continued moving forward in silence a few meters ahead of Archer; though his rifle was discreetly shipped across his back, his hand never moved very far from the holster that held his phase pistol. Corporal Peruzzi and Private Money, both similarly equipped and equally attentive, followed alongside his flanks.

Slightly behind Kemper, Major Hayes turned back toward the Starfleet trio and favored O'Neill with a lopsided grin. "That's what we're here for, ma'am," he said. Reed noticed that Hayes's disposition seemed to have improved considerably since the mission briefing back aboard *Enterprise.* Though he looked just as sharply vigilant as any of his MACO subordinates, he, too, was keeping his rifle slung across his back, obviously in order to avoid provoking panicky responses among the locals.

O'Neill responded to Hayes with a sour-milk scowl. *I think she was actually pretty much on your side, Major,* Reed thought, suppressing a chuckle. *Until you called her "ma'am," that is.*

The group walked on in silence, following Grakka's directions to the southeast section of the spaceport. The rabbit warren of a street narrowed even further, bringing closer the powerful aromas radiating from the dilapidated stone inns and eateries and the busy, awning-covered food-and-beverage stalls. Reed found the odors at once intriguing and objectionable; the street was a whirling olfactory carousel that changed from moment to moment as they moved along a hard-packed roadbed that they shared with sparse crowds of buyers and sellers, most of whom wore clothing that had clearly seen better days. Rag-clad arms reached toward Reed from the stalls as he passed, imploring him to partake of the proffered bowls of alien meats and vegetables, in exchange for the oddly denominated precious metals the locals were using as currency.

Many of the people they passed offered no food, however, but instead held out beggar bowls, pleading for alms, some wordlessly, others loudly. All of these were studies in misery and desperation. Revulsion for the society—or lack of same—that had produced such circumstances seized Reed as the group continued forward. *How can such squalor exist on a world covered with spaceports and warp-driven vessels?*

The narrow road soon widened, and the density of the stalls, inns, and ramshackle shops abruptly thinned out. Away from the crowds of vendors and beggars, the horizon once again became visible. A flat, sunbaked field stretched into the distance, beyond which lay a collection of wide, stone buildings arranged in a rough semicircle. A motley collection of perhaps a dozen space vessels—all of them much smaller than *Enterprise*—sat with their landing legs splayed across the hard, desolate ground. Reed didn't recognize any of the ship configurations, though he noted that some looked truly baroque and alien. The antigravs on one of the ships activated then with an earsplitting howl, raising the vessel slowly skyward on a rapidly dissipating cloud of brownish-gray dust as a pair of conspicuously armed, uniformed men—local police or private security personnel, Reed surmised—looked on.

At least the spaceport's actually here, he thought, eyeing some of the larger buildings that lay horizonward. He was relieved to learn that the information their informant had provided had been accurate, at least so far.

"Those big structures out in the distance must be ship hangars," Archer said.

"Too bad we couldn't get more information about our Xindi-friendly pilot's vessel," O'Neill said. "Like the exact location of the hangar it's parked in, or even a registration number."

Reed nodded. "It would be nice to at least know where Trahve's ship is, in case he tries to make a run for it after we catch up to him."

They walked onward toward one of the nearer structures, a low-slung wattle-and-daub building that seemed to have been extruded aeons ago out of the planet's very crust.

"We might not know exactly where he moored his ship," Archer said, pointing toward the ancient-looking edifice. "But we do have the next most important piece of information: We know where he drinks."

Assuming, Reed thought as the group walked through the crooked, arched entrance, *that we can continue to trust the source of our information.* Though the captain had paid handsomely for a supposedly secure parking space for the shuttlepod, Reed was beginning to regret Archer's decision not to leave at least one member of the team behind to guard the ship.

But he knew there was no time to worry about that now; he was much too busy searching the random farrago of semidarkened booths and tables for the face of the man they sought. Aliens of every description—some humanoid, some corresponding to no phylum Reed had ever seen before—drank, ate, and conversed. On a corner stage, a quintet of hairless, vaguely humanoid aliens tortured unfamiliar tubular and stringed instruments into producing atonal music, which a ceiling-mounted speaker system amplified far too loudly for Reed's taste. He was distracted from this nuisance by a thickening miasma of recreational smoke, which seared his lungs and forced him to suppress a wheezing cough.

Archer gave the group a silent nod, and the four MACOs instantly peeled away in different directions. *Covering the exits,* Reed thought as Archer, O'Neill, and Chandra also melted into the shadows, each obviously intent on their own searches.

Reed reached into his native-style traveling cloak and withdrew the small handheld scanner and padd he had brought with him from the shuttlepod. Using the padd's small display screen, he briefly summoned up the best of the pictures of La'an Trahve that Ensign Chandra had recorded at Grakka's spaceport and studied it as he loaded it into the padd's biometric recognition program. Because of the dim illumination—and because his quarry might well be in disguise, or might have hidden his features behind a hat or a cloak—human eyesight alone simply wasn't a reliable guide for this kind of search.

Holding the scanner discreetly at waist level, Reed turned very slowly in place in a complete circle before moving closer to the bar that was located at the center of the dim chamber. The scanner sent out invisible, low-intensity transtator pulses across the booths and tables and bar stools. The reflected signals returned instantaneously to the scanner's pickup, collated the resulting biometric data, and fed it into the padd for comparison with Trahve's recorded image.

No match yet, Reed thought, still staring at the

bland, mild-looking male humanoid face displayed on the backlit padd. Walking quietly, he moved on, stepping aside to allow a rather scary-looking, saber-fanged felinoid drink server to move past him with a heavy tray heaped high with beverages and fragrant, disconcertingly raw-looking meat. Reed did his best to return his focus to the hunt, pointing his scanner toward the next group of tables and booths.

"Who the hell are you? Some kind of constable?"

The voice, or at least the English version of it, was issuing from the translation matrix Hoshi had installed into his padd. The voice's hulking owner, however, was suddenly standing before Reed on four bandy legs topped by a bulbous torso that was adorned with three oddly jointed and hugely muscled upper limbs. The creature's chalk-white face was ringed in delicate growths that resembled feathers, and its four dark eyes glared balefully.

Perhaps I did make it a wee bit too obvious that I'm here looking for someone, Reed thought, taking a single cautious step backward.

The alien advanced on him, closing the gap, and reached for the padd in Reed's hand. A tentacle-like limb seized Reed's wrist in an iron grip, making good on the threat that Grakka had made a little earlier.

Reed sincerely hoped he wouldn't have to try to shoot his way out of his current circumstances, partly because he wasn't at all certain he could reach his phase pistol in time if he needed to do so.

He decided instead that the safest way to handle this situation was to temporize.

"Easy, friend. I'm only looking for a, ah, missing person." Where were Archer, O'Neill, and Chandra?

Where are the bloody MACOs? he thought, though he knew they were all still probably preoccupied securing and watching the building's exits.

The creature held Reed immobile just long enough to grab the padd with one of its other two upper limbs, which moved with surprisingly whiplike speed. "I'm not your friend. And before you begin canvassing among the customers, you should at least speak to the management."

Reed clung tightly to the small scanner in his hand, determined not to allow the device to escape his grasp. "And who might that be? You?"

"Near enough, off-worlder." The alien studied the image that was still displayed on the padd, then abruptly released its grip, nearly causing Reed to fall down in the process. "Now get out, while you can still walk under your own power."

It occurred to Reed then precisely where Archer and the rest of the Starfleet contingent had to be at the moment: they must have taken seats at one or more of the tables, blending in with the rest of the patrons as they conducted their searches. Since he hadn't heard any sounds of struggle, they had evidently managed to avoid attracting the hostile attention of the bar's staff.

Reed's sense of embarrassment immediately overtook whatever fear the alien bouncer probably should have inspired in him. *There's no way I'm going to let myself foul up this badly. Not on a mission as important as this one.*

And certainly not while serving in the same landing party as Hayes, who had from day one made no effort to conceal his differences with Reed about the tactical and security aspects of the ongoing Xindi hunt in the Delphic Expanse.

"How about showing me to a table so I can order something expensive?" Reed said aloud.

"I've got more than enough customers who *aren't* here just to make trouble for me. Now leave. There's no scanning of the patrons without asking permission first. That's tavern policy."

Sure, Reed thought. *That way, your most favored criminal barflies end up getting fair warning—and continue to stay just one step ahead of whoever might be after them.*

The alien grabbed Reed by both wrists and the back of his cloak. His feet left the floor, and he nearly dropped both scanner and padd as he flailed to get his boots back beneath him. "Now. Get. Out."

This is bloody humiliating, Reed thought as the creature hauled him effortlessly back toward the very door through which he had originally entered.

"Easy there, Rekna. This gentleman's with me. Got a table for us?"

Because of the slight echo effect generated by the translator, Reed had some difficulty locating the owner of the voice. But it was deep, male, and not entirely unpleasant.

The alien bouncer stopped, then dropped Reed unceremoniously onto his feet. Recovering his balance—if not his dignity—Reed glanced to the bouncer's left, where a slightly-built humanoid male dressed in a one-piece flight suit stood and regarded him with a wry expression.

"Follow me," the hulking alien bouncer said, then turned and led the flight-suited humanoid toward a low table located in a dark, smoky corner. Still feeling somewhat disoriented after his near-ejection, Reed followed and took a seat directly across the table from the newcomer, who Reed noticed had taken care to keep his back to the corner rather than the nearest door.

Reed laid his scanner and the padd on the tabletop and studied his rescuer's pale, unassuming humanoid face. It superficially resembled the image displayed on Reed's padd, but was also the countenance of someone for whom the ability to blend into a crowd seemed to be a basic survival tool. The insistent beeping coming from the padd, however, indicated that the scanner's biometric comparison matrix hadn't been fooled by the man's obviously finely honed gift for appearing nondescript. A low-volume secondary alarm began sounding on the padd as well, evidently the result of one of the chemical trace scans he had been running in the background. Silencing the padd's alarms with one deft keystroke, Reed decided he would have to wait until later to evaluate the results of the chem scans.

He faced the alien and met his mild gaze squarely. "La'an Trahve, I presume."

The other man nodded, his voice echoing slightly as the translator rendered his words in English. "At your service. It's already come to my attention that someone was looking for me."

Reed nodded. "Word travels fast around here."

"In a place like this, if one doesn't discover such things quickly, one can end up very dead even *more* quickly."

Good point.

Reed didn't like sitting with his back to the door any more than Trahve did; his scanner, which he had covertly set to monitor the space directly behind him, suddenly began giving off another series of urgent beeps. Reed tensed, then turned, ready to spring on whoever it was the scanner had caught trying to sneak up on him.

"Nice work, Malcolm," Archer said. Reed quickly reset his scanner, heaving a sigh of relief. The captain and O'Neill, their own padds and scanners in hand, took seats across from one another at the table Reed and Trahve were sharing. Reed saw that Chandra had appeared as well, and was standing nearby.

"Next time, though, you might want to try to be a little bit less obvious about it when you're running your scans," O'Neill said from behind a tight smirk.

Reed noticed a moment later that he had begun grinding his molars involuntarily. "I'll try to remember that, Lieutenant. Thank you." *And thank goodness she probably doesn't share gossip about me with Hayes,* he thought, grateful for this one small mercy.

Archer was facing the humanoid, his brow furrowed in evident impatience. "My name is Captain Jonathan Archer."

Trahve nodded. "La'an Trahve," he said, placing an identifying hand across his chest. "It's a pleasure to meet you, Captain."

"What do you know about a race called the Xindi?" Archer said without further preamble.

Trahve scratched his smooth chin and looked thoughtful. "Xindi? A little, I think. Of course, I'm no expert." The echo effect caused by the padd's translation matrix seemed to be fading steadily away as the device's self-correcting heuristics refined their parsings of his words.

Archer looked as though he might be about to grab the man by the throat, and seemed to have to work very hard to keep from raising his voice. "I know that you work for the Xindi."

A shrug. "Occasionally. Why?"

Because the Xindi killed several million of us, Reed thought, his own emotions vibrating in sympathy with the captain's. *Because that atrocity demands a response. And because the bastards are cueing up another attack intended to wipe out our entire planet—*

Archer seemed to need a moment to compose himself, probably because he was having very similar thoughts. "Because we have . . . business with them."

Trahve raised an eyebrow. "Hmmm. *Unfinished* business, from the sound of it."

"Which is none of *your* business," O'Neill said, her eyes flashing daggers. She looked as though she wanted to go on, but Archer silenced her with a hard gaze and a quick shake of the head.

"Then I suppose I'd best be on my way," Trahve said, rising. "After all, I wouldn't want to intrude on *your* busin—"

Archer's hand came down firmly on Trahve's shoulder and he shoved the man back down into his seat, interrupting him. "Why be in such a hurry, Mister Trahve? Stay awhile. Get comfortable. Let's chat."

Trahve no longer seemed quite so congenial as he had moments earlier. "I caution you, Captain, I have many friends here."

Reed bared his teeth, but somehow managed to

keep his voice level and his tone civil. "Then let's all agree right now to keep our conversation friendly."

"Tell us about the work you do for the Xindi, Mister Trahve," Archer said.

The pilot replied with a hard, silent stare, then shrugged as if what he was about to say really didn't matter. "There's not all that much to tell, really. After all, it's not as though I have an exclusive working relationship with them. I am a simple courier, and the Xindi are merely one client among many."

Most of whom probably wouldn't appreciate your revealing the details of your dealings with them to strangers, Reed thought. *Especially if those strangers came from a planet your clients are planning to annihilate.*

"We're only interested in the Xindi," said Archer.

A crooked grin appeared on Trahve's otherwise inexpressive face. "Why? Do they owe you some latinum? Did they break a contract?"

"That's between us and them, Mister Trahve. I'm sure you can appreciate the need for confidentiality in business relationships."

The humanoid nodded knowingly. "Ah. So they are customers of yours as well?"

Archer ignored the question. "I need to speak to your Xindi employers. Where is their homeworld?"

Trahve shook his head in an almost pitying fashion. "I have no idea. They aren't terribly forthcoming with such information, you understand."

Reed was having trouble believing that. "Then how do you maintain contact with them?" he asked.

"I don't. Officers from a Xindi construction concern contact me whenever they require my services.

Freight running, courier assignments to intermediaries, and so forth." Trahve tipped his head slightly to the side, and regarded Archer with evident curiosity. "Say, where are you from, anyway?"

"Let's just say we're from far enough away not to have any Xindi within easy reach," Archer said.

"Hmmm. It doesn't sound as though you've developed a terribly solid business relationship with them."

"There are a few things we still have to . . . negotiate with them," Archer said, nodding slowly.

Trahve suddenly became flinty-eyed. "You haven't come to negotiate. I don't believe you're being very candid with me, Captain."

"We could say the same thing about you," Reed said, feeling heat rising under his collar. The man's continued evasions and diversions were growing tiresome.

Trahve chuckled. "No doubt you could."

Archer again placed an arm around Trahve's shoulder, and smiled a smile that was all lances and knives and did not completely reach his eyes. Reed noticed then that his scanner's proximity alarm had begun beeping again. Shutting off the sound, he looked to the side, where the multi-limbed Rekna stood by gazing at the group, suspicion clearly evident in his four dark eyes.

"What if I were to tell you that the Xindi recently launched a sneak attack against my homeworld?" Archer said to Trahve, his words dripping with acid even as he smiled and nodded in Rekna's direction. "Suppose I also told you that they murdered more than seven million of my people with a particle-beam weapon?

"What if I went on to tell you that the Xindi are

now building a far more powerful version of that weapon—and that they plan to use it to finish off the *rest* of my race?"

Archer released his grip on Trahve's shoulders, then slapped him convivially across the back. The alien blanched, all of his worldly insouciance abruptly vanishing as he sat heavily, dropping backward into his seat.

"You say the Xindi contact you when they have work to offer you," Archer said, leaning forward, an intent, earnest expression on his face. "When was the last time you heard from them?"

Trahve seemed to be recovering his composure, though he still seemed far less confident than he had before; the revelation about the Xindi attack on Earth seemed to have blindsided him. He nodded and said, "Very recently, Captain. Maybe four—no, five local daycycles ago." That seemed to square with Grakka's account, Reed realized; perhaps Trahve wasn't an inveterate liar after all.

Perhaps.

"So they've given you a new assignment?" Archer asked.

After a moment's hesitation, Trahve said, "Yes."

"Can I assume you've made plans to meet with them again soon?"

Trahve nodded again, though his eyes were darting to and fro like trapped animals. Reed surmised that his employers were rather unforgiving of blatant security breaches.

Well, that's his *problem,* Reed thought, glancing down again at his padd. The display still showed a diagram of the results of the chemical trace scan he had run on Trahve earlier. The complex, snowflake-like energy pattern was clearly unusual, like nothing produced by Starfleet technology. And yet it also looked strangely familiar.

Reed suddenly remembered exactly where he'd seen it before. An almost volcanic wave of outrage surged deep within his chest.

"You're going to take us to them," Archer said, his gaze boring into Trahve like a pair of mining lasers.

Trahve looked mortified, and lost even more of his scant coloration. "I can't do that, Captain. I already told you, I don't know where their homeworld is located."

"Assuming that's true, you can still take us to your Xindi business contacts," Reed said. He glanced again at the energy signature displayed on his padd, and a growing sense of certainty raced to catch up with his escalating anger. The two emotions seemed to fuel one another. "*They'll* know how to reach the Xindi homeworld."

"I can't simply . . . sell out my clients like that," Trahve said, looking distressed. "Discretion is very important to them."

Archer's smile was quickly becoming a transparently angry rictus. "The Xindi committed a massacre on my homeworld, Trahve. I can't afford to let them launch any further attacks."

"I don't know anything about any of that, Captain."

"Captain, he's lying," Reed said. "I believe he knows a good deal more about the Xindi attack than he's admitted to."

Archer turned toward Reed. "Why do you say that, Malcolm?"

Reed pushed the padd across the tabletop toward Archer. "This is from a chemical trace scan of Trahve's clothing, Captain. Look at this energy signature. Do you recognize it?"

Archer studied the diagram on the padd for a lengthy moment. His eyes widened in surprise, then narrowed again in barely restrained fury.

Trahve stood, pushing the table over and knocking Reed's chair onto its side, along with Reed, who landed in a winded heap on the dust-caked floor, along with his padd and scanner. Taking advantage of the group's collective surprise, Trahve leaped over the scattered furniture and made for the rear of the tavern as though the entire Andorian Imperial Guard were right on his heels.

Rekna approached menacingly as O'Neill helped Reed get to his feet; Reed could see that Chandra was already chasing after the fleeing alien, and Reed quickly moved to follow.

"Let him go!" Archer said, grabbing Reed's elbow. A few meters ahead, Chandra stopped and stared in shock at the captain. Trahve ran for the exit like a man being chased by the Furies.

"What?" Reed felt every bit as incredulous as Chandra looked.

Archer produced a fair approximation of Trahve's carefree grin. "You heard me."

Rounding the corner and cutting across the alley, Trahve thought his lungs might burst at any moment; he was unaccustomed to such bursts of extreme exertion, especially in the relatively high gravity of this thrice-cursed frontier world. He spared a moment to glance over his shoulder. No sign of pursuit.

He grinned as he caught his breath. These strangers were evidently neither as dangerous nor as competent as they seemed to fancy themselves. There was apparently little reason to take them seriously.

But had they really been telling him the truth about the mass fatalities their home planet had sustained, allegedly because of the Xindi?

There was no time now to worry about such things, however. He had a ship to get ready for launch, and he knew it would be prudent to do so quickly.

But if he were to turn up alone to meet with his Xindi contacts, what would he have to say for himself? He decided he'd simply explain that the humans must have gotten sidetracked searching one of the smaller spaceport towns. Or perhaps they would simply follow him to the appointed place in one of their own vessels.

Trahve ducked around another corner and the back side of Hangar 43 immediately hove into view. Moments later, the automated retinal scanner verified both his identity and his clearance credentials, and admitted him to the secure portion of the launch bay, where his small vessel patiently awaited his return.

Seven million people. Did the Xindi *really* murder seven million people?

And were they actually planning on doing it again? Or were they simply acting to protect themselves against these humans? Archer and his people did, after all, appear to be capable of a great deal of aggression.

He continued to ponder these questions as he crossed the hangar and approached his ship. It wasn't until he used his handheld remote unit to open the hatch and lower the gangplank that he began to wonder what had happened to the security guards the spaceport usually posted at the hangar entrances.

Just as he reached the gangplank, a quartet of gray-uniformed figures armed with rifles landed all around him, lowering themselves swiftly on long cables suspended from the hangar's vaulted ceiling.

Trahve raised his hands in a gesture of surrender as one of the troopers pulled something from Trahve's back. The transmitter that Archer must have placed there, he realized belatedly.

He smiled appreciatively as they bound his wrists and marched him aboard his own ship. "You people are more accomplished than I gave you credit for." He doubted whether they had understood his words, since they were holding weapons rather than translation gear.

Seven *million* people?

Trahve tried to put all such doubts out of his mind. He told himself yet again that everything would work out just fine, so long as everything continued going exactly to plan.

"I want at least one MACO guarding the gangplank," Archer said, taking care to use his most no-nonsense command voice. With the entire team now aboard La'an Trahve's captured vessel—which was still standing on its landing legs in the hangar, and thus was extremely vulnerable—there could be no question as to who was in charge of this mission. "Just in case the spaceport security personnel start getting curious about what's going on aboard this ship."

Hayes nodded, first to Archer, then to Kemper and Money, both of whom immediately disappeared into the still-open gangway of Trahve's ship. Corporal Peruzzi remained standing a short distance from Hayes, keeping vigil over the cramped cockpit.

Archer's feelings of grief and rage were every bit as strong now as they had been back in March. Tamping down his emotions with a ferocity that he suspected T'Pol would applaud, he accepted the padd that Malcolm was holding out to him. Then he walked past Hayes, O'Neill, Chandra, and Peruzzi and took a seat beside Trahve in the alien courier's own cockpit.

Archer raised the padd so that the manacled Trahve could see its display easily.

"We found this energy pattern in the remains of the weapon the Xindi sent against our planet," Archer said, holding the padd like an indictment. "My tactical officer just found traces of the same energy signature on your clothing.

"Your courier duties wouldn't happen to take you anywhere near a facility where the Xindi are building a large-scale particle-beam weapon, would it?"

Trahve merely sighed, slumped in his chair, and stared down at the deck.

Archer thought the man's guilty-looking silence spoke volumes.

SIX

Enterprise NX-01

IF WE FIND THIS, *we find the Xindi.*

As she looked through the scanner at the elegant, snowflake-like energy pattern, T'Pol suddenly became acutely aware of the preternatural silence that had descended upon the bridge. The quiet wasn't the result of inadequate staffing—despite the day's anomaly-related trauma, she had filled all the bridge positions handily—but had been caused instead by a simple lack of noise. None of the crew members present were conversing, and even the regular pings and beeps produced by the ship's computers, sensors, and various other systems seemed to have paused as though in contemplation.

T'Pol appreciated the stillness, which gave her study of the energy signature an almost meditative quality. But she also knew that eventually this transient moment of serenity would end, and the ongoing press of ship's business would whisk her back into the unending babble of starship life, in this environment dominated by overly emotional and sometimes too-gregarious humans.

Not fifteen minutes had passed before T'Pol's prediction came true.

"Sub-Commander T'Pol," Ensign Felipe Marcel said from the combined helm-navigation station located behind her, in the forward section of the bridge's center. "I think we've found something."

T'Pol crossed over to his station. "Would you care to be more specific, Ensign Marcel?"

He pointed to the numbers that were scrolling across the screens atop his station. "It's from one of our long-range probes. Telemetry is showing significant residual quantities of the Xindi compound. A highly refined isotope, to be specific. It lies along a straight line that might be light-years long. My guess is that it's an exhaust trail from a warp-driven ship."

But *whose* ship?

T'Pol glanced back at her own console display, where the snowflake pattern—the energy signature of the fuel residue found with the wreckage of the first Xindi weapon on Earth—continued its slow rotation. Turning forward again, she studied the data that were scrolling across the ensign's station. There could be no doubt that the probes had discovered more of the same substance, and that it formed a trail—a trail that might lead to a Xindi base, or perhaps even straight to the Xindi homeworld itself.

But she could also see that the trail might not be easy to follow, according to the coordinate data. "The Xindi isotope trail doesn't appear to intersect either with Kaletoo, or with the trajectory of the captain's shuttlepod." *Enterprise* had taken up a long orbit about Kaletoo's distance-dimmed sun, hiding her presence in the far reaches of the system's Kuiper belt; the apparent Xindi trail seemed to begin much farther into the depths of interstellar space.

"No, ma'am," Marcel said. "The probe picked up the trail nearly six light-hours from our present position. *Enterprise* could be there in minutes." The ensign gazed up at her expectantly. "Should I lay in a course?"

"Not yet," T'Pol said, having no desire to scuttle the entire Xindi hunt by leading *Enterprise* right into the jaws of a trap.

As she considered her course of action, T'Pol crossed over near the captain's chair, though she didn't sit in it. She preferred to stand when she had command of the bridge; taking the captain's chair always felt a bit presumptuous, regardless of her rank or position.

"Is the chemical signature remaining constant?" she asked, addressing Marcel.

Marcel studied his screen for another moment. "No, ma'am. It appears to be diffusing and fading, just like the exhaust trail of a moving vessel."

A Xindi vessel, T'Pol thought. *Unless it turns out to belong to a different civilization that happens to use precisely the same propulsion method.* Though she found herself doubting the latter scenario, T'Pol had to concede that it was certainly possible. Even after having spent more than twelve weeks in the Expanse, *Enterprise*'s crew still knew precious little both about the region and about the many races that traveled it. They didn't even know what the Xindi called the compound they were seeking, much less whether any other starfaring species utilized it. For all she knew, the energy signature that the probes had found could lead them to some vacationing family's pleasure yacht.

Instinct was not a trait that T'Pol was fond of considering; her Vulcan background told her that decisions should be based on logic and fact, and instinct was based on feelings and suppositions. But in this matter, she had little factual material to go on. And with the trail decaying, she had little time to gather more data.

Compounding the issue was her inability to discuss the matter with key members of the command staff. With Captain Archer, Lieutenant O'Neill, and Lieutenant Reed currently off-ship—and unavailable because of the com silence that Archer had ordered—as well as Tucker and Sato incapacitated, she had few options. Lieutenant Hess was in engineering, but she had her hands full with Tucker out of action, and Lieutenant Salvatore's astrophysical talents had proven disappointing of late. She resigned herself to making this decision all on her own.

T'Pol crossed over to the captain's chair and pressed a button on the armrest, opening a channel to a particular set of crew quarters. "Sub-Commander T'Pol to Ensign Mayweather."

A moment later, a voice came over the com system, though it didn't belong to Mayweather. *"Corporal Chang here, Sub-Commander. Mayweather is not here in our quarters right now. I'm not quite certain where he is."*

T'Pol raised an eyebrow. "Thank you, Corporal."

She toggled the comm off and turned to Crewman Baird at the communications console. "Crewman Baird, please locate Ensign Mayweather."

Baird's fingers tapped at his console, and he concentrated for a moment. "Ensign Mayweather is in Commander Tucker's berth, sir."

Curious, T'Pol thought. She adjusted the com controls again. "Sub-Commander T'Pol to Ensign Mayweather."

This time, after a few moments, she heard Travis's familiar voice, though he sounded tired. *"Mayweather here."*

"Ensign, please report to the command center."

"I'll be right there, Sub-Commander."

Curiosity flitted briefly through T'Pol's head yet again. *Why was Ensign Mayweather sleeping in Trip's quarters?*

"Charles Anthony Tucker, you march back in here!"

Trip cursed under his breath. He had almost made it out of the house without getting caught.

"What, Mom?"

Elaine Tucker stepped out from the kitchen area, her hands planted firmly on her hips. "Don't you 'What, Mom?' me. You know you're supposed to be taking care of your sister today. I have to take your father in for physical therapy."

"But Lizzie's old enough to keep herself entertained."

His mother looked exasperated. "She's eight. Honestly, Charles." She paused, glaring at him, her expression turning dark. "Sometimes I think you don't really care about her, or about anybody in our family. Sometimes I think you don't want any of us around."

Trip was stunned. "What?"

"Don't act so innocent," his mother said, waggling her index finger at him. "I know you'd rather go to the movies without her. But not today. I'm having a hard enough time without having to hear her wail like a banshee just because you abandoned her."

"I didn't *abandon* her, Mom. I just wanted to go to the theater alone," Trip said. His little sister came around the corner, looking forlorn, her brown eyes large and pleading.

His mother walked past him, talking as she went. "Just deal with your responsibilities, Charles. How do you expect to make it through engineering school or astronaut training if you can't even handle your baby sister?"

Trip looked back at Elizabeth, to tell her to get ready, but she was gone, as was the back half of the house. In its place was a huge, smoking chasm. He could smell the air now, choking him, full of char and sulfur and ozone. Coughing, he called out. "Lizzie?"

"I'm right here," she said, from behind him. "What's wrong?"

He turned to look, and saw that they were both already standing in line at the old revival movie house. Elizabeth was in her favorite red jacket, the one decorated with lion cubs, and her long hair was braided on either side of her face.

"Nothing's wrong," he said, not knowing how they'd gotten there, or even what film they were about to see. "I just lost sight of you for a moment."

"Well, I'm right behind you, dummy," she said, speaking in a singsong cadence. Suddenly, they were sitting side by side inside the theater, Lizzie's gangly body almost lost in the plush, retro upholstery. "It's not like when I grow up and you go off into space and leave me to be exterminated by those aliens."

He turned in his seat and faced her as the lights went down and the movie started. "Lizzie, what made you say that?"

An angry man sitting in the row in front of them leaned over the back of his seat, putting a finger to his lips. "Shhhhhhhhh! Some of us are trying to watch the movie."

"Sorry," Trip said, hunkering down in embarrassment as the movie progressed. It was an action film of comparatively recent vintage, made during the brief 2-D revival of the 2120s.

"I don't like this movie," Elizabeth whispered some time later, speaking around mouthfuls from the bucket of popcorn she kept braced between her bony knees. "There are too many people getting hurt. It scares me."

Trip looked up at the screen. The flickering light of the vintage projector showed a group of men and women clad in dark steel-blue jumpsuits, shooting lasers back and forth at blue-skinned aliens with antennae. *Andorians,* Trip thought. He recognized them. He couldn't quite remember the plot of the film, or even what it was called, but he recognized most of those people in the jumpsuits.

Suddenly, a new alien came onto the screen. It was a tall and scaly reptilian with armor and spikes. It seemed to face the audience and look out at them, and Trip experienced a visceral sensation of belly-clenching dread. The creature stalked forward toward them, its head getting larger and larger as it approached.

Finally, it opened its mouth and roared, sending a gout of very hot, very real flame out of the movie screen and into the theater. Trip ducked to the side, rolling onto the floor between the seats, feeling the heat roil over him. He heard screams and sickening popping sounds, and then, utter silence.

It was only then that he remembered his sister. Quickly struggling to get up, he found that the floor was hot and sticky, clutching at his feet like a puddle of quicksand. At first he thought it was gum, but it seemed more like black tar sucking him downward as though he were a Cretaceous dinosaur. Using every ounce of strength he could summon, Trip pulled himself up out of the mire, and back onto the nearest empty seat.

He looked next to him, but found the adjacent seat empty; there was no trace of his sister, or her remains. "Lizzie!" he yelled out as he surveyed the rest of the theater, most of which lay behind him. He could neither see nor hear anyone else. The rows of seats went on for as far as he could see, their backs illuminated by the flickering blue light of the projector. They reminded him of a vast graveyard full of identical tombstones, ranks of monuments set up to commemorate centuries of wars, and the soldiers who fought and died in conflicts initiated by others.

He turned back around and looked at the movie screen. The reptilian alien, the Andorians, and the jumpsuit-clad people were all gone now, both replaced by a tranquil scene of a woman lying on the neatly manicured grass of a storybook meadow.

She had a large art pad with her, and as the camera slowly zoomed in on her, he could see that she was drawing a building. The design was fantastic, combining sleek modern designs with Old World eighteenth-century European architecture.

A shadow fell across the girl, and she turned and looked up. She was pretty, with long, free-flowing, blond hair, cut to flat-bottomed bangs above her wide, brown eyes. A man crouched into the frame, handing her a glass of yellow liquid in which ice cubes clinked.

"Thought you might like some lemonade," the man said.

"Why, thank you," the woman said, and Trip suddenly realized it was Elizabeth, all grown up now. *But she's still a little girl,* he thought, still caught up in the absurd logic of his dream. *And we came here together to see a movie. And she was scared about . . . something.*

"So, when are you gonna tell your family?"

Elizabeth held up her hand, looking at the engagement ring on it, almost as if appraising it. "I dunno. When I finally decide it's real, I suppose." She grinned up at the man then, her face glowing. "I want to tell Trip, but he's off in space somewhere. Probably on some secret mission."

"You think he'll come to the wedding if we give him enough notice?" the man asked.

Her expression suddenly becoming serious, Elizabeth turned her face further upward, her gaze pointed toward the skies. "Maybe. It's hard to say. He's a pretty busy guy, thanks to Starfleet. Doesn't even have the time to save my life."

And in an instant, a fire from above engulfed Elizabeth and the grass and the drawing and the lemonade and the man and everything around them.

In an instant, all that was left was a smoking chasm that smelled of char and sulfur and ozone.

Trip could feel hot tears sliding down his cheeks as he reached out for his sister. But his hands began to vibrate, and he could feel himself shaking so badly that he felt as if his very body would dissipate and drift away, like the clouds of smoke that had wafted over the huge wound the Xindi weapon had inflicted on his home planet. His hometown.

And as the blackness and stench and shivers finally overwhelmed him, he heard her voice again, accusing and hurt:

"You'll never see me again, Trip."

"I apologize for disturbing your rest, Ensign Mayweather," T'Pol said. "You *were* resting, weren't you?"

Travis Mayweather tried to maintain his composure, but he was too tired to be certain he was succeeding. And the unfamiliar surroundings—specifically the state-of-the-art, monitor-screen-festooned command center that Starfleet had recently installed in what had formerly been B deck's storage bay for conduit housings—were anything but soothing.

"Yes, ma'am," Mayweather said with a nervous smile. "Was there something else I was supposed to be doing?"

T'Pol tilted her head, clearly not amused. "You were in Commander Tucker's quarters when I summoned you. Since he is incapacitated in sickbay, I have no idea what you were doing."

Mayweather could see that his attempt at easygoing charm had fallen completely flat. *Am I in some sort of trouble?* he wondered, though he was at a loss as to why that might be. By his own reckoning, he had been off duty when the sub-commander had called him to the bridge, and his next shift wasn't due to start for another several hours.

Then he realized that his use of Commander Tucker's quarters was the issue.

"I didn't think Commander Tucker would mind me using his quarters for a little while, and neither did the quartermaster," he said, and immediately winced at how callous he must have sounded; after all, he sincerely hoped that Commander Tucker, Ensign Sato, and everyone else who'd been affected by the latest spatial anomaly would make speedy recoveries.

In a more formal tone, he added, "Sub-Commander, because of some recent MACO duty-roster changes, my own sleeping quarters were . . . temporarily unavailable."

T'Pol nodded. "I see." It occurred to Mayweather that she must have known about every reassignment of shipboard living space that the quartermaster made. Perhaps she merely enjoyed seeing human junior officers squirm. "Do you feel you've had enough rest to be effective on an off-ship mission, Ensign?"

That question was surprising enough to jolt Mayweather to full alertness. "What? A mission? You bet. I mean, yes, ma'am." Not only would an off-ship assignment break up the monotony of the last several interminable weeks, but it just might put millions of kilometers between himself and Corporal Chang's oppressive presence in Mayweather's personal living space.

Before T'Pol could begin explaining the details of the upcoming assignment, the hatchway slid open and a quartet of parade-ground-ready MACOs stepped into the command center. As they turned, Mayweather felt his mounting excitement drop a notch. Corporal Chang was one of the four, along with Corporals Guitierrez and McCammon and Private Eby.

"Good evening," T'Pol said by way of greeting. "I was just about to discuss the mission with Ensign Mayweather."

"We're ready for the mission briefing, ma'am," Chang said crisply. Travis noted that the MACO hadn't even bothered to acknowledge his presence. Might that mean that he had gotten on Chang's nerves as much as Chang vexed him? He allowed himself to hope so.

"One of our long-range probes has found a quickly dissipating chemical trail that contains significant residual quantities of the fuel compound found on Earth in the wreckage of the first Xindi particle weapon." T'Pol pointed to a data graph displayed on the command center's master systems display console. "While it is certainly possible that non-Xindi ships might use this compound, given that it is one of the few leads that we have found thus far, we would be remiss not to follow up on it."

"I agree," Mayweather said, leaning against one of the room's many bulkhead-mounted consoles.

T'Pol looked at him blankly. *Stupid. Why the hell did I say that?* He resolved to keep his mouth shut for the rest of the briefing, to avoid looking any more foolish in front of Chang than he did already.

"Because the captain has ordered com silence, we cannot contact him while he and his team are off the ship," T'Pol said, continuing to address the entire group as if she'd never been interrupted. "Nor can we gauge the success of his mission so far. I have decided that it would be injudicious to divert *Enterprise* from her present position, in the event that the captain and his team break com silence to request backup, supplies, or medical attention."

She looked Mayweather straight in the eye. "Thus, I am assigning you to investigate this matter, Ensign Mayweather. Your mission is to determine whether this trail leads to the Xindi, and to take whatever action is most appropriate, prudent, and logical."

Mayweather grinned. Even though piloting the ship was one of his greatest joys, he never felt that he spent enough time participating on piloting assignments away from *Enterprise*. He could feel his pulse already starting to race. A reconnaissance mission could be just the diversion he needed from his conflicts with Chang.

T'Pol turned to address just the MACOs. "Because this mission may involve contact—or perhaps even combat—with whoever is aboard the vessel that left the chemical trail, I'm assigning all four of you to accompany Ensign Mayweather. I have just consulted with Corporal McKenzie, whom Major Hayes has placed in temporary charge of the MACO company during his absence, and she concurs with my personnel recommendation."

No! Mayweather's feelings of elation dropped away suddenly and precipitously, like an asteroid colliding with a planet. Chang *will be going with me? There's nearly three dozen other MACOs aboard* Enterprise *right now who could have taken his place, and T'Pol decides to cram me into a shuttlepod with* Chang? His mind raced for a legitimate reason to ask T'Pol to leave the strutting MACO behind, but in the scant moments he knew remained in the briefing, he couldn't think of any objection that the Vulcan might consider logical.

"Understood, Sub-Commander," Chang said a moment later, bowing his head and smiling slightly. "We'll make certain to return Mayweather *and* the shuttle in full working order. And we'll get all the information possible about the Xindi ship, or whatever it is that we're chasing."

"Thank you, Corporal," T'Pol said, then turned to face Mayweather. "Can you be ready to depart in thirty minutes?"

Mayweather was about to respond, but Chang preempted him by speaking up first. "We'll be ready in *twenty* minutes, ma'am."

"Me, too," Mayweather said, braving a smile. Inwardly, he was seething.

As the MACOs turned to leave, Mayweather once again considered appealing to T'Pol to find some reason to reassign Chang, but thought better of it. *Sometimes you just have to suck it up, Travis,* he thought. *Maybe he'll be too busy cleaning his weapons to get really annoying. Besides, what's the worst thing Chang could do on this mission?*

He wasn't sure he really wanted an answer to that question, though he was determined to remain prepared for any threat, whether from Xindi marauders or cocky MACO sharks.

SEVEN

Kaletoo

"I WANT YOU TO GET back to the shuttlepod as soon as possible, D.O.," Archer said to Lieutenant O'Neill. They both stood just inside La'an Trahve's captured ship, near the interior hatch. The cavernous hangar beyond remained deserted.

For the moment, Hayes thought, anxious to get off the planet and under way.

The MACO commander nodded silently as the captain calmly issued his orders. He thought Archer's plan made perfect sense; keeping the entire landing party concentrated aboard the captured alien vessel could well put the mission in jeopardy. O'Neill, however, evidently had a very different take on the matter—and was also displaying the poor judgment to speak up about it.

"Respectfully, Captain, are you sure that splitting the team up is such a good idea?" O'Neill said.

"I understand your concern, Lieutenant," Archer

said. "But somebody has to get back to *Enterprise* to make a full report in the event the rest of us end up on a collision course with one of those 'worst-case scenarios' you're so fond of warning the junior officers about."

Lieutenant Reed nodded soberly. "I agree completely."

O'Neill gave the captain and Reed a smile that conveyed little happiness. "So on my first away mission ever, you're sending me back to stay with the wagon. Why not put Ensign Chandra on that job instead?"

Hayes glanced at Chandra, and noted that he looked unhappy as well. The ensign, like O'Neill and most of the others who crewed the NX-01, evinced not nearly enough discipline under fire, in Hayes's opinion. Not for the first time, the MACO leader wondered whether Archer's Starfleet crew, despite its collective expertise, was being hampered by its own lack of focus on the chain of command. How could they hope to deal with the Xindi while such basic personnel breakdowns occurred so routinely?

Archer glared at O'Neill. When he spoke, his tone was stern, almost admonishing. "Right now the shuttlepod is our vulnerable flank, D.O., and I want it protected. Our cooperative Mister Grakka might have warned Trahve that we were coming, so there's no telling who else he might have talked to, or what whoever he spoke with might be planning to do to us."

"I understand, sir," O'Neill said, though she still looked mightily displeased about her redeployment.

"But I agree that you shouldn't go alone," Archer said. "Ensign Chandra."

Chandra snapped to attention. "Sir?"

"I'd like you to accompany Lieutenant O'Neill to the shuttlepod."

Chandra's dark eyes grew huge with what Hayes could only interpret as apprehension. But he really couldn't blame the man. "Aye, Captain," Chandra said.

Hayes found that Chandra's fear affected him on an almost instinctual level. "With your permission, sir," he said to the captain, "I could send Corporal Peruzzi along with them. Just in case."

Archer appeared to weigh the main mission objective's need for firepower against the possibility that O'Neill and Chandra might run into trouble that they couldn't readily handle without MACO cover.

"It makes sense, Captain," Reed told Archer, apparently surprised to find himself in agreement with Hayes.

Hayes had to admit to himself that he, too, was surprised—and more than a little suspicious of finding himself on the same page with a man who had always seemed more concerned with protecting his own job than with accomplishing the mission.

"All right, Major," the captain said at length. "You, Kemper, and Money should be able to supply all the muscle we'll need after we get under way."

Hayes grinned at Archer. *"Semper Invictus,"* he said.

The MACO leader saw that O'Neill was aiming a high-amplitude scowl directly at him; just for a moment, he was absurdly tempted to dive for cover behind one of Trahve's passenger seats. "Thank you, Major, but I think Chandra and I are capable of hiking back to the shuttlepod without a babysitter," she said frostily.

Before Hayes could respond, Archer spoke in a tone that both soothed and chided. "It's just a precaution, D.O."

"Don't worry," Hayes said. "I promise that Peruzzi won't get in your way. Unless she has to." *Which I know she'll do in a heartbeat,* he thought, *if your party encounters anything half as scary as you are when you're pissed off.*

"I understand, Captain," she said, evidently beginning to get hold of her emotions, though she was still clearly reluctant to take a side trip away from the main mission force.

"It's too bad Trahve's ship isn't equipped with a transporter," Chandra said, scratching his chin. "Couldn't we make a quick detour to the shuttlepod *first?* Just drop all of us off using *this* ship before getting under way."

"Too risky," Reed said, shaking his head. "We have to get Trahve's vessel off the planet immediately, before the spaceport authorities figure out that somebody's hijacked it."

Hayes considered the security guards he and Kemper had knocked unconscious and concealed in a large nearby tool locker after they had tracked Trahve to this particular hangar; those men couldn't be counted on to remain quiet and undetected for more than another hour at the most.

"Are you sure you're going to be all right, D.O.?" Archer asked O'Neill, lines of worry corrugating his brow. It occurred to Hayes then that he would never have thought to ask any of his people that question; the notion that, say, Corporal McKenzie might not be able to handle herself solo on a simple five-klick hike, even in a desiccated hellhole like this one, simply would not have crossed his mind.

"I'll be fine, Captain," O'Neill said, now regarding the captain with a deferential expression. "I'm not the one who's about to fly straight into the proverbial lion's den. Have a safe journey, sir."

Archer smiled gently. "Thanks, D.O."

"And if you let yourself get eaten by the proverbial lion, you and I are going to have *words,* believe you me. Sir." She grinned.

Archer grinned in response as the lieutenant turned and stepped into the gangway, then vanished from sight. Corporal Peruzzi and Ensign Chandra quickly followed.

"Seeing the mood she's in, I almost feel sorry for any unsavory characters they might run into on their way back to the shuttlepod," Reed said quietly a few seconds later, a rueful smile crossing his lined face.

Archer nodded grimly. "Right now, I think we'd be better off paying some attention to one of those unsavory characters. . . ." The captain trailed off as he gestured toward the fore section of the ship.

Hayes followed the Starfleet pair forward into the small vessel's crowded cockpit, where a sullen-looking La'an Trahve sat manacled in one of the chairs that fronted a tertiary control console.

Sergeant Kemper, his phase rifle at the ready, stood watching the prisoner with a raptor's attentiveness, silently discouraging him from trying to touch any of the console's myriad toggles, buttons, and switches.

"Pirates," Trahve said, his voice still echoing slightly through the Starfleet language-translation gear Chandra had left running atop one of the consoles. "You're all nothing but common pirates, the lot of you. You realize that, don't you?"

Archer approached him very closely, his craggy features taking on an almost mournful cast.

"We're only doing what we have to do, Mister Trahve. Now you're going to help us get this ship into space—discreetly."

Standing behind Trahve and Archer—who were seated, respectively, in the pilot's and copilot's seats—Reed's eyes were drawn to the forward cockpit port. He heaved a quiet sigh of relief as bright blue sky gave way to blackness, and the sere brown world dropped away until the curvature of its daylit limb was clearly visible.

Trahve's vessel had made it to orbit, and there was no pursuit in evidence. So far.

Despite the extremely attentive presence of the very armed and vigilant Major Hayes, Sergeant Kemper, and Private Money, Reed was still more than a little surprised that Trahve had answered Archer's questions about the ship's systems and instrumentation as forthrightly as he had; after all, he might just as easily have tried to trick the captain into setting off some sort of cockpit alarm, or triggered a hidden security system before the ship had even cleared the spaceport hangar. Instead, he had simply walked them through the spaceport clearance procedures, including communications with the local traffic-control authorities (such as they were), as though they were paying passengers.

But he might still have a trick or two up his sleeve,

Reed cautioned himself. He knew it wouldn't do to let his guard down around the alien courier, even for a moment. Trahve surely had an agenda of his own, and that agenda most assuredly did not include saving the people of Earth from destruction at the hands of the Xindi.

Archer turned his chair toward Trahve. "We're free and clear to maneuver, Mister Trahve. All we need now are the coordinates of the facility where the Xindi are building their particle-beam weapon."

Trahve's normally bland face now looked drawn and haggard. "Look, I know you claim to have some sort of debt of honor to settle with the Xindi. But how do I know you've been telling me the truth about them? How do I know they've really attacked your homeworld?"

"Do you really think we'd cross fifty light-years and start scouring a forsaken waste like the Delphic Expanse as some sort of *prank?*" Archer said, the impatience beneath his words becoming clearly audible.

"I truly don't know what you would do, if you really believed it to be necessary," Trahve said, shaking his head. "Or if you were desperate enough. But I *do* know that my Xindi employers won't be very happy with me if I start leading perfect strangers to their secret construction sites."

Reed sighed. Just as he had surmised would happen, Trahve's easy cooperation seemed to be coming to an abrupt dead end. *Sometimes I really, really hate being right so much of the time,* he thought.

"You'll notice that the Xindi aren't the ones standing here with their weapons locked and loaded,"

Hayes said, raising the barrel of his own phase rifle for emphasis. Kemper did likewise, taking steady, pitiless aim at Trahve's head. Since both MACOs stood only a little more than a meter from their target, the likelihood of their shots going astray was negligible.

In spite of himself, Reed was impressed by Trahve's coolness under pressure, though he could have done without the courier's infuriatingly insouciant smile.

"Shooting me won't help you find what you're looking for, gentlemen," Trahve said. "Even if your weapons have a stun setting. Besides, even stunner fire might damage the flight-control console, or compromise one of the forward windows and space us all. *Then* where would you be?"

He's right, Reed thought, his own sense of frustration steadily rising. *If he won't cooperate, there won't be a lot of good options open to us.*

"The Xindi slaughtered millions of innocent people on my planet," Archer said, his eyes narrowed, his body as taut as a bowstring. He gripped the headrest of a nearby chair so hard that Reed thought it might snap in half. "And they're planning to wipe out billions more. Even as we speak."

"I have only your word on that, Captain," Trahve said, recoiling slightly from the captain's barely constrained rage.

"Everything you've told us about the Xindi so far supports our story," Reed said. "Do you really think we've been lying to you?"

Trahve shrugged. "Whether your story is true or not, it has nothing to do with me."

"Really?" Archer said. "Even if the work you do for the Xindi makes you their accomplice in an act of mass murder?"

Trahve's composure wavered momentarily; his winsome smile reappeared almost instantly, however, though Reed thought it looked more than a little forced.

"I'm just a courier trying to make a living in a quite nasty part of the galaxy, Captain," he said at length. "I don't know anything about any attack."

"Then you're about to get a crash course," Hayes said curtly. His rifle barrel remained pointed squarely at Trahve's head, as were the weapons of Kemper and Money.

"Talk to us, Trahve," Archer said. "Tell us whatever you know about the location of the Xindi weapon."

Trahve's smile crumbled again. Now he looked almost pitiful, a man who had been cornered and now faced a truly untenable Hobson's choice. "I can't, Captain. At best, the Xindi would never hire me again. At worst, they'd get annoyed enough with me to vaporize my ship, and me along with it."

Hayes raised his weapon so that the butt faced Trahve, and loomed menacingly over him. Reed realized all at once that the MACO was about to smash the alien across the face with it.

"Stand down, Major," Archer said a split second before the surprised Reed managed to find his voice.

Hayes lowered the weapon stock, but with clearly evident reluctance. Reed considered the instant dislike he had felt for this man from the moment he and the rest of the MACO force had first come aboard *Enterprise* months ago. He felt a curious blending of satisfaction and disappointment as he realized that his initial instincts had been correct. Being from a family with a centuries-old naval tradition, Reed understood the ancient, ingrained rivalry between sailors and marines—"squids" and "sharks," in ancient naval parlance—whenever they were billeted together; now he wondered if the antipathy he felt toward Hayes was rooted in a much deeper, even more fundamental place.

"With respect, Captain, this prisoner is clearly going to require some additional persuasion," Hayes said in clipped, formal tones. Reed gathered that the man was quickly reaching the end of his limited fund of patience. Perhaps the last several weeks of enforced inactivity had taken more of a toll on the MACO leader than was immediately apparent. *Is Hayes bored and restless because he's such an obnoxious martinet?* Reed wondered silently, pondering the imponderable. *Or is he an obnoxious martinet because he's so bored and restless?*

"We don't know for a fact that he actually knows how to find the exact site where the Xindi are building their weapon," Archer said.

Reed nodded. "I had the same thought."

Hayes spared a dismissive glance at Reed before turning his hard gaze back upon Archer. "May I remind the captain of the trace energy signatures Lieutenant Reed found on the prisoner's clothing? And the images of Trahve and the Xindi we found back on Kaletoo?"

"He might have handled some of the weapon components on behalf of the Xindi," Reed said, feeling more than a little anger toward the MACO. "But we don't know for certain that he took them directly to the Xindi construction site. He could just as easily have delivered them to intermediaries. For all we really know, the delivery we saw him involved in on Kaletoo might have been the end of his contact with the Xindi."

Hayes turned back toward Reed. "Just whose side are you on, Lieutenant?"

"That's enough," Archer said to Hayes, his voice pitched in a low tone that Reed knew meant *Don't poke the bear.* Reed tried his best to suppress a triumphant smirk, though he suspected that he hadn't been entirely successful.

"Sir?" Hayes said, glowering at Archer, yet still deferential.

"At ease, Major," Archer continued. "You're probably right in assuming that this man knows a hell of a lot more than he's telling us."

Though cornered, Trahve apparently wasn't entirely cowed. "So you're further assuming that I know precisely where the Xindi are assembling this weapon that frightens you so?"

Archer smiled, but in a manner that suggested anything but benevolence. "Let's just say I'm assuming that you're the kind of man who goes out of his way to gather every piece of information that might conceivably turn out to be profitable to have."

"All right. Let's suppose I have the information you seek, and that I decide to divulge it. What sort of 'profit' are you offering me in exchange for it?" Trahve asked, his tone dripping with insolence.

"Maybe 'profit' isn't the best choice of words," Archer said, his gaze locking with that of the alien like a ship-to-ship grappling line. Then he turned toward Hayes and favored him with a silent but eloquent nod.

No! Reed thought, taking a single step toward Hayes.

But it was already too late. Responding to Archer's wordless signal, Hayes raised his rifle again and struck the manacled alien courier in the abdomen with the butt of his weapon. Trahve cried out in pain and surprise and slumped forward in his seat. Kemper kept him from sliding onto the deck, shoving him backward into his chair using one of his booted feet. The alien lay there, slumped and gasping.

"Captain!" Reed shouted. "Since when has inflicting torture become part of our mission profile?"

Archer whirled on Reed, his eyes ablaze. "If you know of a more efficient way to secure the prisoner's cooperation, Lieutenant, I'm ready to hear it."

Reed knew he was treading on very dangerous ground at the moment; he'd seen this very same look in the captain's eyes all too frequently these past dozen frustrating weeks.

But he felt he had to press on regardless. "This man still might not know where the weapon is being built, Captain. In fact, he might simply be a decoy, deliberately misinformed by the Xindi just to throw us off their trail." Reed recalled the bitter disappointment he'd felt several months earlier when he'd been similarly fooled, his efforts to free the captain from a Tellarite bounty hunter foiled by a piece of hardware designed to leave a false trail.

Hayes apparently wasn't having it. "But the chemical trace scans—"

"Only prove that he's been in contact with the

same material that powered the weapon the Xindi used in their first attack," Reed said tartly.

Hayes seemed none too pleased about being interrupted. "This man works for the enemy, Lieutenant. Why are you *defending* him?"

"If I'm defending *anything,* Major, it's simple decency. We still have to stand up for that, whether this man can help us find the Xindi or not."

"Not finding the Xindi is simply not an option, Malcolm," said the captain.

"I never suggested that it was, Captain. But using methods like this . . ." Reed trailed off, momentarily at a loss for words. "Frankly, it's beneath us, sir."

"You are out of line, *Lieutenant,*" Hayes said, holding his weapon in a death grip.

"I'll thank you to leave that to the captain's judgment, Major." *And you'd better hope you never find out just how much further "out of line" I'm capable of getting.*

"I have, Lieutenant. And the captain has judged that current circumstances warrant applying a degree of coercion."

"'Coercion.' That's a fine euphemism for a rifle butt in the belly. Where will you apply your 'coercion' next? To his skull?"

Hayes turned menacingly toward Trahve, who flinched in response. "He's in bed with the Xindi—the murderers of seven million human beings. We haven't come all this way to put on a high tea for our enemies' friends, Lieutenant."

Reed certainly understood the anger Hayes harbored toward the Xindi; he shared it, after all. But the brutality he had just witnessed had ignited within him another kind of anger that was perhaps every bit as primal.

"Overcoming the Xindi doesn't mean we need to become as *bad* as the Xindi," he said.

The cockpit fell silent then, except for the low moan that escaped from Trahve.

"Let's hope you're right about that, Malcolm," Archer said finally. "But overcoming the Xindi also means we're going to do whatever we have to do to find and destroy the Xindi weapon. For the sake of everyone on Earth. Is that clear, Lieutenant?"

"Yes, sir," Reed said, clenching his jaw tightly.

Reed saw that tears stood in the captain's eyes as he grabbed Trahve by the front of his shirt and hauled him roughly to his feet.

"No more. Stop. *Please.*"

Archer felt an enormous sense of relief sweep through his soul, though it only partially cleansed him of his mounting feelings of guilt and self-disgust. Still, he was thankful that he'd only had to strike Trahve four times—twice in the abdomen and twice across the face. Hayes, however, had hit the man at least that many times, while Kemper and Money stood by mutely, their weapons at the ready, their youthful faces carefully schooled into emotionless masks that T'Pol might have envied.

But T'Pol would probably do a much better job of keeping her hands from shaking, Archer thought as he glanced aftward, where Malcolm stood by watching. He looked pale and ill. *Disgusted with me.* Archer couldn't blame him.

"Why should we stop?" Archer said to the prisoner,

hoping that his own face was as inscrutable as those of the MACOs.

"Because I'll tell you what I know." His hands still manacled together before him, Trahve used his palms to wipe a trickle of orange-hued blood away from his chin.

"I'm listening," Archer said. *So you* do *know where the weapon is being built. Damn you straight to hell for forcing me to do this just to make you tell me that much.*

Trahve nodded. "Perhaps twenty daycycles ago, I delivered some electronic targeting components and fuel to the Xindi arboreals and insectoids."

Arboreals, Archer thought. *Insectoids.* The words sparked his curiosity on some very deep level. Thanks to a Xindi humanoid named Kessick, a former slave who had died from injuries sustained during an escape from the slave-labor camp on Tulaw, Archer knew that the Xindi were composed of five distinct intelligent species. He had never seen a Xindi arboreal or insectoid, and for a fleeting moment found himself wishing that he were on the kind of mission that would allow him the time to satisfy his natural curiosity about the unknown, to slake his inherent thirst for exploring and asking questions.

But no one knew for certain just how far away the Xindi were from completing and deploying their terror weapon. Therefore the weapon's location was the only question he could afford to pursue at the moment.

"You delivered fuel?" he said. "Let me guess: It was the same compound we found when we scanned your clothing, right?"

Trahve coughed and nodded. "I remember that

some of my Xindi associates mentioned that the fuel was supposed to power a new, large-scale piece of ordnance they were in the process of building."

"Go on."

"There's not much more to tell," Trahve said, chuckling ruefully around a bulbous, swollen, and bleeding lower lip. "It's not as though they showed me the blueprints to their weapon. In fact, they seemed downright secretive about certain aspects of it. Such as exactly where they intended to deploy it."

Archer nodded. *Maybe that's because it hadn't been completed yet. That might mean it's still vulnerable to a carefully executed surprise attack.*

"We already know where the Xindi intend to deploy their weapon," he said aloud. "What I need to find out is where the damned thing is *now*. I don't suppose they told you."

Trahve stared upward in an unfocused manner, apparently considering just how much he could afford to keep concealed even now. Hayes scowled and raised his rifle butt again. Nearby, Kemper and Money appeared to blanch slightly, as though their MACO discipline was grappling with their own private doubts about the "coercion" they were witnessing. Out of the corner of his eye, Archer saw Reed turn away in undisguised disgust.

Archer hated himself. But he had a mission, and knew he had to do whatever was required to accomplish it—no matter how ugly it might be. He closed his eyes briefly, opening them after his mind's eye greeted him with the gently accusing face of his late father. He had been a gentle yet determined man, a builder rather than a destroyer.

How would Henry Archer have dealt with a situation like this?

"Wait," Trahve said.

Hayes froze.

"Did your Xindi contacts reveal the weapon's exact location?" Archer asked, reiterating his question. Glancing down at the prisoner's manacles, he saw that dark orange blood had spattered across their metal rims. The blood was already drying, darkening into the precise color of shame.

"Not intentionally, I'm sure," said the alien, a little bit of his earlier carefree demeanor returning. "But I did take the liberty of doing a little . . . surreptitious investigating of my own a few turns later."

"Why would you do that if you're as concerned as you say you are about not offending the Xindi?" Reed asked from the aft part of the cockpit.

Archer suppressed a smile. Malcolm might have been concerned about how their prisoner was being treated, but that didn't mean he trusted him.

Trahve smiled again, around his bloody ruin of a lower lip. "It's as your captain said: I'm the kind of man who goes out of his way to gather all the potentially profitable information he can."

"Then let's have those coordinates," Archer said.

"I, ah, I'm afraid I can't quantify the location quite so specifically as that."

"He's playing with us again, Captain," Hayes said, brandishing his rifle butt once more.

Trahve's eyes grew large, fearful, and appeared utterly sincere; his gaze remained desperately fixed on Archer's. "There's a gravitic particle cloud located not very far from the Kaletoo system. The weapon construction facility is located near the cloud's center."

"'Gravitic particle cloud'?" Malcolm repeated. "That sounds rather dangerous."

Trahve chuckled. "Perhaps. If you don't know what you're doing, that is. Or if you lack a qualified guide—or a ship as well shielded as mine."

"It also sounds pretty damned vague," Hayes said, his gaze stony as he lifted his rifle yet again. Archer looked toward each of the MACOs and saw the question on all three grim faces.

He also saw that Hayes's mottled gray-and-white uniform tunic was spattered with livid orange blood. Archer decided then that he wanted no more blood spilled, unless doing so proved absolutely unavoidable. *If I really need to see alien blood, I can wait until we finally catch up to the Xindi themselves.*

Archer took a seat behind the conn console, right beside Trahve. He looked out the forward window into the infinite, star-bejeweled void that lay ahead. Somewhere in all of that unimaginably vast expanse lay the device with which the Xindi planned to lay waste the planet Earth.

"Dangerous and vague will have to do," he said, tentatively taking the controls and powering up the console in front of him. "Let's make best speed for the particle cloud."

"Shouldn't we send a coded message to *Enterprise?*" Reed asked. "Let them know where we're headed? We may end up needing their help, after all."

Archer considered Reed's question for a moment, then shook his head. "Unfortunately, we'd run the risk of alerting the Xindi that we're coming, Malcolm.

We're going to have to maintain com silence, at least until we know we've lost the element of surprise." He nodded toward Trahve. "Get us under way, Trahve."

Though still manacled, Trahve entered a course for the cloud with surprising grace and deftness. Archer noted that the cloud's boundaries appeared to lie only a few light-hours away, past the outskirts of the Kaletoo system's Kuiper belt. And within that cloud's boundaries lay . . . what?

"Ahead, full impulse," Archer said once the course showed as laid in on the navigation console. He was well aware that relying on Trahve's impulse engines rather than his warp drive would make the journey take a good deal longer. But with her warp drive powered down, Trahve's ship would also maintain a much lower profile on any Xindi scanners that might be pointed their way.

The impulse drive engaged at full power, and the brown orb of Kaletoo suddenly fell away into the midnight deeps. And as the bright pinpoints that lay before Trahve's vessel shifted toward blue, with those on the periphery lengthening into multicolored, relativistic silver and gold streaks, Archer allowed himself to hope that their quest to save humanity might finally be nearing its end.

Kaletoo

O'Neill watched anxiously as Ensign Chandra pointed his scanner toward the shuttlepod, which gleamed with the reflected light and heat of the merciless afternoon sun.

"There she is," Chandra said as Corporal Peruzzi, her rifle at the ready, approached the little auxiliary ship. "The shuttlepod is right where we left her."

"Everything seems to be in order inside the shuttlepod," Chandra said. "I can find no evidence of any attempt to gain entry, or to access her systems remotely."

O'Neill heaved a mental sigh of relief, took another swallow from her nearly depleted canteen, then wiped yet another muddy waterfall of sweat and dust away from her forehead. *I would kill for a two-minute shower,* she thought as she glanced again at Peruzzi, whose long, red-brown hair and fair skin looked all but immaculate. *Don't these MACOs even sweat?*

Placing the canteen back inside the pouch on her cloak, O'Neill opened her communicator and pointed it toward the shuttlepod. She heard the whirr of the servo motors as the gull-wing hatch on the small spacecraft's port side obediently opened. Chandra walked toward the beckoning hatchway.

At that precise moment, something large and heavy struck the tarmac directly behind O'Neill, startling her into nearly dropping her communicator. An unfamiliar voice shouted something guttural that she interpreted as "Don't move!" or something similar. Something unseen zinged loudly past her ear, and O'Neill heard a nearly simultaneous cry as well as the discharge of a phase pistol.

Peruzzi didn't hesitate, throwing herself onto the ground while barking a time-honored MACO curse. She rolled almost more quickly than O'Neill's eyes could follow, her phase rifle giving off several quick pulses in an eyeblink's time.

O'Neill wasted no time either, diving to the ground beside the ditch as she drew her own phase pistol and turned toward the intruder who had appeared so unexpectedly behind her, probably from one of the other small ships parked nearby. She fired as a weapon held by one of the attackers made a series of loud, staccato reports. An old-style metal projectile weapon, O'Neill decided as she returned fire through the smoke cloud that was swiftly rising around the site of the ambush.

The noise ceased abruptly and the smoke began slowly clearing. O'Neill could see now that there were four attackers—at least so far—each of whom had apparently hidden themselves earlier in or behind at least two other nearby spacecraft, or perhaps on the roof of the closest of the spaceport's outbuildings.

They could have been watching us ever since we landed here, she thought as she moved toward the bodies, kneeling beside the nearest supine form. *Either that, or our oh-so-cooperative Mister Grakka set up this ambush right after we left.* She paused to look quickly around the tarmac again, and noticed that the slug was currently nowhere in sight; she wondered if that fact attested to his guilt, or demonstrated his instinct for self-preservation. *Too bad I don't have time to find out.*

O'Neill removed the hood of the alien's cloak—he was male, and apparently barely out of adolescence—and checked his neck for a pulse. She noted with some relief that he seemed to be merely unconscious. The stun setting on a phase pistol, after all, was calibrated to human physiology; there was no way to guarantee its nonlethality to every unknown species.

O'Neill picked up the boy's long-barreled pistol—a small though surprisingly heavy hand cannon, really—then looked over at Peruzzi, who was busy disarming the other three bodies while checking them for signs of life. The MACO's single affirmative nod indicated that the rest of the hostiles had also been rendered safely insensate rather than killed outright.

These aren't warriors, O'Neill thought, feeling a surge of sympathy for these people despite the harrowing, if brief, firefight they had just provoked. *Whether they're working for Grakka or not, they're probably just desperate, poverty-stricken young people willing to risk everything to steal a ship so they can get off this hellhole. They must have known the shuttlepod wouldn't have been spaceworthy if they'd just blasted their way inside.*

As Corporal Peruzzi moved cautiously into the roadway in search of any other assailants that might be about, O'Neill reminded herself that these four weren't the only desperate people on the planet.

"Ensign Chandra," she said as she began ejecting several unspent metal shells from the unconscious alien's weapon. "Scan the area to see if there are any more hostiles hiding nearby. I don't want any more surprises before we get safely under way."

Hearing no response from Chandra, O'Neill dropped the now-empty weapon in the dust and turned back toward the shuttlepod.

Then she saw why Chandra hadn't replied. His limp body lay askew across the threshold of the shuttlepod's open port hatchway, and a blackened, bloody hole gaped in the young man's chest. His unseeing eyes were frozen in a mask of surprise, and his hand clutched a phase pistol. He had evidently opted to defend the shuttlepod rather than taking the more expedient route of using the shuttlepod's hatch for cover. O'Neill saw immediately that he was already far beyond the help of the vessel's emergency medical kits. Even Doctor Phlox, with all the resources of *Enterprise*'s state-of-the-art sickbay at his disposal, probably couldn't have saved him.

Dammit! "Corporal, we're getting out of here. *Now!*"

O'Neill felt simultaneously pained and numb, as though she had just received a crippling body blow. As she and Peruzzi carried Chandra's corpse all the way into the shuttlepod, O'Neill was seized by a nearly irresistible urge to shout imprecations at the corporal. She somehow managed to restrain herself as they carefully laid the dead man onto the deck behind the cockpit.

But she couldn't suppress the hard, cold glare she cast at Peruzzi. *If you MACOs were anywhere near as good as your rep, we wouldn't have just got done carrying Ravi's corpse.*

Then O'Neill saw the stunned, haunted look in Peruzzi's eyes, and instantly hated herself.

Because it was obvious to her that the young MACO was having the very same thought.

EIGHT

Shuttlepod Two

"SO, WITH ONE HOVER engine down, we couldn't outrace the Blagees anymore," Corporal David McCammon said. "That's when I pulled out all the tricks they *don't* teach you in combat flight training."

"Officially, anyhow," Corporal Hideaki Chang said, grinning at the others sitting in the back of the shuttlepod. It had been about three hours since they had departed from *Enterprise*'s Launch Bay 2, and while they had started out completely STRAC—Skilled, Tough, and Ready Around the Clock—with four hours or so more to go before they reached their destination they had relaxed into casual mode and had finally yielded to the urge to start telling one another "war stories." Chang had heard McCammon recount this same tale to others at least two dozen previous times, and like the anecdotes of many of the other MACOs he knew, this story had grown ever-so-slightly bigger and bolder with each subsequent telling.

"I'll bite," Private Colin Eby said, leaning forward, his blue-gray eyes sparkling. He was one of the newbies in Chang's platoon, fresh out of basic before he passed muster in the MACOs and subsequently joined the Xindi hunt aboard *Enterprise*. "*What* tricks?"

"Stop and drop," McCammon said, his lips curved into a roguish smile beneath his graying mustache. "After making sure our harnesses were secured, I hit reverse and cut power to the grav plating about a nanosecond later. We stopped so fast, it was like slamming into a wall. Then we fell straight down." He gestured with his hand, pantomiming a falling hovercraft. "Our Blagee pursuers shot right past us before they had time to realize what had happened. Their tail gunners couldn't get us in their sights because our sudden vector change had forced their weapons locks into starting another random search-pattern cycle."

"Damn," Eby said, an envious smile on his youthful face. "You didn't burn out your one good engine with that stunt?"

"Well, there was a tense moment or two after we went into freefall through the fog below us, and we knew that a rock-hard ocean surface was rushing up to meet us," McCammon said. "My copilot couldn't get the propulsion system back on-line, but eventually we jumped that baby back to life."

Corporal Selma Guitierrez winced and turned away.

Chang had noticed her distracted behavior ever since they'd both reported for duty in the launch bay. He leaned toward her, concerned, his voice lowered. "What's the matter?"

Smiling grimly, Guitierrez said, "Nothing. Just a bit of spacesickness or something." She looked at Eby and Chang. "I haven't been feeling steady since we left the launch bay."

"The ride hasn't been *that* bumpy, Corporal," Eby said, grinning. "Maybe you're pregnant."

Chang saw a brief flash of angry surprise in her eyes, and wondered if it had passed too quickly for anyone else to have noticed it.

"Yeah, right, with quadruplets," she said, waving her hand as if to shoo Eby away. "I'm *fine.* It's probably just Mayweather's driving. Or the smell of industrial-grade bullshit in here from Dave's story."

Guitierrez stood up and stepped past McCammon, who responded to her remark with an exaggerated, theatrical pout. "I'm gonna go sit up front," she said, "and see if I can give our squid driver some pointers on keeping this tub level. Besides, I already know how this story ends."

Chang watched her go, studying her movements and her shape, watching both for anything out of the ordinary. He knew she probably wouldn't confirm his suspicions during this mission, but if Selma really *was* pregnant, he knew that Hayes would have to be informed about it. *Hell, she would have told me about it,* he thought. *I* am *her squad leader, after all.*

"So, as I was saying, we got our propulsion back up again," McCammon said, scratching the top of his shaved scalp. "We pulled up in a steep forward curve. The Blagees had already turned around and were headed back and down, skimming the fog where they *thought* we had gone. Instead, we ended up behind them, on *their* tails. We pulled through a cloud bank with enough time to tag their weapons and hover systems. Both of their ships went down into the big briny. *All* the way." He smashed his fist into his open palm.

Eby grinned, displaying a disciplined parade ground of even, white teeth. "So you're really a veteran of the Battle of Blagee?"

Chang rolled his eyes at the exaggeration. "Some *battle.* Malcontent uprising is more like it." The event was actually where he had met McCammon. A host of anti-human extremists on one of Blagee III's three large continents had attacked several human mining settlements. Chang and McCammon had both been part of the four MACO companies dispatched to the scene, responding to a distress call after numerous humans had been killed, attacked, or kidnapped.

"Yes, 'battle' is definitely a misnomer," McCammon said. "What we found once we reached the surface was that the Blagee extremists were pretty poorly organized, had only a handful of usable ships, and not much in the way of real weapons or defenses. The Blagee government said it wanted to maintain its trade relationship with Earth, but wouldn't intervene against the attackers for religious reasons. Once we caught up with the terrorists ourselves, though, the Blagee apparently got a little bit stricter in enforcing their own laws."

"What do you mean?" Eby asked.

McCammon tilted his head, hoisted his arm as if holding a noose, and stuck out his tongue as if gagging.

"Wow," Eby said, chuckling under his breath. "I

don't have any cool stories like that. Guess I haven't really seen all that much action yet."

Chang playfully slapped the younger man on the side of the head. "We'll wash the green off your hide soon enough, mister."

"I hope so," Eby said. "So far my time in the Expanse has been pretty freaking boring. I mean, I came here because I wanted to come kick some Xindi butt."

Chang nodded in silent agreement. With the exception of some minor skirmishes, the most serious of which had been brought about by the *Enterprise* captain's colossal ineptitude down in the trellium mines on Tulaw, the months the MACO company had spent bunking among the Starfleeters had produced exactly squat in terms of results. Even Captain Archer's Starfleet crew seemed to be losing their patience and were itching for some real action.

He hoped they'd get some, and soon.

"You want some coffee?" Corporal Guitierrez asked, holding up the canister that she had brought up to the front of the shuttlepod with her.

Still stinging from her words, Mayweather looked over at the corporal, one eyebrow arched in a manner that he thought would have done Sub-Commander T'Pol proud. "What, you think you can trash my flying and then offer me coffee as a peace offering?" he asked, his tone bantering though his meaning was at least half-serious.

"Sorry, Ensign," Guitierrez said, looking embarrassed. "You *heard* all that?"

"We squids have very acute hearing," Mayweather said. He looked over his shoulder toward the aft end of the small passenger compartment. "You have to remember that this is a Starfleet shuttlepod, Corporal, not a cruise ship. It's going to be pretty tough for you MACOs to keep secrets from me while you're telling tales out of school—even if you whisper when you do it." He briefly considered telling her that the cramped upper airlock chamber was relatively soundproof, then decided against it.

Guitierrez gritted her teeth and grimaced, still shamefaced. "Sorry," she repeated, sounding awkward. "Didn't mean to slam your piloting. I suppose I was just trying to blow off some steam."

Mayweather sighed, feeling a surge of compassion for Guitierrez in spite of himself—and in spite of his not overly fond relationship with Chang. She suddenly didn't seem nearly as bad as Chang and most of the other MACOs did. *Maybe I can afford to lighten up with her, at least a little.*

"I hear that," he said. "And, yeah, I'd love to have some of that coffee. Thanks."

After pouring him a mug of the dark, not-quite-steaming liquid, Guitierrez handed it to him. "I really don't mind your flying, you know."

"Uhm-hmm," Mayweather grunted as he took a cautious sip, then decided that the stuff was at least marginally potable. He looked at her, determined to change the subject to something other than the relative merits of his piloting skills. "So how long have you been with the MACOs?"

"Coming up on my sixth year since I first donned the gray cammies," Guitierrez said. He couldn't tell if she sounded proud, disappointed, tired, or some combination of the above.

"And have you accumulated a pile of wild and woolly war stories yet, like McCammon?" He looked aftward as he spoke, and saw that the other MACOs seemed to be utterly absorbed in some other tale of MACO derring-do. Catching Guitierrez's eye, he was more than a little glad to see her smile at his question; she definitely seemed more human than most of the others.

"I don't know. I've been in ten or twelve small engagements. Nothing too heavy, though. Mostly endless patrolling on border worlds or frontier settlements." She took a sip of her coffee and added, "I was deployed in the Janus Loop for about six months."

"And you *still* get spacesickness?"

"Oh, you heard that, too, huh?" He saw her look out the forward window, off into trackless space.

He waggled his finger toward the spacecraft's aft section. "Remember, there's no privacy aboard a shuttlepod," he said very quietly, smiling. "Don't get too confessional."

She grinned in response. "Yeah." She paused to glance backward, as if to confirm that Chang, McCammon, and Eby were all too busy with their bull session to eavesdrop on her. "I dunno," she said finally. "Lately I've been getting sick some. Maybe it's my diet, or something to do with being out in the Expanse. I hope it's not some strange new anomaly thing."

"Me, too," Mayweather said. Her comment reminded him that Trip and Hoshi and over a dozen other crew members were even now lying in sickbay, victims of some bizarre burp of Delphic space. He sent them a quick "get well soon" thought, though he knew from his long experience hauling freight with his family aboard the *Horizon* that a bag of kind wishes was worth exactly the price of the bag.

"How 'bout you? What's *your* story?" she asked. "Sub-Commander T'Pol must trust you a hell of a lot to put you in charge of this mission."

Mayweather tried not to smile too broadly at the comment. The Vulcan was rarely complimentary to anyone, so the fact that a relative stranger to *Enterprise*'s bridge hierarchy had interpreted his assignment to this mission so favorably made his chest swell with pride.

"Well, for starters I *don't* get spacesick," he said, letting a bit more of his smile creep out. "I was born in zero-g, and grew up behind the consoles of various cargo ships."

"Ah, you're a boomer," she said, not really asking, but instead merely making an observation.

"Yep. My dad was the captain of the *Horizon*. It was a J-class freighter ship that used to run dilithium between the Vegan colonies and Draylax." He looked out the forward window for a moment, focusing on the beckoning Delphic stars even as he suppressed an unbidden gulp. His father had been dead for nearly nine months, and the loss still felt like an open wound; after Travis had left the family business to join Earth's Starfleet, he had never really reconciled with his father, Paul, Senior.

"Ships were pretty slow back then, huh?"

"Yeah, they were nothing like the new NX-class," Mayweather said, looking down at his flight controls. Not being warp-capable, the shuttlepod was traveling at its top velocity of point eight c, a speed that made even the *Horizon*'s lumbering maximum seem enviable; he couldn't help but wish he could push the impulse engines just a little bit harder. "Fastest we could go in those days was warp one point eight."

Guitierrez grimaced. "Santa Maria! Must have taken you forever to get anywhere."

Mayweather looked back on his growing-up years, when he'd spent endless hours exploring the ship and bedeviling its crew, and secretly plotting courses to all the star systems and planets that he wanted to visit when he was finally old enough. Back then it *had* seemed like forever.

He nodded. "Yeah, I didn't realize it at first, but even our top speed wasn't nearly fast enough for me. I wanted to see more than I could see going back and forth on those mining runs. The first time I heard of the United Earth Space Probe Agency, I figured *that* would be the path for me to take. But by the time I was old enough to leave the ship—against my family's wishes—Earth's Starfleet had been established as well. Starfleet seemed like the best way to see the galaxy, so that's where I signed up."

Guitierrez cocked her head to the side. "So, why an Earth agency? I mean, had you ever even *been* to Earth?"

Mayweather looked at her incredulously. Nobody had asked him that question since his own family had back when he was a teenager.

He sighed and shrugged his shoulders. "I'm *human*. My great-grandparents came from Earth. They were some of the first humans to leave the solar system. Just because I wasn't *born* on Earth doesn't mean it's not part of my heritage."

"I know that," she said, nodding. "I'm not exactly a

bug-eyed alien myself. And I didn't mean that to sound harsh. My father's family comes from Rosarito, in the northwest part of Mexico. Even though I was raised in Pittsburgh, my *abuela*—my paternal grandmother—and my mom always wanted me to remember 'the old village.' I always thought that was weird. Sure, I'm Latina, but I'm not Mexican." She laughed behind her hand for a moment. "Funny thing is, when I finally went back to 'the old village,' it was all high-end housing and gated communities, and the desert had all been landscaped. I doubt my nana would have even recognized it."

"They always say you can't go home again," Mayweather said. He knew that well. When he had visited the *Horizon* immediately after his father's death, his mother had welcomed him; his brother Paul, however, had been significantly less enthusiastic about Travis's return. The old family dynamic had changed forever.

"Seeing the things we get to see, who'd *want* to go home again?" Guitierrez turned to smile at him, her brown eyes crinkled at the edges.

Mayweather smiled broadly, even as he realized that the distaff MACO might be a reasonable choice to ask for a date on a ship with limited options. His mind raced to see if he could recall having seen her sharing meals or recreation time on *Enterprise* with anyone in specific, male or female.

In a moment, he decided to ask. "I wonder if you—"

She spoke at the same time. "I think I'm going to—"

They both laughed at their mutual interruption.

"You first," Mayweather said.

Guitierrez motioned toward the rear of the shuttlepod. "I was just going to say that I think I'm going to sack out and try to catch a few zees in the back. Might help settle my stomach."

"Oh. Sure. Yeah." Mayweather tried to keep the smile from slipping off his face like a blob of tetralubisol. "That's probably a good idea. We still have about two hours left before we make a close approach to the blip the sensors say is at the end of the trail."

She stood up. "What was it were you going to say a moment ago?"

Mayweather grabbed his coffee mug. "I, ah, was just going to ask if you had any more coffee. I need to stay sharp up here."

"Oh, sure," Guitierrez said, uncorking the canister again. She topped off Mayweather's mug, and turned to go.

Then, she turned back, setting her hand lightly on his shoulder. "I enjoyed talking to you, 'boomer.' We'll have to do it again sometime."

Before he could stop himself, Mayweather grinned widely. Too widely, he thought belatedly. "That would be great."

As the female MACO walked away from him, Mayweather felt his blood creep up to his ears and cheeks as he blushed. *Am I* that *hard up?* he thought, mentally chastising himself for seriously contemplating a liaison with one of the sharks with whom he'd been forced to share *Enterprise.*

But a part of him knew that that wasn't the issue at all. He didn't really care whether she wore the uniform of the MACO company or of Starfleet. And her appeal wasn't merely her looks or her manner, or the easy way they made conversation. Perhaps instead it was his instinctive recognition that she loved space, and exploring it, as much as he did, spacesickness notwithstanding.

He sipped his coffee, reveling in its slightly scorching sensation against his tongue. Selma Guitierrez certainly didn't strike Mayweather as a typical MACO. They would definitely have to talk again sometime. Of that, he was certain.

"That's what the readings show," Mayweather said, pointing to the screens on the consoles. He reduced the shuttlepod's speed until the best way to proceed became clearer.

Standing next to Mayweather's chair, Chang leaned over to look at Mayweather's readouts, though he didn't bother to sit in the copilot's chair as most other crew members would. Mayweather tamped down his mounting annoyance.

"This *entire* dust cloud is made of the Xindi isotope?" Chang asked, sounding incredulous. He looked out the forward window at the approaching yet still far-off spatial vista. The view of the approaching dust cloud was less than dramatic, however, consisting mainly of a slight but noticeable dimming of most of the background stars.

Mayweather shook his head. "Not entirely, but the stuff forms a large proportion of the debris that makes up the dust cloud. Most of it is infused with at least trace quantities of the same energy signature that led us here."

"So we've been on the trail of a cosmic dust cloud all this time, instead of a Xindi ship?" Eby asked.

The other three MACOs had all crowded forward to look.

Mayweather turned, annoyed. "Would one of you just take the damned copilot's seat? I don't need all four of you breathing down my neck."

Displaying a gentle smile that Mayweather supposed was visible only to him, Guitierrez moved forward and took the chair beside him.

"Thank you," Mayweather said, turning to face Eby. "Now to answer your question, Private, the trail we've been following contained a much more refined form of the isotope. And it was clearly left behind by an object moving at warp, which pretty much has to have been a ship. I'm sure you've noticed that this dust cloud *isn't* moving at warp."

"So, if there are ships out here using this isotope as a fuel, then this might be where they mine the stuff in the first place," Guitierrez said, peering at the data scrolling across the shuttlepod's computer screens.

"I think that's a pretty good guess," Mayweather said, impressed. "But we won't know for sure until we get closer."

"Then take us on in, Ensign," Chang said.

Mayweather couldn't tell whether Chang had spat out the last word as though it were an epithet, or if he was simply projecting his own dislike for Chang back onto the man. As he took the manual controls in hand and guided the little ship forward, Mayweather decided that he wasn't terribly comfortable with either scenario.

Fifteen minutes later, the shuttlepod was well within the dust cloud's boundaries, and Mayweather immediately regretted it. The volume of space surrounding the ship seemed to be growing thick with ice particles and rocky debris. The material not only contained substantial quantities of the Xindi isotope, it also played host to hundreds of organic and inorganic compounds. The particles whirled around the shuttle like snow in a blizzard, at times greatly obscuring the forward view of the Delphic starfield.

Thankfully, the shuttlepod's sensors still seemed to be working perfectly, so although Mayweather was flying essentially blind from the front, the sensors were keeping them from pancaking into some of the larger pieces of debris that tumbled at irregular intervals across the ship's path.

"Where could this dust cloud have come from?" McCammon asked, addressing no one in particular.

"I guess it could be what's left of a planet or moon that got clobbered by some giant impact," Guitierrez said. "The stuff out there doesn't look quite like the contents of your garden-variety cosmic dust cloud."

"I wonder if this was another planet that the Xindi attacked," Chang said. "Maybe they needed to try their weapon out before they unleashed it on Earth."

The thought chilled Mayweather to the bone, though he regarded Chang's speculation as unlikely. "The weapon the Xindi attacked Earth with didn't have that kind of power," he said, not bothering to look up toward Chang. "Why would they build something that could pulverize an entire *planet* and then bring the pop-gun version to Earth?"

"Maybe it was a different type of weapon," Chang said, his tone as icy as the dust particles dancing just beyond the shuttlepod's skin. "Maybe the Xindi targeted this planet because it was so rich in the isotope they're using for fuel. We've certainly seen dilithium-rich planets targeted by exploiters and pirates before."

A sensor alarm on the primary conn panel suddenly began beeping and flashing; a cursory read of the incoming data told Mayweather everything he needed to know about the reason.

"Brace yourselves," he called out as he slammed the impulse drive into an abrupt deceleration, matching the shuttlepod's velocity to that of one of the house-sized debris particles that drifted nearby.

Despite his warning, the MACOs struggled to maintain their footing without toppling forward as the ship lurched.

"What the hell are you doing?" Chang roared.

Mayweather was flipping switches, shutting systems down all over the shuttlepod. He hoped that they hadn't been detected.

"Calm down, Corporal. I'm trying to save our asses," Mayweather said. A moment later, satisfied that he had done all he could, he turned to glare at the MACO. "That alarm," he said, pointing to the beeping panel, "just told me that we've found what we were looking for. There *are* Xindi ships inside this cloud. *Three* of them at least, just coming out of warp, from the look of their isotopic trace patterns. And unless I'm reading the cloud's density and chemical profiles all wrong, there's some kind of base or facility in here as well. If I had to take a wild guess, I'd say it's some sort of processing plant."

"So they *are* mining the isotope here," McCammon said. "And maybe refining it into fuel here, too, right inside the dust cloud. And those ships could be picking up cargo to take to other Xindi facilities."

"It certainly looks that way to me," Mayweather said. "We'd have to get a bit closer to absolutely confirm that, but I think those are all safe assumptions to enter into our report to Sub-Commander T'Pol." He was eager to return to *Enterprise* in order to do just that.

Chang stared at Mayweather for a moment, his eyes switching from side to side like those of a predatory animal considering its prey's next move. "You stopped us from plunging right into the center of the cloud so we wouldn't show up on their sensors. Good idea, Ensign."

Mayweather nodded. *Score one for me,* he thought. "According to our sensors, they haven't run any active scans on us yet. And they can't find us from our warp-drive emissions, because we're only equipped with impulse engines. So unless we've somehow given ourselves away to some unknown type of passive scanning technique, they don't know we're here. But if we keep moving toward them at high impulse speed, they're bound to notice us sooner or later, with or without the debris cloud obscuring our motion."

"But we need to go after the bastards," McCammon said to Chang. "These are the *Xindi.* We've actually *found* the Xindi. We've gotta shoot at 'em with something other than cameras."

As Mayweather looked at the pair of MACO corporals, his incredulity finally got the better of him. "You think we should attack them? The five of us? One shuttlepod against *three* ships, with unknown firepower or speed? Does your MACO bravado really make you *that* stupid?"

McCammon frowned, and Mayweather realized he'd stepped on a nerve. "Since when was running away part of the plan? Maybe that's how you squids do things, but we MACOs—"

"That's enough," Chang said, cutting off his shaven-headed colleague. Then he looked down at Mayweather. "What *is* your plan, Mayweather? Turn tail and head for *Enterprise?*"

"Yeah," Mayweather said, though he was aware that this single word had come out sounding more like *no shit.* "We can't risk breaking comm silence, but we still need to report back so that *Enterprise* can get here to do something about those Xindi ships and that isotope refinery, or whatever it actually turns out to be. We don't know how well armed these Xindi vessels are, or how many more of them might be nearby or on their way. In fact, we don't know much of *anything*—other than the fact that we're outnumbered and probably outgunned."

"You're exactly right," Chang said. "That's why we need to get in closer—so we can eliminate as many of those unknowns as possible before returning to *Enterprise* to make our report."

Mayweather shook his head. "If we get too close, *we're* liable to be 'eliminated'—by the Xindi. I don't care *what* sort of battle training you've had, Chang, all we have to bring to bear against the Xindi is the four of you, me, and the shuttlepod. That's *it.*"

Chang grinned a barracuda smile. "Then you'd better use all that space-boomer expertise to keep our profile low."

"Sub-Commander T'Pol ordered us to do whatever is 'most appropriate, prudent, and logical,'" Mayweather said. "We *can't* go in there without backup from *Enterprise*. It would be suicide. And suicide doesn't strike me as very prudent."

Chang placed a surprisingly gentle hand on Mayweather's shoulder, but the gesture made the helmsman feel more patronized than mollified.

"Ensign, anything we can accomplish out here—up to and including finding a way to blow everything inside this cloud to quarks—could be a huge setback to the Xindi plans to destroy Earth. Even if whatever we do in the next few hours only succeeds in buying Earth a couple of extra days, that's a couple of days we wouldn't have had otherwise."

Mayweather had been tempted to swat the corporal's hand away from his shoulder, but resisted the impulse—probably because he realized that Chang wasn't wrong. Every hour they managed to steal from the Xindi could indeed make all the difference in terms of the survival of the human species.

Mayweather offered Chang a small smile. "All right. You're in command of the tactical phase of the mission, so I know I can't countermand any order you give your people—even if I think you're taking unnecessary risks. So please promise me one thing."

"Name it," Chang said, releasing Mayweather's shoulder.

"Just remember what Sub-Commander T'Pol said about doing what's 'appropriate, prudent, and logical.'"

Chang grinned. "That's what I'm relying on *you* for, Starfleet. You can start by finding us a nice rock to hide under until we're done here."

Mayweather could feel his anger boiling up inside him again, swirling around his consciousness like the blizzard of particles raining outside the shuttlepod; it seemed that Chang was ordering him around as though he was a MACO private. He clenched and unclenched his fist atop the flight console, and heard his knuckles pop.

A rock to hide under.

An idea revealed itself to him then, and he suddenly knew how he might deliver Shuttlepod Two right to the Xindi's doorstep without giving the enemy any advance warning.

He knew *exactly* how.

NINE

Courier Ship Helkez Torvo

THEY HAD BEEN TRAVELING for three hours now in La'an Trahve's captured vessel, the name of which they had learned was *Helkez Torvo*. According to the linguistics software running on Reed's padd, the alien words translated roughly to "Fortunate Waterfowl."

Now, as they navigated their way through the gravitic particle cloud, Malcolm Reed hoped that their luck would continue. But despite the reluctance of Trahve to help them—and the painful, though thankfully brief, beatings the alien pilot had endured at the hands of the captain and the major—Reed felt increasingly that something was very wrong. Despite the alleged dangers inherent in this so-called gravitic particle cloud—according to Trahve, an insufficiently shielded vessel could easily be hulled, or even torn apart by the cloud's abundance of tiny, undetectable singularities—everything seemed to be going almost *too* smoothly. In fact, the mission had proceeded with surprising ease ever since they had made planetfall on Kaletoo.

Kemper, Money, and Hayes had all taken turns guarding Trahve as the pilot flew the small ship onward, and for the most part—Trahve's interrogations excluded—the trip had been a rather quiet one. Whether sulking or hurting, the alien had only communicated when spoken to, his glib pre-beating quips no longer in evidence. The MACOs were as taciturn as Trahve had become, alternatively concentrating on watching the alien courier for signs of treachery, and repeatedly checking that their phase rifles were armed and at the ready in the event that the smuggler tried to deliver them to evil.

While the cockpit of Trahve's courier vessel felt rather cramped with more than two people in it, the rest of the ship was a good deal roomier and replete with cargo spaces. *Lots of cargo spaces. And lots of hidden smuggling spaces,* Reed thought. Leaving the MACOs to tend to Trahve, Archer and Reed were already in the midst of scanning those stowage compartments for more traces of the Xindi isotope, while searching for any signaling devices that Trahve might have concealed as a security precaution.

"Malcolm. In here." Archer was calling from an alcove that lay beyond a small, tubular corridor.

Reed stooped to move through the tube, entering the chamber. Several deck plates had been moved aside, and Archer was standing inside a previously hidden floor compartment, which came up to his shoulders.

"This is where he carried the Xindi compound," Archer said, looking up at Reed. "I barely even need a scanner to detect it."

"Well, I wouldn't wade too deeply in the isotope's residue, if I were you," Reed said. "Who knows what the radiation might do to your descendants-to-be?" He crouched and held out his hand to help Archer up.

"You're right," Archer said, looking down into the compartment, a wistful look on his careworn face. Placing his padd off to the side on the floor where the bronze-hued deck plating was stacked, the captain reached up and clasped his hand around Reed's proffered wrist. Bracing himself against the side of the compartment, he allowed his tactical officer to help pull him up.

Setting down his own instruments, Reed helped Archer replace the pieces of plating in their previous position over the hidden compartments. The pieces fit together almost seamlessly. *Quite a good hiding spot,* Reed thought. *I wonder what other sorts of contraband our industrious Mister Trahve has handled over the years.*

Slipping the final plate back into place, Archer yelped and hurriedly withdrew his right hand from harm's way. He flexed his slightly mashed fingertips for a moment, scowling at them.

"Are you all right, sir?" Reed looked quickly for the small medical kit that the team had brought along, but realized it was out near the cockpit area. "Do you want me to get the medkit?"

Archer rubbed his injured fingers with his left hand. "Don't bother, Malcolm. My hands were both a bit sore anyway. That deck plate really didn't make the damage any worse."

Reed saw the bruises that had blossomed on the

captain's knuckles; it was obvious that he hadn't received them while exploring Trahve's smuggling holes.

"When did we come to this, sir?"

Archer stared at him, his eyebrows knotted in the center—more in confusion than anger. "Come to *what*, Malcolm?"

"This," Malcolm said, gesturing with his hand toward the corridor and the cockpit beyond it. "That," he said, gesturing again, this time toward Archer's hands. "When did we stop being the civilization and become the anarchists? We used to be explorers, and now we're thugs."

Archer glared at him for a moment, then finally spoke, his voice even and practically inflectionless. "*We* didn't start this war with the Xindi, Malcolm. Stop trying to hang this over our heads."

"I'm not—" Reed stopped and let out an exasperated sigh. "It's not the *Xindi* I'm talking about. I'll gladly tear them limb from limb when we find them, assuming that we can ascertain that they really *were* behind the attack on Earth. I'm talking about *him*." He pointed in the general direction of the cockpit again. "La'an Trahve. *He's* not Xindi. He's a freelancer, a smuggler. *He's* not the enemy."

Archer stepped closer, looking into Reed's eyes with a steely gaze. "He's a collaborator with the Xindi, Lieutenant. I wonder if you would feel differently if you knew that Trahve had delivered the very same batch of the Xindi compound that fueled their attack on Earth?"

Reed didn't flinch. "Do you have any proof of that, sir?"

"Unfortunately, this stuff apparently doesn't come with a serial number stamped on every molecule," Archer said through clenched teeth. "But Trahve very well could have loaded the gun that killed seven million people back home. Whether or not he did, he's been delivering war matériel that the Xindi could easily use in their next attack against us, or against some other world. And Trahve's efforts will have helped make it possible."

"So we respond by lapsing into savagery? Is that what all our training has taught us? Is that what we've learned these past two years exploring parts of the galaxy where no man has gone before?"

Archer's nostrils flared wide as Reed's invocation of Zefram Cochrane's famous words sank in. Every schoolchild was required to memorize those words, which Cochrane had delivered more than thirty years earlier during the groundbreaking ceremonies for the Warp Five Complex, where the pioneering work of Cochrane and the late Henry Archer had eventually yielded the mighty superluminal engines that now powered *Enterprise*. For a fleeting moment, Reed was sure that the captain would actually strike him, but after several heavy breaths, Archer turned away. He stooped to retrieve his scanner, and stalked away toward the corridor.

The captain stopped abruptly and turned back in Reed's direction. "Did you manage to complete the other task I gave you?" he asked, his voice sharp. "Or did you need to give me a critique of *that* decision as well?"

"Yes, I did," Malcolm said, then corrected himself. "No. I—" He drew a quick breath, and exhaled it forcefully through his nose. "Yes, sir, I *completed* the task. And no, sir, I have no further comments."

Archer spun on his heel and marched away, saying nothing further.

Reed exhaled sharply again, aware that his hands, at his sides, were balled tightly into fists. *I can't allow either the Delphic Expanse or the Xindi to turn me into a bully,* he thought. *And I can't let it happen to the captain, either.*

Leicester, England,
Wednesday, April 11, 2136

Malcolm Reed was skirting the outer edge of Grayton Hall when he heard the sounds. They were unmistakably the sounds of both laughter and weeping, and they were coming from behind the gardener's cottage.

Clutching his monogrammed schoolbag to his shoulder, he crept forward as quietly as he could. Even before he had drawn close enough to the sounds to see what was happening, he knew who the laughter was coming from: Leslie Morris and his two thuggish friends. Why they hadn't been expelled from Evington Academy before now was a mystery he couldn't fathom. Like most of the other boys, he did his best to stay away from them.

"Eat it!" He heard Gerald Balinsweel shout, glee in his voice.

"No, please!" Malcolm didn't recognize the voice, but he could hear that it belonged to someone younger, and its owner was clearly the one who was doing the crying.

"Hold him down," Leslie said. "Hold his mouth open."

Malcolm froze in his tracks, aware that with the sun in the position it was in, if he stepped forward any further, his shadow would crest the side of the cottage, and his presence would be revealed. *But they're tormenting one of the other boys,* he thought. Although his flight instinct was in overdrive, he knew he couldn't just leave. *If I run to get a teacher, they'll be gone by the time I get back. And who knows what they'll do to him.*

Looking back, he saw a rake leaning against the side of the cottage, near its front door. Placing his bag on the ground as quietly as he could, he crept back and grabbed the implement. Grasping it cleanly between his hands, upended like a cricket bat, he dashed back toward the rear of the cottage.

"Let him go!" he yelled, even as he came around the building.

On the ground lay Victor Renslow, a rather simpleminded boy who was in the next form down from Malcolm. His school uniform was torn and soiled, and his face was muddy and streaked with tears. Leslie was squatting on him, straddling the prone boy's chest and holding a wriggling and dirty worm in his muddy hand. Terrance Bishop was holding Victor's struggling hands above his head, while Gerald stood nearby, grinning sadistically and obviously greatly enjoying the show.

The three older boys looked up as Malcolm screamed at them. *"Get off of him!"* Malcolm shouted, trying to remain calmer than he knew he must have sounded. He was aware that his words had rushed out of him in a quick, torrential burst that must have sounded more like *"Getoffofhim!"*

"Get out of here, fish-boy," Leslie said, his tone contemptuous. "Before we make you sorry you turned up here."

Morris's nickname for Reed the last two years had been "fish-boy," apparently because Reed's family had a nautical background. Malcolm tolerated the name mainly because it was almost nonsensical; he wasn't on a ship, and he didn't particularly enjoy fish, and couldn't even swim particularly well. Now, the words coming out of the sneering, pubescent torturer's lips seemed beyond stupid. But Malcolm perceived them to be every bit as malicious as the simpleton who had delivered them must have intended.

"No, *you* get out of here," Reed said. He swung the rake in an arc, its pointed metal tines slicing through the air with a whoosh.

Malcolm's quick scything motion actually caused Terrance to back away from Victor, and the teenage tormentor dropped the smaller boy's flailing hands in the process.

Emboldened by Terrance's retreat, Malcolm stepped forward and swung again, aiming a little closer to Leslie's face. "Move off."

A third swing, and Leslie Morris also scampered backward, dismounting from Victor. "You've just made a big mistake, fish-boy," Leslie said, sneering. He seemed to be taking care to keep his distance from the rake, however.

"I don't care, Leslie," Malcolm said, and at that moment, he truly didn't care what repercussions might result from what he'd just done. A swell of pride ballooned within him at his act of heroism. Still holding the rake aloft like a weapon, he glanced down as Victor flipped over onto his back and moved to sit up. The crying boy wiped a filthy sleeve across his mouth, spitting out mud and gravel.

"Are you all right, Victor?" Malcolm asked, even as he saw Gerald Balinsweel throw something toward him.

An instant later he felt the something hit his head, striking hard and sharp against his left temple. He shouted in pain, and closed his eyes, his equilibrium swimming and a kaleidoscope of colors bursting behind his eyelids. He tried to swing the rake again, but being aware that he might inadvertently hit Victor, he aimed to the side.

He heard the other boys shouting, and he felt them pile onto him in a rush, their fists pummeling, their feet kicking. Pain flared, and Malcolm tasted dirt and blood, even as he curled protectively into a fetal position, trying to protect his most vulnerable parts.

The beating continued for an interminable time, and then Malcolm felt them picking him up from the front, his limp body dragging behind him. They were bearing him away, but in his pain-addled confusion, he couldn't even begin to gather why or where.

As if from a great distance, he heard Leslie Morris shout at him, but recognized nothing other than several occurrences of the term "fish-boy" before a sharp sensation of cold enveloped his battered head.

The shock of the chill water all around him snapped Malcolm back into full consciousness, and he began to struggle against the bullies. But all three of them seemed to be holding him down, and they were stronger, and he couldn't get any leverage against them anyway.

His cheeks bulging as he struggled, Malcolm felt as if his lungs were on fire, felt his blood hot beneath his skin. He opened his eyes and saw moss-covered concrete deeper in the water. He struggled further, and as his vision became hazy again, felt the absurd sensation that the air that remained in his lungs was what was actually suffocating him. He pushed it out in a steady stream of bubbles, and gulped to breathe again.

But there was no oxygen beneath the surface of the old fountain to the southeast rear acreage of Evington Academy.

And so, Malcolm Reed began to drown.

Leicester, England,
Friday, April 11, 2138

Two years had passed since the incident behind the Academy, more than enough time for stern lectures to be thought proper punishment and for expulsions to be reversed.

Mistress Linscott, who had, unbeknownst to the other faculty, been carrying on a torrid affair with Mister Taupin, the greensman, had been coming to call on the man who was her secret shame when she had discovered the trio of youths bullying Malcolm Reed near the fountain. Luckily, she had paid attention in her health class two decades prior, and thus was able to use cardiopulmonary resuscitation to bring young Malcolm Reed back from the brink of death.

Morris, Bishop, and Balinsweel had escaped the grasp of the law—and permanent expulsion—owing mainly to Emily Linscott's nearsighted inability to positively identify Malcolm's tormentors, and to the wealth and influence of the families of all three boys. A new surface to the sports field and a set of padded chairs for the staff lounges had bought the churlish trio much forgiveness from all—save from those they had harassed over the years. Still, the teachers now watched the three boys with hawklike acuity, and the three offenders were not allowed to take any classes together.

Their punishment, such as it was, provided scant comfort to Malcolm. Now through the throes of puberty himself, and all the discomforting newness that that rite of passage toward adulthood entailed, Malcolm also had to deal with psychological baggage from the assault. He had never been particularly outgoing to begin with, but now he was even more reticent about talking to people and making new friends. He also found himself fantasizing about destruction often, dreaming of great explosions that would collapse the school around his enemies.

But most tellingly, he now had a nearly pathological aversion to water. He couldn't explain to his father or grandfather why he didn't want to join them on the sea this summer, nor did he wish to admit to his physical education teacher why showering after gym class held such terror for him.

The one area in which Reed really excelled was in his academic schoolwork—the mathematical disciplines most especially—and he had become one of the Academy's top students.

It was then, precisely two years after the incident at the fountain, that he had finally hatched his plan.

Several of the students in the class one form above his were performing poorly. He got to know a handful of the worst of them that year by offering to help tutor them, then ingratiated himself further to the teens by helping them produce some of the work that they turned in as their own.

By now, he had accumulated a group of boys around him who were, if not exactly his friends, at least loyal to him for as long as he continued to help them academically. They were all larger than he was, some significantly so, and a good deal rowdier as well.

Two years to the day since his near-death experience—his near-murder, really—Malcolm arranged with a quartet of his academic acolytes to take Leslie Morris out for a joyride in Leicester's dockside district. They brought him to a darkened pier area, ostensibly to partake of some Irish whiskey that they had pilfered from their parents' liquor cabinets. And then, very much to the young bully's surprise, they had descended upon Leslie like a pack of wild animals.

Malcolm watched for several moments as blows rained down on his enemy, relishing the fact that the usually noisy teen was barely able to make any coherent sounds as he was beaten.

Finally, he waded into the fray, and landed more than a few blows on his erstwhile torturer. He felt his knuckles break open as he hit the jaw of the boy who had nearly drowned him, and in a flash of insight, understood that the painful reality of fisticuffs was significantly different than what the books, holofilms, and his own very active imagination had led him to expect.

"Take him out on the pier," Malcolm said, trying to keep his voice sounding strong and confident.

He heard Leslie crying and pleading as he was dragged out onto the darkened pier toward an empty section that lay between a pair of tall boats. If anyone on the decks had heard the sounds, they weren't showing their faces or raising their voices to object.

The group neared the end of the dock, and Morris's pleading became more frantic, becoming a high-pitched, keening wail.

Malcolm struck him again, then again, in the face and the stomach, feeling satisfaction as Leslie's body clenched inward.

"Should we throw him in?" one of the older boys asked, and Malcolm could hear the unfettered, stupid glee in the other boy's voice.

"No!" Morris gasped through the blood and tears that stained his florid face. "I can't swim!" He struggled to lift his lolling head, involuntarily flinching at the blows that he knew were imminent.

Malcolm grabbed him by the hair and pulled his head up.

"Neither can I," Malcolm said, looking into Morris's frightened, darting eyes. "Not anymore."

He was going to push him over the side of the pier, the boy who had almost killed him out of sheer, brutal pleasure.

And then, despite the pier's dim lighting and the moonless night, Malcolm saw his own reflection in the wet, terrified eyes of Leslie Morris.

In that instant, he knew that *he* was no better than

the object of his hatred and resentment, and that his actions were only serving to perpetuate a vicious, ugly cycle. The Ouroboros serpent swallowing its own tail.

He exhaled heavily, throwing his head back as the anger and violence and rage poured out of him, into the dark cloudless skies above him.

He saw a light in those skies, far away.

A star. Or a starship, orbiting high above.

Better than this.

Better than us.

He turned to one of the thugs. "Take him to the hospital," he said firmly, ignoring their surprised stares. "He's been hurt enough."

As they dragged their hapless victim away, Malcolm Reed sat alone on the edge of the pier. He listened to the night-enfolded waters of the River Soar as they lapped with a gentle rhythm against the pilings and boats. Staring out across the river's gray, fog-shrouded expanse, he could sense the water's desire to embrace him once again, felt its overwhelming need to consume him.

But above him, dominating the river and the sea into which it flowed, spread openness and infinity.

Air. And beyond that, space.

Limitless possibility.

And maybe even redemption.

Courier Ship Helkez Torvo

Standing in the corridor of a commandeered alien vessel, Lieutenant Malcolm Reed wistfully remembered his past. And he wondered why it was that space itself was now what seemed to be consuming him, drowning him.

And not for the first time, he wondered whether becoming the very threat that the Xindi evidently feared so much was truly the best way to defend the people of the planet Earth.

TEN

Shuttlepod Two

THE LITTLE AUXILIARY CRAFT arced forward through the cloud of dust and debris, her impulse engines running at half power as her pilot guided her toward the strike team's quarry.

Chang had to admit that Mayweather's plan seemed to be working well, at least so far. The ensign had electromagnetically polarized the shuttlepod's hull so that it would attract significant quantities of the dust cloud's abundant ionized granules and debris of both the organic and inorganic variety. The combined effects of ionization and magnetism were sufficiently strong to coat the little ship in several centimeters of dust, but not so strong as to attract larger, more hazardous chunks of debris. Mayweather had commented that it would be hell on the paint job, though even he agreed that it was doing a spectacular job of providing camouflage.

As the shuttlepod glided forward toward the mission objective, Chang watched as Mayweather worked at the flight controls, adjusting and stabilizing the hull's ad hoc camouflage field, allowing some new, lighter particles to take hold while letting other, heavier ones drop away. To anyone outside the shuttlepod, the craft most likely would have appeared to be nothing more than a peculiarly shaped piece of icy shrapnel on a broadly elliptical trajectory through interstellar space, just beyond the confines of the Kaletoo system. During the shuttlepod's occasional close passes with asteroid-sized bodies, Mayweather simulated random gravitational interactions by randomly spinning the ship. Between the thick coating of flotsam, Mayweather's flight maneuvers, the ship's systems being pared down to the bare essentials, and the natural damping effect that the dust cloud seemed to have on active sensor signals, Chang hoped any scans from nearby Xindi ships would fail to detect the shuttlepod's presence—or would at least lead the Xindi to conclude that Shuttlepod Two was an utterly non-noteworthy natural object, tumbling without volition or intent for all eternity through the endless deeps of space.

At least until it's too late for them to stop us from doing what we have to, Chang thought. *Or until we're able to figure out some way to take* them *out.*

"We're looping around one of the larger asteroids," Mayweather said, peering intently at several consoles and displays arrayed in the shuttlepod's forward section. "I'm starting to get a specific read on the facility they've placed inside the cloud."

Chang leaned in closely, studying the readings; astrometrics wasn't his strong suit, but he didn't see any point in letting the ensign know that. He glanced up at the forward window, through which he could see a dark, tumbling rock illuminated only very dimly by the far distant, dust-shrouded Kaletoo sun.

"We need to get within half a kilometer of whatever structures the Xindi are hiding here," Chang said as the great rock dropped away and another object loomed in the distance.

Mayweather frowned. "Why risk getting that close? The sensors won't be able see all that much more than they can from here."

Chang grinned. "Because if you park us much farther away than half a klick our tether lines won't be long enough."

"Tether lines?" Mayweather said, sounding incredulous. "You can't be seriously considering going aboard a Xindi facility."

"Of course I can. Haven't you been paying attention?"

"Whatever happened to only taking action that's 'appropriate, prudent, and logical'?"

Struggling to keep his mounting irritation in check, Chang said, "I thought you agreed with me that anything that could slow the Xindi down is worth trying."

"Sure, but only if it stands a real chance of working. Laying siege to a Xindi fuel station could get everyone on this shuttlepod killed without even giving us a chance to report back to *Enterprise* with what we've found so far. Seems to me an outcome like that would slow down *our* mission a lot more than it would the Xindi's."

"I say it's worth the risk, if we can cripple one of their fuel depots, since that's got to be what they're hiding here," Chang said, unexpectedly relishing the fact that a so-called space boomer could be so fainthearted in the face of danger—even though a tiny voice in the back of his mind asked if Mayweather's overcautious impulses might not be warranted.

Chang turned, making brief eye contact with each one of the other MACOs. Seeing nothing other than faith and resolve in the faces of his people, he dismissed that small voice of doubt and redoubled his own resolve.

Mayweather, however, remained unconvinced. "Corporal, when you mentioned blowing all the Xindi hardware here to quarks a while back, I thought you were just . . . boasting."

Noting that McCammon had visibly reddened at that remark, Chang turned his gaze back upon Mayweather. "Well, now you know better, Ensign," he said tartly.

He pointed at the front windows, toward the growing but still dim and distant pinpoint of light that the sensors had marked as the probable site of a Xindi fuel-gathering facility: their target. "Ensign, I want you to take us to a position just inside a half-klick's distance from the Xindi structure. Then we can launch our tether lines and ride them all the way down to the thing's exterior."

"That might be a little tougher than you're making it sound," Mayweather said, still looking annoyingly skeptical. "For starters, how's your team rated for environmental suit operations?"

"*We'll* worry about handling our suits," Chang said, weary of Mayweather's second-guessing. "*You* keep your eyes on the rudder."

"What do we do if the Xindi decide to shoot us down, thinking we're just some dumb chunk of rock about to crash into their platform?" asked Guitierrez, who was still seated in the copilot's chair. Chang was glad to note that she seemed much steadier—and looked significantly less green—than she had only a little while earlier.

"From what I can see, they haven't been going out of their way to attack any of the other big hunks of debris," McCammon said from just aft of the cockpit. "And some of those look like they've drifted closer than half a klick to the facility."

"There still could be some sort of shield around the thing," Mayweather said, looking away from the computer controls to set his gaze squarely upon Chang. "Or maybe none of the other large pieces of debris we've seen so far have approached whatever distance threshold might alert the Xindi crew, or trigger whatever security countermeasures they have waiting for us. We really have no idea what tricks they might have up their sleeves, you know."

Chang didn't much care for Mayweather's tone. Had the same words been delivered in the same manner by a friend or a MACO colleague, he might have taken them as good-natured, and perhaps even constructive. But he and the ensign had maintained a barely civil state of mutual coexistence for the past several weeks, and the ice had as yet shown little tendency to thaw. There was still no one specific thing about the pilot that Chang could identify as the flash point for his annoyance, other than his slovenly housekeeping, which didn't make life any easier; it was more an all-around irritation at being forced to share space with someone whose fundamental way of looking at the world was exasperatingly different from his own. Truthfully, he felt the same way toward many *Enterprise* crew members.

But he didn't have to bunk in the same room as any of those others. And none of the other Starfleeters were as proficient as Mayweather—who seemed unable to resist the impulse to brag that he was born and raised in microgravity—at reminding Chang of his own shortcomings as a spacefarer. Mayweather's presence in his life was therefore beyond annoying. After all, it constantly rubbed his nose—not to mention his inner ear and his gastrointestinal system—in an unpleasant yet inescapable truth: *I'm a space marine who isn't quite up to traveling through space.* If it weren't for the space-sickness meds Doctor Phlox had prescribed him—"prosthetic space legs," as Corporal McKenzie liked to call them—Chang had no doubt that somebody else would now be in charge of the MACO side of this mission.

Rather than responding to Mayweather's continued criticisms, Chang instead pointed at some of the monitors that displayed the results of the ongoing passive scans of the dust cloud through which the shuttlepod was moving. "Switch this one over to a three-dimensional view," he said.

As a scowling Mayweather tapped a series of commands into the console before him, the monitor that Chang had indicated displayed an unusual sight, magnifying the swath of space along their heading and rendering its dimly lit vista in various shades of night-vision green. Attached to a large asteroid ahead of the shuttlepod was a conical metallic structure, apparently some one hundred and fifty meters tall, its broad base facing toward the asteroid's ancient, pitted surface. The cone appeared to be held in place by at least a dozen stanchion-like legs, each of which appeared to be rooted deep beneath the giant rocky body's crust.

"Passive isotope scans confirm we've found the end of the trail," Mayweather said, looking up at Chang. "This is definitely Xindi real estate, and we're still heading straight for it."

Chang nodded. "So what we need to find out next is whether or not anybody's home."

"With all the ionized dust and debris out here, there's no way to tell without performing an active sensor scan," Mayweather said. "I'd advise against doing that, unless we want to come right out and announce to the Xindi that we're standing on their doorstep."

"I agree," Chang said. "We'll lay in the weeds for now. In the meantime, I want a tactical assessment."

Guitierrez stepped forward and pointed to the legs that supported the Xindi structure. "Those pilings the thing is standing on look like a serious vulnerability to me. If we could take them all out, we may be able to tip the thing over. That would cripple the whole facility, at the very least."

Chang was about to congratulate Guitierrez when Mayweather spoke up. "I'm not so sure about that," the pilot said, using that "condescending expert" tone that far too many of *Enterprise*'s Starfleet crew used in the presence of MACOs. To Chang, that tone indicated that the squids regarded his comrades-in-arms as little more than undereducated ground-pounders.

"And why is that?" Chang asked, his back teeth grinding involuntarily.

"Because this asteroid barely has enough gravity to keep itself in one piece. Just tipping that structure over probably won't do nearly enough damage to cripple or destroy it."

"All right, Ensign," Chang said, struggling to keep his voice even. "How would *you* attack this thing?"

"I wouldn't, necessarily. Sub-Commander T'Pol didn't order us to take on the whole Xindi war infrastructure all on our own."

Chang was determined not to argue that point yet again. "Noted, Ensign. Indulge me."

"Well, I'd start by trying to figure out *exactly* what they're using this facility for." Mayweather pointed toward the base of the conical facility very close to the asteroid's surface, where several large intake grilles seemed to be inhaling long plumes of dark dust, near a network of ducts that disappeared into holes in the crust. "I'm betting these are their collecting devices and mining shafts. The technology isn't that different from what I saw doing the ore runs from Draylax." He looked up at Chang. "If I'm right, the Xindi are *definitely* mining the isotope, both from inside this asteroid and directly from the debris cloud."

"Maybe when they use up one asteroid, they just disengage from it and sink their teeth into the next one they find," Eby said from beside Guitierrez.

Mayweather nodded. "And in between asteroids, they'd still be able to suck in a whole lot of free-floating dust-cloud material through those intake grilles."

Chang's mind whirled as he considered how he might use the Xindi facility's emerging technological profile against it. "We're pretty certain that this isotope that the Xindi are collecting in this dust cloud—the same stuff that made up the trail we followed here—is what they're using for fuel, right?"

"I'd bet my living quarters aboard *Enterprise* on it," Mayweather deadpanned.

Chang ignored the obvious jab. "So is this facility able to refine the raw material it's collecting?"

"We don't really know *what* technology the Xindi have," Mayweather said, his expression peevish. "For all we know, they've been tracking us for hours and are just luring us into a trap."

Chang saw Eby's eyes grow wide. *I've got to shut him down,* Chang thought. *And right now. Before he plants any more doubts in my people's minds.*

"If that's the case, Ensign, they'll find that we aren't all that easy to trap," he said evenly. "And I think it's better for our mission if you concentrate on positive outcomes and solutions instead of acting like a scared rabbit."

When Mayweather looked away and didn't respond, Chang pointed to a trio of large, rounded objects that were affixed to a side of the mining platform that was just turning into view as the asteroid continued its slow, stately rotation. Though they were still only dimly visible through the forward window, the false-color image on the console monitor showed that each of the football-field-sized objects was tethered in place by long tubes or conduits of some sort. "What are those things? Fuel storage tanks?"

Mayweather tapped some controls, and the scan image zoomed in to provide a closer view. "The lines tethering them seem to be flexible tubing of some sort, probably designed to accommodate geological instabilities on the asteroid's surface. I can't tell you just what the tanks themselves are made of, but they definitely contain large amounts of a liquid or gas that gives off a strong signature of the Xindi isotope we've been tracking. I'd call that proof positive that they're storing the raw stuff here as well as refining and enhancing it into fuel for their ships—and probably for the large-scale beam weapon they're planning to send to Earth."

Even as a red light began blinking on the pilot's console, a muted alarm sounded. Mayweather's hands flew over the controls, and a look of panic crossed his features.

"There's a Xindi vessel closing on our stern," he said, punching another button.

An instant later, the interior of the shuttle went completely dark.

Mayweather found himself praying, something he hadn't done for a very long time. But the situation seemed to merit a call to whatever deity or deities might be within divine earshot of the Delphic Expanse.

He wasn't certain how long they'd been sitting in darkness. It felt like an eternity, and yet he was reasonably certain that it hadn't been longer than a few minutes. The moment the sensors had detected the Xindi ship, he'd shut down virtually every system aboard the shuttlepod other than the grav plating, whose emergency shutdown sequence might have produced a telltale power spike visible to Xindi sensors. Even the main console's life-support indicators were now dark; if the Xindi vessel didn't linger long, Mayweather knew that he and the MACOs could survive for a short time on the breathable air and residual heat that remained in the crew cabin.

"Are they gone?" He heard Guitierrez whisper the question from behind his cockpit chair.

"I don't know," he murmured in response. He didn't turn around, not wanting to tear his gaze away from either the forward cockpit window or the few passive-scan monitors and gauges that continued to glow faintly on the console before him. All he knew was that he couldn't see any movement through the forward windows, and the passive sensors had lost the approaching ship's profile, no doubt because of the profusion of dust and debris that surrounded both the shuttlepod and the Xindi fuel depot. The layer of camouflaging dust-cloud material that caked virtually all of the shuttlepod's hull probably wasn't helping matters.

He heard a sharp clank as someone behind him came into sudden unexpected contact with the crew cabin's port-side wall.

"Don't move!" It was Chang hissing an order to whoever had made the noise. "Everybody stay still and stay quiet."

Mayweather smiled grimly to himself; the idea that the occupants of the other vessel out there might somehow hear their footsteps across huge volumes of airless space was absurd on its face, a concept that belonged to the days of Earthbound submarine warfare. But he found Chang's impulse toward caution, belated though it was, immensely reassuring. He knew that if the Xindi's sensors had spotted them, then Shuttlepod Two would be a sitting duck, drifting helplessly while the cold-blooded alien killers picked her off at their leisure.

Even worse, the team might be captured. *But here we are, and we'll just have to deal with whatever comes next,* he thought. His earlier exasperation toward Chang returned; even though a part of him had begun to admire the corporal's moxie, he still held him responsible for getting the team stuck in this situation.

Still, he felt fairly certain that if the Xindi had spotted the shuttlepod without summarily destroying her, the well-armed MACOs would put up a fierce fight before being taken prisoner. In that event, he fully expected that *none* of them would survive to be interrogated, even if it meant that many of them ended up succumbing to "friendly fire." It wasn't a very comforting prospect to contemplate.

Time ticked onward, and even though he knew the shuttlepod still had many hours of breathable air, Mayweather noticed that he was instinctively taking shallower-than-normal breaths. He tried to will himself into a calmer frame of mind, but he'd never been particularly adept at forced relaxation or meditation techniques—especially during times of impending doom.

Finally, Chang spoke from slightly behind him, his voice still pitched at a stage whisper. "If they were going to get us, they should have done it by now. I think they must've moved on."

Mayweather's mind flashed to some of the horror films that had been screened a few months back on movie night, prior to *Enterprise*'s entry into the Expanse. It was almost *de rigueur* for the comely heroine to think she was safe even as she turned the lights back on, or retreated backward only to find a knife-wielding killer lurking behind her, waiting for the perfect moment to strike. *Cat and mouse. Let's hope we aren't about to walk right into the jaws of a very patient Xindi pussycat.*

"Do you want me to power our systems back up?" he asked Chang quietly.

"Only the essentials," Chang said, his voice disembodied in the near-total darkness.

Mayweather toggled several switches, his hands guided by memory as much as by the few dials that continued to glow very faintly. The brightness of the console lights intensified, and the unnerving silence that had engulfed the cabin vanished as the almost subliminal hiss and hum of oxygen scrubbers, heat exchangers, and atmosphere pumps returned.

Most importantly, the passive sensors abruptly regained most of their usual acuity. Mayweather blinked and studied the readings on the displays, then let out a heavy breath. "They sailed right past us, on a heading toward one of those fuel tanks."

Chang leaned forward, peering at the display. "How close are we to the tanks?"

"Another fifteen minutes on our current heading and speed and we'll be right in the thick of things." He summoned a tactical image to the largest monitor on his console.

Chang pointed toward the three-dimensional image, on which a wireframe representation of the Xindi ship was steadily approaching one of the three vast fuel cylinders that was tethered to the Xindi depot.

Two more ships had appeared as well. Both newcomers were slightly farther away from the Xindi fuel depot than the first was, but they were definitely on approach vectors as well. Mayweather's breath froze in his lungs, and he only barely contained his urge to point the shuttlepod's stern toward the incoming Xindi traffic and open up the throttle all the way.

"See if you can intercept any of their com traffic," Chang said with annoying coolness. "I want to know if any of these ships are communicating with each other, or with someone inside the Xindi facility."

"Where did these other ships come from?" Guitierrez asked. "Are these the same ones we detected a while back?"

Mayweather studied the sensor readings for a moment while the computer scanned up and down the EM bands in an effort to lock onto any detectable Xindi signals, without any immediate success. Then he turned toward Guitierrez and replied, "It's hard to say. As long as we're restricted to passive scanning techniques, this dust cloud could be hiding a dozen more Xindi ships. Wherever these ones came from, they obviously arrived after we went dark."

"So *more* of them might be on their way?" Eby asked, concern evident in his voice. "Or more might already be here and hiding right nearby, just out of sight?"

"If this dust cloud can hide us, it can also hide them," Mayweather said.

"Look at this," Guitierrez said, leaning in closely to the monitor and its false-color image of the fuel depot and the approaching ships. She was clearly trying to move the conversation past the worrisome point Eby had raised. "The nearest Xindi ship is docking at one of the fuel tanks. Must be fueling up."

"It's definitely sending out a signal, too," Mayweather said. "If I were a betting man, I'd say it was transmitting some kind of access code."

"We're *all* betting men right now," Chang said, smiling grimly. "That ship might have just handed us the keys to the kingdom. How much of their access code did you capture?"

Mayweather examined the readouts on the com monitor, then shook his head in disappointment. "The little bit we picked up was pretty garbled by all the ionized particles floating around out there. I'm afraid they're not going to make it quite that easy for us."

The quintet watched in silence for the better part of an hour as each of the Xindi ships docked and drank its fill of the refined Xindi isotope. Mayweather busied himself at the controls, hoping that the computers might be able to record some useful Xindi information—words, numbers, pictograms, anything at all—despite the dust cloud's abundant electromagnetic interference. But the few bits he received were both embedded in and distorted by a torrent of radio noise. Mayweather also noticed that there seemed to be a near total absence of discernible audio communications between the ships and the depot—a fact that tended to confirm his suspicion that the facility was entirely unmanned and automated. He pondered this as he fed the precious few nuggets of Xindi data he'd gathered into the computer's translation matrix; predictably, the linguistic algorithms had no luck interpreting any of the incoming symbols or sounds.

Hoshi will find a way to crack their language, he thought. He realized in that instant, and to some small comfort, not only that he expected Hoshi to recover from whatever anomaly-induced state she was in, but also that he anticipated success in bringing the captured Xindi signals back to *Enterprise.* Which meant that he expected to get the shuttlepod to safety, despite the odds.

Don't get cocky, flyboy, he chided himself. *You're a long way from home free. Lots of things can go wrong before we're out of here.*

Chang turned away from his study of the monitors and barked an order back to McCammon and Eby. "Get four EVA suits ready. And prep the tether lines and magnetic grapples." He turned back toward Guitierrez. "Corporal, break out the ordnance. We'll want twenty-four heavy-yield tri-thermite explosives, rigged for remote detonation." He hesitated a moment, and Mayweather saw him sizing up the structures on the monitors. "Better make that thirty-six of them."

"Are you really planning what I *think* you're planning?" Mayweather asked. "Are you sure lobbing a few grenades at the Xindi is really the 'appropriate, prudent, and logical' thing to do?"

Chang turned toward him, raising his voice loudly enough for the others to hear clearly; just as clearly, the MACO squad leader had no intention of responding to Mayweather's comment.

"We don't have enough weapons to take on the Xindi ships that are docked here," Chang said to his team. "But we aren't leaving until we take out as much of this fuel distribution operation as possible. We're going to do a surgical ground strike. But instead of targeting the enemy directly, I intend to go after those fuel tanks."

"And instead of striking on solid ground, we're going to be space walking," McCammon said, sounding glum. Mayweather wondered wryly what had happened to the gung-ho spirit with which he had imbued all of his tall tales of his past exploits.

"Once these three ships depart, Mayweather will bring the shuttlepod to position a half-klick above the containment tanks and keep station there," Chang said, ignoring the other corporal's interjection. "We'll launch our magnetic tether lines from that position."

Mayweather was liking this less and less. "Suppose your tether lines trigger some sort of security measure?"

"Then I'll have to depend on you to make us very scarce, and to do it very quickly. But absent that eventuality, the four of us will suit up and ride the tethers down to our respective targets. We will then plant our tri-thermite charges around the perimeters of each of the three tanks. Then we'll evac back to the shuttlepod, and detonate the devices from a safe distance."

Mayweather pointed at the forward window, where the fuel depot lay mostly in darkness, lit only by the running lights of the docked ships. "Let's hope all the interference out there doesn't make that impossible. The 'detonate the devices from a safe distance' part, I mean."

"Our equipment is designed for adverse circumstances, Ensign," Chang said, his eyes narrowing in evident annoyance. "At a minimum, we'll destroy the storage tanks. And I'm betting that the yield of all that volatile fuel will wipe out the entire refinery platform for us."

"What if some other Xindi ship lurking in the dust nearby sees the big 'kaboom' we're about to make and comes after us?" Eby asked, looking up from the preparations he had already begun making to the quartet of dark gray MACO-issue environmental suits.

"I thought I already covered that," Chang said, then gestured in Mayweather's direction. "Under the cover of the explosion, Mayweather will get us the hell out of here as quickly as humanly possible. I don't particularly like running, but as the ensign keeps reminding me, we do need to get back to *Enterprise* with a complete report, at the very least." Chang paused to glance significantly in Mayweather's direction before continuing to address the entire group. "I never planned on this being a kamikaze mission."

Seeing the unshakable determination in Chang's eyes, Mayweather came to the realization that he, Mayweather, might be the one embarking on a suicide errand—if he kept trying to dissuade Chang from his plan.

And despite feeling nettled by Chang's jab, he felt another surge of grudging admiration at the sheer ballsiness of the MACO leader's scheme. While growing up on the *Horizon,* Mayweather had become used to implementing seat-of-the-pants solutions in response to unexpected problems, but only rarely had the stakes been quite this high.

Nevertheless, there were aspects of Chang's plan that still bothered him, and he felt obliged to speak up about them. "We won't have long to pull this off, Corporal. If there's anybody aboard that depot, and if they get the least bit suspicious, they'll probably run some sort of scan of the exterior of the tanks. Then they'll probably spot us."

Chang nodded, a grave expression on his face. "Solutions, anyone?"

"Isn't there some way to camouflage the suits the same way we camouflaged the shuttlepod?" McCammon asked.

Mayweather thought that wasn't a half-bad idea, though he could think of no practical way to do it. "Not unless you want your mobility and your visibility stripped down to almost nil," he said.

"Can we disguise the suits somehow so that anybody scanning them will see them as part of the tanks?" Guitierrez asked, looking up from where she had been assembling multiple stacks of the disk-shaped miniature tri-thermite bombs.

"If we had samples of the hull metal, several extra hours, and a couple of Starfleet engineers, maybe," Mayweather said with a glum head shake.

"Seeing that we apparently have no other options, we'll just have to work hard and fast to get it done," Chang said. "It'll be just like one of our favorite training scenarios. Except this time, it'll be real."

With that comment, Mayweather decided to give voice to another misgiving he had about the mission. "I'm going to prep a fifth environmental suit. I'm going with you."

Silence descended over the cabin, and quickly

became deafening. The MACOs looked first at each other, then at Mayweather, disbelief etched into their faces—except for Chang, whose countenance registered only scorn.

"*Not* an option," Chang said flatly. "You're our pilot, not a MACO."

"Hold on just a minute, Corporal," Mayweather said, twisting around in his seat. "You guys may have had extensive munitions training, but how much work have you done in zero-g?"

"Enough," Chang said, turning away.

Mayweather turned to Guitierrez. "Are those armed?" he asked, pointing to her carefully stacked munitions.

"Not yet," she responded, one eyebrow raised slightly in apparent curiosity.

"Good," Mayweather said, turning back to the controls. He tapped a few of them.

Immediately, the dim illumination inside the shuttle lowered to one-sixteenth intensity, and the gravity plating shut down completely. Mayweather heard the others swearing as their movements sent them pinwheeling aft through the crew cabin, their own momentum and inertia banging them ungently against the walls, the deck, and the ceiling.

Mayweather released his seat straps and pushed his foot against the console, propelling himself gracefully back into the semidarkened cabin that he knew like the back of his hand. It had been months since his last microgravity experience, but having grown up on a ship that frequently lost its artificial gravity meant that he was almost as comfortable in freefall as he was walking—even when carefully dodging flailing MACOs in a relatively confined space.

In the faint light, he reached up to snatch two of the bombs, all of which were drifting aimlessly in the gravityless chamber. He saw Guitierrez above him, trying and failing to keep several of them from spilling out of her grasp in all directions.

"Get the gravity back *on!*" Chang yelled. He had tumbled to the port side of the shuttle's ceiling, and was clinging to it like a barnacle. Mayweather couldn't see his expression fully, but he knew there was no mistaking the anger in the MACO's voice.

"Sorry," Mayweather said. "Must be a glitch somewhere in the environmental controls." He toggled the mag switches on the bombs he had gathered, then adhered them to the bulkhead. Even as the MACOs struggled to right themselves and keep hold of their munitions, their tools, and the drifting pieces of their environmental suits, he adroitly flipped and dived, shoving off from the ceiling in order to grab more of the bombs, which he rendered harmless by attaching them to whatever metallic plane surfaces were handy. Then he began grabbing up and securing the free-floating environmental-suit helmets and life-support packs, hoping to get them all out of harm's way quickly.

Ignoring the ongoing stream of MACO invective, Mayweather finally returned to the forward cockpit area, and made a fine show of studying the systems readouts there. "My goodness, it seems that I *am* able to restore gravity now. Best find something to grab onto, everybody," he said, calling out loudly toward the stern section, his voice dripping with mock sincerity.

A moment later, he abruptly brought the lights back up and switched the gravity plates back on. He heard multiple thumps and thuds behind him as the MACOs, much of their equipment, and various small environmental suit components crashed unceremoniously to the deck.

Chang immediately picked himself up and charged into the cockpit. "I'll see to it you're cashiered out of Starfleet for that stunt!" he said, delivering his words in a single, uninterrupted snarl.

Mayweather shrugged. "*What* stunt? The records will show that there was a temporary glitch in the system—no doubt caused by some Expanse-related anomaly that we haven't catalogued yet—and that I was the most capable person aboard in dealing with the resulting zero-g conditions. It seems to me you should be *thanking* me for helping to make certain that the bombs didn't go off where they shouldn't."

He turned back and looked at the others. Although Eby seemed fine, Guitierrez and McCammon both looked a bit green around the gills from the experience. He felt a twinge of shame for what he'd just put Guitierrez through. *I hope she'll still talk to me after this is all done,* he thought. Fortunately, she seemed to have heeded his warning and thereby avoided taking a fall when the gravity came back on.

Mayweather saw that Chang was also looking over the other MACOs, and noted that the MACO squad leader didn't seem quite so steady on his feet as he had before. *It's awfully hard to look like you're in charge when you still don't quite have your space legs yet,* he thought, trying his best not to grin.

Aloud, he said, "Chang, you should know by now

that I was *raised* a boomer. I've spent probably half my life in freefall. I'm *not* just some glorified pilot. If I come along on this mission, I can help get the job done in half the time. And that time saved will go a long way toward our getting away from the Xindi with our asses attached—and with *theirs* blown to kingdom come."

Mayweather saw a panoply of emotions roll across Chang's face as the corporal considered what he'd just heard.

Finally, Chang turned and barked a terse order toward the rear of the shuttle. "Private Eby. Help Mayweather prep his environmental suit. He's coming with us."

Even as he grinned in triumph at having broken through at least some of the barriers that lay between him and Chang, shadowy thoughts began creeping into the back of Mayweather's mind. Once again, he couldn't help but wonder whether Sub-Commander T'Pol would *really* consider the coming mission to be "appropriate, prudent, and logical."

We still might get blasted by some hidden Xindi ship out there, even after these ones leave. Wouldn't it be smarter to stay aboard the shuttlepod with my hand on the rudder, just in case?

He did his best to push this last-minute negativity aside. After all, how could he live with himself if he *didn't* share the extreme risk the MACOs were all taking?

Besides, he knew he was far better suited for this particular job than any of them. *And if it's my time to go,* he thought, *at least I'll die where I did most of my living—in space.*

ELEVEN

Courier Ship Helkez Torvo

ARCHER STARED OUT THE transparent aluminum windows of La'an Trahve's cockpit, focusing on a pinpoint of light ahead that their captured pilot had assured them was the manufacturing facility where the Xindi were assembling the large-scale particle-beam weapon they intended to deploy against Earth.

"Take us in, but slowly," Archer said, looking down at Trahve from the prisoner's side. "I don't want to announce our presence here." Grudgingly, the smuggler adjusted some of the controls on the console in front of him.

Malcolm Reed sat in the copilot's chair, his brows furrowing in concentration as he studied the controls. "I'll run a battery of passive scans as best I can, Captain, but I can't vouch for the results. We're not on *Enterprise*, and I'm still trying to get a handle on this ship's systems."

Patting his munitions officer on the shoulder,

Archer offered him a gentle smile. "I'm sure your best will be more than good enough, Malcolm."

Archer was still feeling embarrassed about his recent confrontation with Reed, and wanted to avoid getting into another for as long as possible—mostly because he knew that, fundamentally, Malcolm was right. The use of torture to gain information or a tactical advantage was anathema to every principle he held dear . . . except for one. And that one—the preservation of all life on Earth—was what was driving him now. It was the principal force that had driven him mercilessly for months now, ever since Admiral Forrest and General Casey had informed him that *Enterprise* was to be the spear's point in Earth's struggle against the Xindi.

"My initial scans are showing what appears to be a large-scale construction project of some sort, Captain," Reed said. "It's about the same mass as *Enterprise,* though I'm reading it as nowhere near as dense."

Hayes stepped in close behind Archer. "How many crew are on board? How many ships are protecting it?"

"There's no way to answer either question definitively using only passive scans," Reed said. "If I start bouncing sensor signals off of that facility, then whoever might be inside will know we're coming. And I'm sure we'd also attract some unwanted attention from whatever Xindi ships are nearby." He fiddled with a few more switches and buttons, frowning as he concentrated on the alien graphics that appeared on his monitors.

"I am detecting several residual Xindi isotope trails apparently on outbound headings judging from their vacuum dilution gradients. But they seem unusually degraded, as though they were left by vessels that departed weeks ago."

Hayes turned to Archer, his voice low. "I don't like this, Captain. It's all been too easy. Finding *this* reprobate—" He paused as he gestured at Trahve, who winced slightly at the MACO leader's suddenly close proximity. "—getting passage here, and then finding their station apparently undefended. It all smells like a trap to me."

Archer nodded. "I know. But we have to get close enough to find out whether or not this really is the target we need to destroy."

"With all due respect, sir, what then?" Hayes asked, his eyes focusing on Archer's. "If you decide this isn't the target—that it's really some kind of decoy—then do we turn tail and run? If they spot us fleeing, won't that rouse their suspicions? We don't know if we can outrun them back to *Enterprise,* and we don't know what kind of firepower the *Lucky Duck* has. Hell, we don't even know that there isn't a scrimmage line of ships behind us just out of sensor range, waiting for us to turn."

Reed looked up at Archer, his hazel eyes piercing, but said nothing.

Time to put some cards on the table, Archer thought. He put a hand on Hayes's shoulder and turned him away from the forward part of the cockpit. Trahve might hear anyhow, but at least Archer could attempt to be discreet.

"We'd know," he said. "We have backup."

Hayes' eyebrows shot upward in surprise. "What? Who?"

"O'Neill," Archer said. "After Trahve agreed to take us here, I had Reed send her an encoded message burst. She has orders to follow us in Shuttlepod One, and to stay far enough behind us so that she'd notice and warn us of anything pursuing us."

Hayes nodded thoughtfully, and Archer was glad to see that even Kemper—who had his rifle practically touching the back of Trahve's skull—and Money seemed to be more than a little pleased by this revelation. "O'Neill and her crew are also gathering astrometric data to guide *Enterprise* here at top speed, should that become necessary. And she's under orders to maintain com silence unless she discovers a direct threat to this ship. We haven't heard from her, therefore we don't need to worry about watching our back."

"Or else something happened to them after they left Kaletoo," Money said quietly. "Or maybe before they even got off the ground."

Archer and Hayes both turned to look at the private, though Hayes's expression obviously carried more of a reprimand for Money's undisciplined outburst than did Archer, who was used to allowing his people to speak freely regarding mission-related matters. Apparently aware that she had overstepped MACO protocol by failing to ask Hayes's permission to speak, the young woman shifted her weight nervously from one foot to the other, saying nothing more as she concentrated closely on the barrel of the phase rifle she toted.

"So, we're set from behind, but what about what's in front of us?" Hayes asked, pointing toward the forward windows and the slowly growing Xindi facility that floated far ahead of the ship's bow. "If it is some kind of weapons platform, and they decide to lock their batteries onto us, then we're toast. And badly burned toast, at that."

"Sometimes, Major, we have to take a few risks if we expect to make any progress," Archer said, turning back toward the forward part of the cabin. "We're in the ship of a courier who makes deliveries to the Xindi. By the time they realize that he's not here to drop something off, we'll already be somewhere very far from here."

Reed turned to look up at him. "Captain, I *am* reading some life signs aboard the Xindi facility now. It could be as many as a few dozen individuals, though it's still hard to separate them out because of all the particulate matter occluding the readings. But I'm picking up no energy signatures that might indicate the activation of weapons systems."

Archer nodded, then pointed toward the steadily expanding point of light that lay in their flight path. "Can you get us a better visual than what we can see through the windows?" Though it remained small and indistinct, it was already plainly identifiable as an artificially constructed object, rather than a naturally occurring chunk of space debris. But Trahve's vessel was still far enough away from it that no specifics of the design were clearly evident.

Reed looked up at Archer, then over at Trahve. The smuggler squirmed under the tactical officer's probing gaze.

"My long-range visual sensor pickups are all down at the moment," Trahve said, his faintly apologetic voice translated by the linguistics matrix Reed carried. "I was supposed to get those systems repaired while I was ashore on Kaletoo. But I was . . . otherwise detained before I could get around to it." He offered a weak smile.

Hayes released a snort of air from his nose, and Archer thought he could actually hear the MACO officer's teeth grinding. "This is what I *mean,* Captain. This little slug is giving us just enough rope to hang ourselves with, and he's doing everything he can not to tip his hand. He's *playing* us."

Reed looked up at Archer. "I'm afraid I have to agree with Major Hayes, Captain. And as long as the major is using Wild West metaphors, I think it would be in our best interests to get the hell out of Dodge, as you Yanks used to say."

Archer glared at the two men, then at Trahve. The officers weren't being insubordinate, but he didn't appreciate the lack of support he was feeling from them both at the moment.

"Don't look to *me* for advice," Trahve said, turning slightly from his console in order to hold up his bloody, manacled hands, as though for inspection. "Whatever I say only seems to encourage more threats and violence from you people."

"Let *me* see the scans," Archer said gruffly, putting his hand on Reed's shoulder. The young officer quickly stood up from the chair, allowing Archer to sit in it.

As he studied the data in front of him, and glanced at the quickly approaching Xindi construct, Archer realized that the hairs on the back of his neck had been raised for at least the last thirty minutes, and not merely because of the tension of the mission or the disagreements that had been slowly coming to a head between himself and Reed and the MACOs. *Maybe they're right,* he thought, recalling with some embarrassment how he'd carelessly allowed himself to be captured by the Tellarite bounty hunter Skalaar shortly before the Xindi attack on Earth. *Maybe this is just another trap. And no matter how much I want to get back at the Xindi, maybe there's just no way I can manage it in a courier ship captured from some low-life smuggler.*

On the other hand, Archer couldn't dismiss the possibility that this facility was precisely what he hoped it was: something indispensable to the Xindi plan for genocide.

He suddenly noticed something odd about the scan data he was viewing. "Malcolm, did you say that the density of the Xindi facility was significantly less than it should be for its mass and size?"

Reed leaned over his shoulder, pointing at some of the instruments and gauges on the control board. "Yes. See the readings here and here."

"So why aren't we seeing a stronger titanium signature? Or duranium? And regardless of the local sensor interference, if we can read *some* Xindi life signs, shouldn't there be a lot more of them than what we're seeing here?"

"It's a *trap,*" Hayes repeated, his head just behind Archer's as he, too leaned over to look at the instruments. "The whole thing's a trap."

Despite his growing misgivings, Archer still wasn't completely convinced. Gritting his teeth, his mind raced as his anger neared its boiling point. *If you don't have anything new to contribute, Major, kindly keep your mouth shut,* he thought as he cast a silent glower that could have chewed straight through *Enterprise's* polarized hull plating.

Hayes backed away from that glower, but he didn't back down. "With all due respect, sir, you aren't exercising sufficient caution."

Trahve spoke up then, pointing toward the Xindi platform, whose surface details were clearly discernible through the forward windows, even though the facility still had to be several kilometers away. "They're still *building* the weapons facility," he said, his voice pitched higher and faster than it had been before. "I heard them talking about it."

"Right in front of you?" Archer said, scowling at the smuggler, whose credibility was dwindling at least as rapidly as his ship was approaching the weapons platform.

Trahve nodded. "They must have thought I wouldn't understand the insectoid language. They've just got a small crew on site now."

As sure as a klaxon and red lights flashing, alarms went off inside Archer's mind. *That's the first reliable information Trahve has volunteered,* he thought. *He's* lying. *He* wants *us to get closer. The weapons platform really* is *only a decoy, meant to lure us in.*

"Get him *off* the controls," he yelled to Reed, even as he reached across the console in an attempt to stop the vessel's forward acceleration himself. "We really *do* have to get the hell out of Dodge. *Now!*"

But even as Reed and Kemper hastened to snatch Trahve out of his chair, Archer saw the alien pilot slam his palm down on what appeared to be some sort of panic button. *He could have hit that switch any time,* Archer realized, feeling a sick, tumbling sensation deep in his belly. *He really* was *just playing us.*

Perhaps half a second later, the *Helkez Torvo* shuddered, her hull groaning as though in the grip of some angry deep-space deity. Reed and the MACOs struggled to maintain their footing as the deck plating beneath their feet tilted and rocked violently for several moments, while the artificial gravity system struggled to deal with the sudden additional inertial load.

Archer concentrated on the controls before him, and he knew in his gut what one of the sensor monitors was displaying, without being able to read the accompanying alien text and pictograms.

Trahve's ship had just been caught in a tractor beam that originated aboard the decoy Xindi weapons platform. And everyone aboard the little courier vessel, except perhaps for Trahve himself, was being pulled inexorably toward a most unpleasant death.

TWELVE

"YOU *BASTARD!*" growled Kemper, ramming the barrel of his phase rifle hard against the back of the alien courier's neck. "You set us up!"

So much for that unflappable MACO discipline, Archer thought as the deck shifted slightly from starboard to port and back again while the gravity plating struggled against the relentless grip of the Xindi tractor web. Aloud, he said, "Stand down, Sergeant," backing his words with as much calm authority as he could muster.

The sergeant shot a hard glare at Archer, then looked toward his MACO commanding officer for guidance. Hayes, his face a study in businesslike calm, nodded quietly. Kemper immediately took two paces backward until he stood shoulder-to-shoulder with Private Money, whose eyes were wide with apparent shock. Though he had backed away, the sergeant's weapon remained at the ready.

The captain was relieved to note that the MACOs hadn't forgotten that General Casey had placed them under Archer's authority—and that they and

Enterprise's Starfleet crew were still fighting on the same side, no matter how badly they might tend to aggravate one another personally.

At least, they haven't quite forgotten yet, Archer thought.

Glancing out the forward window, Archer saw that the false Xindi weapon platform continued to grow larger as the facility's tractors reeled Trahve's small vessel inexorably closer.

The jaws of the trap would soon spring shut, unless Archer could devise some way out, and quickly. Still seated beside Trahve in the primary pilot's seat, Archer set out immediately to do just that.

Preoccupied as he was studying the ranks of toggles and indicators arrayed on the console before him, Archer couldn't see Trahve's triumphant grin, though it was clearly audible in the alien pilot's voice.

"You really ought to save your energy for dealing with my employers, Captain," Trahve said. "After all, you're going to be seeing them very soon."

Archer ignored the man's gibe, which he knew was calculated to make him lose his cool—and thereby lose his focus. "We'll see about that."

"They're going to reward me handsomely for handing you over to them, you know. The Xindi, I mean."

"If you ask me, they don't seem to be a very trustworthy lot," said Reed, who stood beside Hayes, Kemper, and Money in the aft portion of the cockpit compartment. The tactical officer's voice dripped with unconcealed disgust. "What makes you suppose they're going to honor whatever agreements you've made with them?"

Trahve smiled tolerantly. "Ah, you simply don't know them the way I do, Lieutenant."

And that's a situation we've got to change, Archer thought as he continued his so-far fruitless labors behind the primary pilot's console. *As quickly as possible.*

"So this was your job all along," Hayes said, not asking a question. "To lure us away from our real objective to a decoy weapon site."

"Of course. How better for the Xindi to protect their *real* particle-beam weapon from discovery by *Enterprise?*"

Hayes sounded both incredulous and angry. "And you even manipulated us into beating your decoy's location out of you."

Trahve chortled quietly. "Well, I had to make the entire scenario as convincing as possible for all of you, didn't I? It was a small price to pay for a much bigger reward."

"There's got to be a way to break free of this thing," Archer said, his frustration mounting as he continued working the flight controls to no avail. "And I'm going to find it."

"There isn't, Captain, I assure you. But if it makes you feel better . . ." Trahve trailed off, and Archer glanced toward him long enough to see that he had used his feet to push his chair half a meter or so farther away from the console before him. With his hands still confined in manacles, he made an almost courtly *be my guest* gesture toward Reed, inviting him to join the captain in what was beginning to look increasingly like a completely hopeless task.

Hayes and Kemper wasted no time hustling the

alien into an adjacent seat, and Reed hastened to take the newly emptied chair beside Archer's. Private Money merely watched the proceedings in attentive, and perhaps apprehensive, silence.

No matter what commands Archer and Reed fed into the console, the little ship remained firmly caught in the tractor's apparently unbreakable grip. The Xindi weapons facility—or rather, the large-scale Xindi decoy—now filled more than half of the forward window, and continued quickly increasing in apparent size. Several docking ports, each equipped with multiple spidery grappling arms, beckoned in sinister fashion. Banks of external floodlights mounted on the facility itself made almost the entire football-field-sized platform clearly visible, along with several of its vaulted, utilitarian docking bays.

"We're going to need a lot more thrust than this boat's power plant can deliver," observed Reed, who continued working calmly yet speedily at Archer's side.

"You've noticed that, too," Archer said dryly as he continued manually entering commands. He'd already identified a number of alternative pathways through which he could supplement main power by directly tapping the warp core, though none of these appeared to have any effect on the amount of reverse thrust the vessel was able to produce. *Where's Trip when I really need him?* he thought, though he knew that his chief engineer had been in no condition to join the Kaletoo landing party. And even if Trip had been well, Archer could never have predicted developing such a keen need for the commander's engineering talents during this mission.

"We'll just have to keep at it," Reed said before lapsing into silence as he continued puzzling out the alien controls.

Feeling Trahve's eyes boring into the back of his neck, Archer spared a quick backward glance in the courier's direction.

"You've both come up with some truly ingenious approaches to power distribution, I must say," Trahve said, looking sincerely impressed. "It's too bad you won't have nearly enough time to completely puzzle these systems out."

Hayes moved with the speed of a panther, grabbing the alien by his still blood-spattered tunic, lifting him off his feet, and throwing him bodily into another chair located on the cockpit's starboard aft side.

Hayes cocked his phase rifle and pushed its barrel into Trahve's face until Archer thought he might shove it right down the alien's throat. Standing beside their superior, Kemper and Money both raised their weapons as well, their expressions blank and all but unreadable.

"If you know a way out of this, you'd better share it with us," Hayes said in a foreboding tone that gave even Archer a chill. "*Now,* mister."

Another unpleasant grin split Trahve's face, but he said nothing.

"Did you know that a phase rifle instantly cauterizes the stump when it blows a limb off?" Hayes said. "Unless you start cooperating, you're going to find out the hard way. Now help us get clear of this place."

Archer rose, leaving the console to Reed, who continued working it, though to no apparent effect. He was thankful, at least, that Malcolm hadn't spoken up again in protest against their admittedly unsavory tactics.

Trahve replied with a smug laugh. "Do you really think I can take your threats seriously anymore?"

"You will if you want to keep all your original equipment in place," Kemper said, his warning sounding out of place wrapped in the sergeant's usually easygoing, round-voweled Minnesota drawl.

"You all seem just a little bit too ambivalent about violence to do anything quite that . . . permanent," Trahve said.

Archer pointed at the front of the man's tunic, which was still stained conspicuously orange. "Are you really prepared to take that chance—especially after Major Hayes showed everybody here the color of your blood?"

Trahve chuckled again. "What's a mere beating or two? The major doesn't have the courage to maim me, nor do his guardbeasts here. And you need me too badly to simply kill me outright." Trahve sneered at Kemper, who controlled himself only with an obviously herculean effort. Money was again beginning to look apprehensive, as though the situation was spinning entirely out of her control and away from her expectations.

"I wouldn't make that assumption if I were you," said Archer. "Especially if you keep going out of your way to goad us."

"Oh come now, Captain. Don't be insulting. Do you really think that a clichéd 'sensitive constable and crazed interrogator' routine will actually work on me?"

"We're not doing any sort of 'routine' here. We're as serious as a supernova. Help us get out of this, or you're going to wish you had." *How far is he going to push me?* Archer thought. How close to the abyss would Trahve force him to walk?

Trahve shook his head, still smiling his infuriating smile. "These soldiers—or MACOs, or whatever you call them—obviously answer to you, and they're far too disciplined to act without your express authorization. But I have looked into *your* eyes, my gentle captain. And I've seen that you simply don't have it in you to get really serious about inflicting torture."

Archer forced himself not to wince at Trahve's mention of torture. Did the blows he and Hayes had already struck against their helpless prisoner already constitute torture? And was it actually going to come down to that—again?

Archer glanced over his shoulder once more at the Xindi facility, which now completely filled the forward window. One of the nearest docking ports was beginning to bear an unpleasant resemblance to the mouth of a hungry carnivore.

Turning away from the window, Archer resumed his staring contest with Trahve. "Maybe you're right," he said at length, then returned to the pilot's seat.

Ignoring Malcolm's look of relieved surprise, he resumed the task of rerouting the ship's main power.

After Captain Archer resumed his place at the pilot's console beside Lieutenant Reed, Hayes alternately studied the prisoner and the Xindi trap that continued to grow in the forward window. The immense structure approached like some interstellar leviathan intent on swallowing the entire ship whole.

Semper Invictus, he thought, though the MACO motto now struck him as somehow hollow. He felt anything but invincible at the moment, after all. They had been deceived, and would no doubt soon be captured and interrogated.

Afterward, more than likely, they would all be killed, except perhaps for Trahve, though Hayes found himself hoping that the Xindi would execute the low-life courier too as a possible security risk. *It would serve the sonofabitch right,* Hayes thought.

The mission to find the Xindi and their homeworld would go on, of course, carried out in tandem by the MACO company and Starfleet. Per the sealed final orders Hayes had left behind with his company clerk, Corporal McKenzie would lead the MACO force in his place. Not only would she make a demanding leader—those beneath her in the command hierarchy, not to mention several of her current superiors, privately referred to her as "Corporal Punishment"—she also understood the order and discipline of the troops better than anyone else besides Hayes himself. Command of the ship and the Starfleet contingent that ran her would pass to Sub-Commander T'Pol, whose reserved Vulcan demeanor would probably make for a better fit with the open-ended MACO presence aboard *Enterprise* than had Archer's more emotionally volatile personality.

The mission had to succeed, after all, regardless of what happened to any individual charged with carrying it out. Too many millions of innocents had already died and had yet to be avenged. And billions more would join those millions if either the MACO or Starfleet contingents serving aboard *Enterprise* were to falter now.

Comforted by that assumption, Hayes also felt confident that his family back on Earth would get along well enough after his death. The notion of oblivion held no real terror for him; his time in the MACOs and those bloody battles against the Janus Loop pirates had crushed the fear of death out of him years ago. Not being able to see his kids again, being incapable of reassuring them that he had died pursuing a worthy cause, were his only personal regrets.

It'll be up to McKenzie and T'Pol, or whoever ends up taking over for them if they buy the farm, too, to make sure that my kids have the luxury of mourning me, he thought.

The Xindi structure loomed steadily larger in the window before him. Hayes was pleased to note that even now he felt no personal fear of death, despite his growing certainty of its inevitability. He could only hope that Kemper and Money would also meet their respective ends with a similar sense of equanimity, and would also resist whatever interrogation techniques the Xindi might use on them in the meantime.

But he wasn't quite so certain about Archer and Reed. Certainly, they were as accomplished as any naval officers he had ever encountered. Their skills—such as an impressive ability to make sense very quickly out of utterly alien instrument panels—made them invaluable mission assets, assets that had to be protected at all costs. But Archer and Reed simply weren't the product of the MACO company's elite military training program—a grueling physical and academic ordeal that consistently chewed up and spit out ninety-five percent of even the finest candidates.

Hayes studied Reed, who remained intent on the console before him, on which he continued to work frantically—and so far fruitlessly—to free Trahve's vessel from the grip of the Xindi tractors. Though Reed appeared to be tougher, both physically and psychologically, than most of the other Starfleeters aboard NX-01, he still wasn't MACO material. At least, not quite.

Will he crack under the pressure of sustained interrogation? Hayes wondered. He shifted his gaze toward the captain. *Will Archer?*

Glancing down at his weapon, Hayes hoped he wouldn't be forced to intervene with extreme prejudice before that question was actually put to the test. But he had no illusions about the expectations of General Casey, the officer in charge of the entire MACO organization back on Earth; Casey had made it clear that *everyone* on this mission would be considered expendable, including senior officers in imminent danger of capture and interrogation.

I'll do what I have to do when the time comes, Hayes told himself, though he still hoped fervently for a postponement that he really didn't believe was possible.

A yellow light on Reed's console began flashing, attracting Hayes's eye. The MACO leader watched as Reed and the captain exchanged nods, after which Archer turned his chair so that he faced Trahve. He smiled broadly at the alien, a mannerism that Hayes found perplexing; after all, Archer hadn't succeeded in his efforts to escape the Xindi tractors, as the continued approach of the Xindi trap attested. And yet he didn't have the look of a man who was getting his affairs in order in preparation for death. Nor did Reed, for that matter.

Instead, they both looked like poker players who secretly held all the aces.

Several bright orange alarm lights on the flight-control console suddenly began flashing in a frenzied rhythm. Reed appeared unsurprised by this, and didn't even glance down at the instruments in response. Seeming equally unfazed, Archer merely regarded Trahve with a cool, appraising stare.

Hayes also looked toward the alien pilot, who was no longer smiling, smugly or otherwise. Hayes felt nearly as confused as Trahve looked.

"Maybe you're right about me, Mister Trahve," Archer said, reiterating his exchange with the alien pilot from a few moments earlier. "Maybe I *can't* bring myself to order my subordinates to simply kill you, or torture you. So I think I'll propose something else instead."

Though the manacles remained on his wrists, Trahve tried to rise from his chair, obviously intent on reaching the flight console that now lay behind the still-seated Archer. Kemper shoved the alien back into his seat, where he remained, splay-legged and goggle-eyed.

"Do you have any idea what you're doing, Archer?" Trahve said, his brow furrowed, his eyes darting across what he could see of the forward flight consoles.

Archer nodded. "I think so. If I understood your

instrument panels correctly, your warp core is now building up an internal feedback overload."

Trahve was aghast, and made no effort to hide that fact behind banter. "That's not going to break the Xindi tractor beams, Captain!"

"Of course it won't. But that's not what I'm trying to do."

A knowing look crossed the alien's face. "Ah. So this is merely yet another attempt at persuasion on your part. Either I somehow free us from the tractors, or you blow up my ship."

Archer put on a passable imitation of Trahve's carefree chuckle. "You still don't seem to get it, Trahve. In a few minutes, the rising power levels won't have anywhere to go except back into your multiply-redundant warp-core containment systems. At that point, there's going to be a fairly enormous explosion aboard this ship. One that will rip through each and every layer of core containment."

Trahve's upper lip was beginning to glisten with perspiration. He held up his manacled wrists in a gesture of entreaty. "Listen to me. You've got to let me stop it."

"If I thought I had a chance of breaking the Xindi tractor beam, I'd be tempted to let you try to do that."

"But you'll die, too, Captain. *Everyone* on this ship will die!"

Archer nodded. "And that's just for starters." The captain hiked a thumb toward the *faux* weapons-assembly facility. "Once your warp core loses antimatter containment, that entire structure out there will be blown to quarks, too."

A pair of slender, elaborately articulated mechanical grapples crossed the forward window, then vanished from sight. The little vessel shuddered as the arms grabbed the hull, which in turn transmitted a loud, reverberating clang into the cockpit.

"Why are you doing this, Archer?" Trahve asked, his eyes huge and pleading. "Why?"

"Because there could be Xindi aboard that facility who'll want to interrogate us. And *Enterprise*'s mission is simply too important to risk letting anything compromise it. And I do mean *anything,* including our own survival.

"And yours, too, incidentally, Trahve."

Hayes was impressed. He really hadn't thought that the captain, or even Reed, would have quite enough courage to face death so directly.

Hayes grinned at Trahve, who clearly wasn't made of such stern stuff. Catching the alien's frightened gaze, he nodded toward the front window, through which a second pair of mechanical grapples could be seen heading toward the ship.

"I'd offer you a front-row seat," Hayes stage-whispered in Trahve's ear with a blackly humorous smile. "If I thought any of us were going to be alive to see the fireworks show that's about to begin."

THIRTEEN

Outside Shuttlepod Two

AS THE MEMBERS OF Strike Team Hammerhead continued moving into position, one thought occupied Chang's mind almost to the exclusion of all others: *Gods, how I hate space.* The sentiment turned over and over in his mind, repeating like an endless mantra. Stars whirled with disconcerting speed in the blackness above—or was it below?—his gray-colored helmet. *Hate it, hate it, hate it,* hate *it.*

It wasn't that space was unpleasant to look at; Chang enjoyed looking at the stars through *Enterprise*'s observation windows probably as much as any of the Starfleeters did. He even found the gigantic interstellar vistas inspiring in a way he had difficulty putting into words, though he rarely felt moved to try. *Being* in space, however—specifically in zero-g freefall, no less, with the added handicap of a bulky environmental suit, a workbelt stuffed with equipment, and a conspicuous absence of decks, bulkheads, and grav plating—was a harrowing, gut-heaving sensation for which he simply had no use.

And against which Phlox's antinausea potions no longer seemed to be having much of an effect.

He silently berated himself as he looked through his faceplate at the dizzying starscape that extended toward infinity in almost every direction. And although he knew that Mayweather had been reared in space, he continued to ask himself: How was it that someone as undisciplined as this Starfleet ensign could make this look so easy? And how could Chang himself—who had aced MACO training—come up so short when it came to suiting up and making a damned spacewalk? For perhaps the tenth time today, he reminded himself that his current discomfiture wasn't rooted in any lack of courage; after all, he felt certain he'd amply demonstrated his valor on numerous occasions, in military engagements that stretched from the Martian Freehold Uprisings to the defense of Jupiter Station to the Janus Pirate War.

And now all the way to the backyard of the Xindi, he told himself, closing his eyes momentarily to chase away a furious wave of vertigo. In an effort to keep his belly level, he tried to concentrate on the very slight grinding sound that his movements were transmitting into his suit, thanks to the thin layer of improvised camouflaging material that now covered most of the suit's exterior. Again, he had to marvel at Starfleet ingenuity. While the strike team had patiently waited for the three Xindi ships to depart, Ensign Mayweather had set to work on drawing some of the dust cloud's fuel isotope particles into the airlock; less than an hour later, he had combined it with a portion of the shuttlepod's stock of emergency hull-breach repair foam, fashioning a paste that altered the sensor profile of each of the environmental suits, making them effectively blend in with the dust-caked surface of the Xindi fuel tanks. The stuff had smelled pretty nasty back inside the shuttlepod, something like spent gunpowder mixed with rotten eggs—a problem from which everyone was thankfully spared now that they were sealed into their suits—but nobody could argue with the results, at least so far. Chang could only wonder if either he or any of his people would have tumbled to such a simple yet brilliant solution on their own.

Of course, he wasn't about to speak any of these laudatory thoughts aloud—not with Mayweather himself almost literally breathing down his neck.

His stomach lurched as he opened his eyes again and surveyed the too-close horizon of the sprawling, gray-clad chemical tank, which was illuminated only by the twin beams of the powerful halogen lamps mounted on either side of his helmet, as well as by Mayweather's helmet lights. Chang felt his environmental suit ballooning alarmingly around him as he slowly and laboriously moved his magnetized boots before him across the hundred-meter-wide tank's metallic surface, one foot in front of the other. The sound of his footfalls was swallowed in the airless silence of space, except inside his suit, which picked up and amplified the vibrations created by his boots as they alternately struck and released the tank's thin, gently flexing skin.

Left *(How I hate being out here).*

Right *(God, I hate this).*

Left again *(Please, please don't let me upchuck inside the damned helmet).*

A familiar voice spoke up via a secure, tight-beam channel, echoing slightly inside his helmet. *"If you don't mind my saying so, Chang, you seem to be a little uncomfortable out here."*

Glancing toward his neck ring at the com system's small heads-up display, Chang noted with some gratitude that Mayweather hadn't made his comment on the strike team's open channel; no one else had heard the pilot's comment. Nevertheless, a curse formed on Chang's lips. He bit it back in silence, knowing that there was no point in letting Mayweather see—or, rather, hear—any cracks in his cultivated veneer of disciplined calm.

"Thank you for noticing."

"It's all part of the service," Mayweather said. *"Wouldn't want you to somehow get the idea that I'm just some sort of taxi driver, after all."*

No. Never. A quality taxi driver would have stayed with the cab. "Then I hope you're not expecting a tip."

"Well, one tip would be nice. For starters, I could use a little more advice on the best way to place these charges."

Chang turned to his right, where he glimpsed Mayweather's suited form, which was following along the tank's skin only about two meters behind him. Like Chang and the rest of the MACO strike team, the pilot wore an unwieldy-looking toolbelt over his environmental suit. Unlike the rest of the team, however, Mayweather's suit was one of the russet-colored, Starfleet-issue models. With its large, back-mounted life-support pack, Mayweather's suit was bulkier than those the MACOs wore, since it was intended for extended operations in space rather than for brief engagements in airless, zero-g environments.

Why'd I let him talk me into bringing him along on the EVA? Chang thought, shaking his head within his immobile helmet. After all, Mayweather was a pilot, not a demolitions specialist. He'd been reared among freight haulers, not elite troopers or even asteroid miners; he might know his way around space, but he was clearly lacking in the essential MACO skill of Blowing Stuff Up Real Good.

"Watch and learn, Ensign," Chang said aloud as he made another laborious stride forward before pausing. As he'd done many times since making his initial awkward climb onto the outside of the tank, Chang glanced down at the padd that was lashed to the left gauntlet of his suit. The device's small backlit screen displayed a schematic of the storage tank to which he and Mayweather were magnetically tethered. Thanks to data gathered earlier by the shuttlepod's sensors, the structure's most vulnerable seams were outlined in bright red.

Two flashing green blips, representing Chang and Mayweather, had drawn to within scant meters of the isotope tank's visibly bulging waist.

You are here, Chang thought, just as he began to notice that his nose was beginning to itch fiercely. Normally, that sensation would have been intolerable in an environmental suit, since he couldn't do a damned thing about it without exposing himself to the hard vacuum that lay just beyond his faceplate.

This time, however, Chang decided to be thankful for almost anything that served to distract him from the tortures his stomach and inner ear were suffering at the moment. His belly heaved again briefly, but settled down as the agony in the skin around his nostrils steadily escalated.

He took another step, and another after that, and then glanced down again at the padd to check on his location. Satisfied, he knelt on the gently sloping metal surface, the magnetized tip of his right boot holding him tenuously in place as he carefully opened the Velcro-secured flap of his toolbelt.

He took out the topmost of a short stack of flat, metallic disks, each of which measured some ten centimeters across; though his gloves made his fingers clumsy, he managed to pull out the device's arming pin and push it back down. As he attached the disk's magnetized top surface to the tank, a blinking red light confirmed that the mechanism was now armed and awaiting its terminal countdown-to-detonation signal.

Chang looked up and saw that Mayweather was now standing beside him, showing no obvious signs of spacesickness-related distress as he opened his own munitions bag. Mayweather's gloved hands moved with a stage magician's grace. Chang remained amazed that anyone could maneuver so quickly and confidently in microgravity. Because of the glare coming from Mayweather's helmet lamps, Chang couldn't tell whether or not the Starfleet pilot was laughing at what Chang saw as his own obvious deficits in this area.

With as much confidence as he could muster, the

MACO strike-team leader said, "Let's get the perimeter covered as fast as we can, and then double-time it back to the shuttlepod."

Before anything has a chance to go seriously wrong out here, he thought, squashing down the notion even as it surfaced in his mind.

At Target Charlie, McCammon knelt again and attached yet another explosive unit to the storage tank's wide, curving hull. Ordinarily, he would have been disappointed to have been sent to his target without a buddy—someone with whom he could share a bit of companionable martial chatter. Today, however, he was grateful to be alone.

He wondered how he was going to conceal the evidence of his steadily worsening spacesickness from his fellow MACOs—and particularly from Ensign Mayweather—once he concluded his work out here and returned to the shuttlepod's airlock. *Maybe Archer's squids really do have a good reason to call us "ground-pounders,"* he thought. *Guess I'm a shark out of water out here.*

McCammon's misery remained mostly unrelieved, though he was thankful that Doctor Phlox's drugs had at least prevented him from emptying the contents of his stomach into his helmet, an eventuality that often proved lethal to anyone sealed into an environmental suit. On the plus side, the unrelenting discomfort was keeping him focused like an asteroid-mining laser on the task at hand.

He tried to use his nausea to motivate him to increase his speed as he armed and set a fourth charge, used his magnetic boots to clomp methodically several meters farther along the tank's waist, and then knelt to set a fifth charge. Feeling almost detached from his body, he moved along, circumnavigating the huge storage tank's entire perimeter. As he worked, he began spinning the current mission in the back of his mind, trying it on as a saga of personal valor that he would add to his already highly burnished repertoire of battle yarns, suborbital skydiving tales, and other extreme-sports anecdotes the next time he held court in *Enterprise*'s crew mess.

McCammon grinned and belched simultaneously as he finished placing his twelfth and final charge. He looked backward along the skin of the fuel tank, which was illuminated only by his helmet lamps. Just barely visible above the tank's weirdly foreshortened horizon, the shuttlepod hung in the blackness at an oddly skewed angle. Fortunately, the boat remained unmolested, at least so far, by any Xindi vessels that might have been lurking unnoticed nearby. At this distance the little ship looked as small as a child's toy, making McCammon uncomfortably aware that he owed his life to a few scant millimeters of transparent aluminum, and not many more cubic centimeters of air.

Per MACO mission protocols, he used his chest-mounted compad to send two clicks over Strike Team Hammerhead's open channel, thereby reporting that his charges had all been placed at Target Charlie.

Just don't pop the caps, Guitierrez, until after I get back inside that Starfleet boat, he thought as he pointed his magnetic boots toward the distant shuttlepod and took his first woozy step back toward relative safety.

Several minutes later, as McCammon reached the shuttlepod's tether line to Target Charlie, a portion of the tank's hull shifted very slightly beneath his left boot. But in his haste to leap free of the tank—and into space to reach the shuttlepod—he ignored it.

I've really gotta find a way to spend more time in zero-g, Guitierrez thought, incredulous. There was something liberating about being in freefall, and her only regret was that she had to remain tethered, via her magnetic boots, to the huge isotope storage tank at Target Baker.

But the best part of being out here was that she no longer felt a trace of the gut-clenching nausea she had been experiencing since shortly before she had discovered her pregnancy. *Who would have thought that microgravity was the cure for morning sickness?* she thought. *Maybe Phlox will want to write a paper about this.*

After he helped her figure out what to do about the damned pregnancy in the first place, of course. Naturally, that couldn't happen until after she finally gathered up enough courage to tell him about it.

Which, she knew, was effectively the same as telling Major Hayes, who would have to be informed, since the Xindi-hunt mission protocols would surely trump the sanctity of any doctor-patient relationship aboard *Enterprise.* And that would no doubt summarily end her MACO career, as well as Nelson's.

Whether I bring the baby to term or not, whether I keep the baby or send it away, Hayes will have to cashier us both. He won't care that we don't serve in the same squad. He's going to say, "Fraternizing is fraternizing," and that'll be that.

"You okay up there, Guitierrez?" Eby said, the sudden appearance of his sharp voice inside her helmet startling her into almost losing her grip on the last of her half-dozen magnetized explosive disks. *"You need to stay focused, Corporal."*

"Don't you worry about *my* focus, Private," Guitierrez said, nettled at what sounded uncomfortably like an order coming from a trooper she outranked. "Right now I've got more focus than I know what to do with. Any sign of countermeasures?"

"Negative, either active or passive."

Guitierrez was relieved to hear that, but she expected her current, relatively nausea-free state of combat-ready nervousness to continue for at least as long as they remained out here, exposed to whatever surprises the Xindi might decide to throw at the strike team. As gently as she might lay an infant down into a bassinet, she set the final disk in place on the skin of the storage tank, where it sat armed and ready. Next, she double-checked the timer-detonator control padd strapped to her left gauntlet, examining the readout that confirmed the successful deployment of each and every one of the radio-linked explosive charges in all three target areas on the Xindi facility. Then she keyed in the INITIATE command. At her signal, each explosive device would independently begin its final thirty-second countdown to detonation.

Using Strike Team Hammerhead's open channel, she sent a pair of clicks that declared to the entire group that her task was now complete. "Race you back to the shuttlepod, compadres," she said, speaking into the silence of her suit rather than either of the voice channels; there was no point in unnecessarily risking com-signal interception by the Xindi. "It's showtime."

The rest of the team acknowledged remotely, also using clicks, and while Guitierrez and Eby began retracing their cumbersome steps back toward the shuttlepod, something deep in her belly seemed to kick.

But she felt certain—or at least *almost* certain—that it was nothing more than a warrior's natural apprehension about engaging a thus-far invisible enemy.

Back at Target Abel, Chang noted the bomb-deployment confirmation signals that were coming in on his padd, and clicked his acknowledgment to both. Relief was racing through him like an endorphin; his ad hoc plan was going to work. All the strike team had to do now was get out of harm's way as quickly as possible, board the shuttlepod, and then double-time it back to *Enterprise* to make their after-action reports. With the explosion of the fuel tanks to provide a covering distraction, he thought they had a fair chance of evading any Xindi ships that might have lingered unnoticed nearby. He cast a quick grin in the direction of Mayweather, who was walking alongside him, his expression as unreadable as ever in the glare of both men's helmet lamps.

"How much farther to the shuttlepod?" Chang asked over the secure, tight-beam com channel, his eyes sweeping the close, rolling horizon of the cylindrical storage tank as they continued their slow, methodical walk along its duranium spine. The shuttlepod itself was out of sight.

"We should be able to see her after we cover about another thirty meters in this direction," said Mayweather, who was consulting the padd on his arm without slowing his pace. *"We'll reach our tether line, and start pulling ourselves back aboard, about twenty meters after that."*

A seeming eternity later, just as Chang was about to ask Mayweather to check his directions again, the shuttlepod hove into view just above the gleaming metal horizon. Another enormous gust of relief blew across the corporal's soul, not only at seeing the shuttlepod again, but also because he could see a member of the team—McCammon, probably, since he was the only trooper who had been working unaccompanied—drifting quickly toward the airlock that lay atop the shuttlepod, using both leg power and inertia for propulsion, and guiding his trajectory with one of the tether lines that connected the spacecraft to each of the three Xindi storage tanks. Very soon, the entire team would be back aboard the little ship, and then the bombs could all be sent into their final countdowns.

Chang felt a sudden, unfamiliar vibration beneath his grav boots. Then, after he disengaged the right boot's magnet, he discovered that he couldn't raise either of his feet from the tank's surface; even with the magnets shut down, both boots remained stubbornly locked in place, as though he were an insect caught in tree sap.

"What the hell?" Chang said. He looked toward

Mayweather, who had come to a stop beside him, evidently every bit as rooted to the fuel tank as Chang was.

"I can't move, either," the ensign said.

Shit! Chang thought. *One of us must have triggered some sort of security countermeasure somehow. Or maybe we've been seen by actual Xindi.*

Just over the horizon, McCammon was vanishing into the open outer airlock hatch on the shuttlepod's dorsal surface. The spacecraft itself now seemed impossibly distant, as unreachable as the Andromeda Galaxy.

Chang's com system crackled to life, carrying McCammon's not-quite-so-confident-as-usual voice. *"Shuttlepod Two to Strike Team Hammerhead. I'm back in the boat. Where the hell is everybody?"*

Corporal Guitierrez spoke up a moment before Chang could find his voice. *"Shuttlepod Two, we have a problem. Eby and I are both stuck in our tracks. Looks like some sort of electromagnetic security trap, but the field's getting so strong it's interfering with my scanner."*

Then it could interfere with Guitierrez's remote detonator-timer controls, too, Chang thought, his stomach once again pitching and yawing, just as his and Mayweather's suit lamps abruptly cut out, and the icy fingers of interstellar space began tracing feather-light touches along the length of his spine. *Not to mention our environmental suits.*

With a shock of horror, he realized that everyone in Strike Team Hammerhead except for McCammon was fixed in place here, like a pod of Rigelian root-grubs.

"*—orporal Chang?*" Guitierrez's tone was beseeching, though her signal was becoming distorted by static.

"*—ame over!*" Eby was shouting, his cries almost entirely swamped by the rising tide of static. "*We're f—*"

Setting aside his own mounting fear, Chang said, "Hold it steady, people! We just need a new plan."

Chang only wished he actually had one.

Enterprise NX-01

The wedding was quite probably the largest catered affair Trip had ever seen.

His great-grandniece was finally to be married. One of the granddaughters of his beloved sister, Lizzie, was all grown up and starting a life of her own, amid hundreds of family members and friends. The guest list spanned at least four generations.

The warm scent of hay and peach blossoms filled the air under the azure canopy of a fair May afternoon. Well-wishers arrayed themselves in happy, semi-orderly ranks on either side of the wedding party. The bride, escorted by her father down a verdant green lawn in the shadow of a centuries-old church, was radiant.

Then the bride vanished abruptly in a blaze of light that scorched the air, tingeing it with the harsh metallic odor of ozone. The ranks of wedding guests reacted, tumbling quickly from exultation and joy into chaos and panic. One by one, the guests, from elderly ladies to toddlers, flared into short-lived nimbi of brilliance and vanished as well, disappearing by the dozens until Trip stood essentially alone.

"Lizzie!" Trip shouted, moving as quickly as he could through the rapidly diminishing crowd, desperately seeking his closest living relative. He ignored the pain in his tired old bones as he made haste toward the small white gazebo where he had last seen her.

And there she was, turning toward him, speaking to him, though he couldn't hear anything over the escalating tumult that surrounded him. Nor did he seem to be making much headway in getting to her; she seemed to remain perpetually ten meters or so out of his reach, as though he were trying to swim toward her through gelatin.

"Lizzie! Elizabeth!"

Lizzie was still looking toward him, but was no longer trying to speak. An immensely sad expression now clouded her lined, elderly face. When had she gotten so old? When had he? Trip couldn't remember.

Then he suddenly understood why he couldn't remember.

Lizzie never got this old, Trip thought, still unable to reach his baby sister. *She never got anywhere* near *this age.*

She waved at him one final time, looking both rueful and resigned. Then she vanished in a blaze of scorching, blinding light.

Along with generations of others who either died at the hands of the Xindi or were never born in the first place because of the aliens' cowardly sneak attack all those decades ago.

A moment later, the horrible light engulfed Trip as well, and he screamed.

• • •

"Welcome back to the world of the living, Commander Tucker," the voice said. Though he couldn't see anything just yet, Trip could sense the underlying benign smile that propelled that voice.

"Phlox," Trip rasped as his eyes at last opened and began to focus. "What the hell happened to me, Doc?"

"You've been unconscious for about a day and a half, Commander," said the Denobulan chief medical officer, who then turned and nodded toward another nearby sickbay bed, on which Hoshi Sato lay; beyond her lay several others. Though Hoshi looked pale and tired, the young woman seemed uninjured and fully conscious, and most of the other patients seemed to have begun stirring as well. "You, Ensign Sato, and twelve other crew members have been in a coma-like state ever since the sudden spatial anomaly swept through E deck. Thankfully, everyone who was affected already seems to be reverting to normal."

E deck, Trip thought. *The mess hall.* It occurred to Trip then that the last thing he remembered was being in the mess, sitting at one of the dining tables across from T'Pol. Then the dreams had come, visions even more disturbing than the ones that still visited him routinely during his normal sleep shifts, in spite of T'Pol's nearly daily Vulcan neuropressure treatments.

"I think I'd better talk to the captain and get myself up to date."

Phlox's only response was an uncomfortable-looking smile as he handed Trip a glass of water to alleviate his hoarseness.

Trip drank thankfully, but before he could inquire further about the captain's current whereabouts, and whatever else had been happening aboard *Enterprise* over the past few hours, the transparent sickbay doors slid open. T'Pol strode into the room, taking graceful, purposeful steps. Trip realized that Phlox must have called her down to sickbay when he had first begun showing signs of regaining consciousness.

As T'Pol came to a stop in front of him, Trip set down his glass on the bedside table and favored her with a small, wry smile. "Sounds like I'm in need of a pretty damned thorough briefing."

He got one, and he absorbed it in unsurprised silence.

Two landing parties off the ship at once, he thought, resting on his elbows. Both shuttlepods had carried some of *Enterprise*'s very best people off into two separate sets of dangers. Not only was the captain walking into what might well turn out to be a Xindi trap, but so had Malcolm, Travis, D.O. and Ensign Chandra—friends and colleagues whom he now couldn't safeguard by trying to go on one mission or the other in their place. Whatever the outcome of either team's efforts, everything that happened would be a pure *fait accompli* now, for better or for worse. And the die had been cast while he'd been summarily dealt out of the game. *And all because of a whim of Delphic Expanse fate.*

Trip exchanged a wordless but sympathetic glance with Hoshi, who seemed to be having similar thoughts. After all, if they both hadn't been KO'd simultaneously by the E deck anomaly, might not his engineering skills, and her gift for languages, be making some crucial difference between life and death for one or the other of the away teams—perhaps right this very minute?

Even T'Pol seemed to be sensitive to his misgivings, albeit in her uniquely cold, Vulcan way. "There's nothing you can do to affect the outcome of either mission, Commander," she said very quietly. "Even your presence among one of the shuttlepod crews would not necessarily guarantee a successful outcome. It is illogical to dwell on it."

Trip nodded in grudging agreement, though the thought still didn't sit well with him. "I know that, T'Pol. I just hope they're doing all right out there. I guess it's really all I can do at this point."

"Both teams are extremely competent," T'Pol said impassively. "And with their complements of MACO troops, I'm certain that they have matters well in hand."

Trip nodded again. But T'Pol's bland assertion of confidence sounded suspiciously like somebody's famous last words. Even on a milk-run mission, after all, there were simply too many damned things that could go wrong.

Trip lay back against the biobed's single hard pillow, fervently hoping that neither Murphy nor Finagle were enforcing their respective laws today.

Outside Shuttlepod Two

Mayweather tried once again to lift his boots, the left one first, followed by the right. It was a useless gesture, as he'd expected; like Chang beside him, he remained rooted in place, shivering as the heat inside his suit steadily dissipated.

"I wonder what else can go wrong? What's next, a sneak attack by a hidden Xindi ship?" Chang said after he'd ignited another brief string of caustic, clearly MACO-minted epithets. The intermittent but frequent blasts of static that were coming over the com channel—obviously originating from the very magnetic trap that continued to hold four strike-team members in place where they stood on the outer skin of the Xindi fuel tanks—were already making conversation difficult.

Working hard to keep his own rising anxiety at bay, Mayweather registered some surprise at Chang's increasingly emotional outbursts. People born and raised in space simply didn't speculate about possible disastrous outcomes while in the midst of an extravehicular activity; all such discussions were supposed to take place sometime before or after, and in far safer places than in untethered environmental suits surrounded by hard vacuum. *And these guys really consider* us *undisciplined?*

Still, Chang's concerns about the sudden appearance of another Xindi vessel resonated with Mayweather, who once again felt the stomach-sinking fear that he had compromised the mission by convincing Chang to bring him along on the EVA. Once again, he had to remind himself of the futility of this line of thought; even if he had both hands on the shuttlepod's rudder right at this moment, he still wouldn't be able to outrun an attack by a warp-driven Xindi ship, if one should appear.

Turning his helmet in Chang's direction, Mayweather

breathed a silent prayer of thanks that at least the suits' radios still seemed to be working, however marginally. Then he said, "Maybe we ought to concentrate on whatever we have that's still working properly—and put it to good use. After all, that's really the only hope we have of finding a way out of this mess."

Chang remained silent for a lengthy moment, and in the absence of both suits' helmet lamps Mayweather was beginning to be able to see the MACO squad leader's face as he carefully schooled his expression back into its customary mask of inspection-tour stoicism.

"All right," Chang said finally, speaking around yet another bacon-frying crackle of static. *"Why don't you giv—me an—nventory?"*

"Well, we have our radios." Another sudden oceanic swell of electromagnetic noise prompted Mayweather to think, *For now, at least.* "And we have a fully operational shuttlepod, with one member of the strike team already back on board her."

"But that shuttlep—is still connected to these storage tanks by our tether lines," Chang said. *"And McCammon isn't rated as a pilot. I never should have let you suit up and leave the boat."*

But you did, *didn't you?* Mayweather thought. Despite his irritation, and his own regrets, he understood that pointing this out would have been just about as useless as Chang's own comment had been.

"Chang, we have to stay focused on getting ourselves out of this situation," he said finally, willfully inflecting his voice with patience. "I mean, the explosives aren't armed yet, the camouflage layer on our suits still seems to be intact, we still have air, and there's been no sign of other Xindi vessels since we began the EVA. So we can probably afford to devote a few hours to solving this problem if we have to."

A moment later, an alarm flashed through the strike team's open com channel, interspersed with a steadily rising tide of static. Mayweather tensed, looking toward the fuel tank's dark horizon, where he expected to see the running lights of a swooping Xindi vessel appear at any moment.

But no such apparition met his searching eyes. Instead, he heard the voice of Corporal Guitierrez coming over the strike team's com loop, and her words sounded flash-frozen with fear. "*—think we must have tripped another Xindi countermeasur—*

"*Repeat, Guitierrez,*" Chang said. "*We—idn't copy that.*"

"*—said that the explosives all just started their final—ountdown to detonation.*" Another quick, uncomfortably loud blast of electromagnetic hash reverberated painfully through Mayweather's helmet. "*—all by themselves. We have —ust under thirty seconds.*"

Though he knew it was pure superstition, Mayweather wished he could move his feet just for a moment—not to escape, but to kick Chang for violating the boomer's taboo against tempting the fates that ruled the great uncaring universe.

FOURTEEN

Courier Ship Helkez Torvo

CLANG.

The second set of grappling arms engaged, holding fast to the hull of Trahve's ship. Meanwhile, the cockpit console readouts, the noisily flashing alarms, and the persistent rumbling from the bowels of the vessel confirmed that the ship's engines were still progressing inexorably toward containment failure. Internal stresses continued to build energies and pressures that would shortly seek their level via a catastrophic engine overload.

This sudden "reequilibrium" of the warp core's vast energies would, of course, be followed by a tremendous, annihilative matter-antimatter explosion that would momentarily burn as hot and bright as the photosphere of a G-type star.

Reed hadn't been so certain that his own death was imminent since nearly two years earlier, when he and Commander Tucker had nearly been frozen and asphyxiated aboard the very same shuttlepod that had ferried him and his current teammates to Kaletoo. But his growing certainty of his coming demise was accompanied this time by a surprising sense of tranquillity that he hadn't experienced on that previous occasion, possibly because this time he had far less time to fret over his many missed opportunities, alienated family members, neglected personal affairs, and lost loves. As he vainly worked the alien console alongside Archer, continuing to seek a means of breaking Trahve's ship loose from its confinement, he regarded his final moments with the wry, detached amusement of a condemned prisoner who had already been granted more stays of execution than he could count.

"Is there any sign we've gotten the Xindi's attention yet?" asked Archer, who paused in his labors over the pilot's console to stare resolutely out the forward window at the Xindi weapons platform.

Reed quickly consulted the alien characters that scrolled frenetically across the instruments on his side of the console. Though he still couldn't read the text, it wasn't hard to intuit the meanings of most of the graphics, which denoted various systems gauges and indicators.

"No, sir," Reed said, shaking his head with a resigned sigh. Then his back stiffened as he noticed a sudden change on his board. "Wait—I'm detecting a large falloff in the energy output of their tractor beam generator."

At that moment, the shuttlepod trembled and rattled slightly, as though it had been struck amidships simultaneously by small objects on its port and starboard sides. A heartbeat or two later, the sounds and vibrations repeated themselves.

Archer turned toward Reed and grinned. "They've just released all four of the docking arms. They must have figured out what we're up to."

"And they're inviting us to kindly blow ourselves up someplace else," Reed said, answering the captain's grin with one of his own.

"Fine, good, great!" Trahve babbled behind them, clearly agitated almost to the point of coming unhinged. "We might still have enough time to bleed off our excess power and stop the engine overload you've started!"

Working the pilot's console before him, Archer addressed Trahve without turning around. "We might, but only if we shut down the whole propulsion grid right now."

"So *do* it!"

"And let the Xindi just grab us again with their tractor beam? I already told you, I'm not going to allow the Xindi to capture any of us. And the best way to ensure that they can't do that is by keeping them worried."

"You don't think they're sufficiently worried?" Trahve said, his voice raised almost to a shriek. "They're trying to turn you *loose!*"

"Control yourself, Trahve," Archer said with exaggerated calmness. "Or your head will explode before your ship does."

"That's precisely the fate I'd like to avoid, Captain. For *all* of us." Though his hands were still shackled before him, Trahve struggled to get to his feet, only to be pushed back down by Sergeant Kemper, who was standing closer to the alien courier than was either Major Hayes or Private Money.

"Please *don't* bother the driver," Kemper said.

Hayes moved up into the cockpit area, a concerned look crossing his otherwise taciturn features as he leaned forward between the pilot's and copilot's chairs. "Have you received any response to that signal you sent to the shuttlepod, Captain?"

Archer shook his head. "I ordered Lieutenant O'Neill to maintain com silence, so she wouldn't risk announcing her presence to the Xindi."

"So she either heard us and headed straight for us, or she didn't," Kemper said with admirable calm. Reed glanced back in the major's direction, and noted that Kemper and Money both looked quietly terrified behind him.

"Then I suppose a nick-of-time cavalry rescue is probably a little too much to hope for," Hayes said with a small smile.

"Not necessarily," Reed said, looking up and sideways at the MACO leader.

Hayes seemed surprised. "When did you become such a reckless optimist, Lieutenant?"

"I simply meant that a last-minute reprieve wasn't too much to *hope* for, Major. But I also think it's not a good idea to *count* on it."

"That's the spirit," Hayes said wryly, patting Reed on the shoulder. The whine of the overstrained engines grew ever louder and more ominous. Since Reed's specialty was blowing things up, he knew that it wouldn't be long before Trahve's vessel vaporized itself.

"You people must be insane," Trahve said, the

translation equipment rendering his words in suitably fearful and incredulous tones. "Do you *want* to die?"

The ship abruptly shuddered again, this time far more roughly than it had when the Xindi docking arms had released it. The jarring noise and vibration, coupled with the screaming of the alarm klaxons and overtaxed propulsion components, momentarily convinced Reed that the end had indeed come at last.

But half a beat later he noticed that Trahve's courier ship hadn't yet disintegrated, in defiance of the escalating noise and tumult.

"What was that?" Hayes said, shouting to be heard over the din.

Archer got out of his chair and faced Hayes. "Get everybody into the airlock, Major!"

Reed rose and grinned at Hayes, savoring the major's look of confusion. "I think the cavalry has just arrived."

Archer had never much enjoyed placing himself in extreme physical jeopardy. But over the past two years he had discovered that he could make the sensation far more tolerable if he pretended he was merely engaged in a particularly cutthroat water polo match. The sport had been his principal athletic pursuit during his university years, and he had been a serious competitor, always playing to win.

But today, with La'an Trahve's ship perhaps only moments away from violently immolating itself, the stakes were far higher than Stanford U.'s standing in the championships. Today, he would either win the match, or he would die, along with his entire team.

As well as, quite possibly, his mission to safeguard the planet Earth from the Xindi.

Archer allowed Hayes and Kemper to lead the way from the cockpit into the single narrow corridor that ran along the spine of Trahve's courier vessel, and around a corner that led to the ship's single, utilitarian airlock bay. Assisted by Money, the two senior MACOs hustled Trahve along with them down the corridor.

As the MACOs moved forward, Archer glimpsed their faces in profile, then focused on Hayes in particular. While he appeared markedly less nervous than did his two subordinates, even the MACO commanding officer couldn't conceal his apprehension entirely.

While Archer couldn't say he was exactly enjoying their discomfiture, he made an even greater effort than usual to appear cool and confident whenever any of the MACOs were watching him. *There's no harm in letting them see they're not the only branch of Earth's services that receives expert training,* he thought.

The team came to a stop a moment later at the corridor's end. Through the slender observation port located to the side of the airlock chamber's inner door, Archer could see portions of the hull of Shuttlepod One, angled so that its dorsal surface—specifically, its already-open airlock hatch—was facing the starboard-side external airlock door of Trahve's vessel.

"I don't suppose there's any reason to continue maintaining com silence now," Reed said, barely managing to outshout the alarm klaxons that the acoustics of the corridor were amplifying slightly past the point of pain. "If we can just look out the window and see the shuttlepod out there, then so can the Xindi."

"Agreed," Archer said.

"Can't they just slap *another* tractor beam on the shuttlepod?" Money asked.

"Maybe," Archer said as he withdrew his communicator from his field jacket. "But I think they may have their hands full trying to get rid of the ticking time bomb we're about to leave at their front door."

Archer flipped open the communicator's antenna grid with practiced ease, and the little transceiver's distinctive activation chirp was completely lost in the ambient noise. Cranking the gain all the way up, he shouted into the tiny audio pickup, "Archer to Shuttlepod One. We're at Trahve's airlock, ready and waiting to come aboard."

The reply was audible, but only barely. *"O'Neill here, Captain. Message acknowledged. It's good to hear your voice, sir."*

"We can hug and kiss later, Lieutenant. This ship's engines are overloading. She's getting ready to blow herself apart. Are you hard-docked with us yet?"

She replied after a slight pause. *"No, sir. I just made an attempt, but something went wrong during the docking capture procedure. I'm going to pull back a few meters and give it another try."*

Archer watched with mounting anxiety as the shuttlepod moved backward several meters. Small, silent puffs of compressed gas blossomed momentarily along its bow as the craft's maneuvering thrusters fired. Very slowly, the shuttlepod's hull closed again with Trahve's outer airlock, until the two hulls met with a brief clang that was audible thanks to the vibrations being transmitted through Trahve's hull.

Archer noticed that Money and Kemper were both eyeing him with undisguised nervousness, which he no longer found the least bit entertaining. The tense frowns exchanged by Reed and Hayes reinforced his growing suspicion that something was going terribly, terribly wrong. All the while, the keening of the alarm klaxons and the scream of the forcibly overloaded engines increased in both urgency and volume.

"Docking status?" Archer shouted into the communicator.

"Dammit!" O'Neill said. *"Sorry, sir. The docking capture procedure failed* again. *I'm not sure why."*

Archer felt a single bead of sweat free itself from his hairline and begin rolling onto his forehead. "Lieutenant, this ship isn't going to last much longer."

"I need a few minutes to get this snag worked out, sir. Can you shut down the engine overload?"

"Not without letting the Xindi capture us all, Lieutenant. If you can't get us aboard the shuttlepod, I'm going to have to order you to get clear of us, and make best speed back to *Enterprise."*

Assuming that the Xindi don't intercept the shuttlepod on its way back to the ship, he thought.

Archer could barely hear O'Neill's reply, and tried to boost the gain on his communicator further as she spoke. *"Understood, Captain. I'm scanning to try to figure out why I can't achieve an airtight seal with Trahve's ship."*

"We only have a few minutes left at most, Commander. You've got to dock with us *now."*

Eternities passed during which Archer waited for O'Neill to slay whatever gremlins had assailed her. Despite the alarms, the sound of his own pulse thundered in his ears, drowning out everything except for the silence that blared from the communicator he clutched in his sweat-slicked hand.

Archer abruptly became aware that Hayes was speaking to him, sounding agitated as he struggled to outshout the din of the klaxons. "Even if we do manage to get aboard the shuttlepod and get away from here—"

"We will, Major," Archer interrupted, in no mood for negativity. *Somehow.*

Hayes looked irritated. "Fine. *Once* we get away, can't the Xindi just follow us?"

"I suppose that depends on how thoroughly Trahve's ship destroys this place when it goes 'boom,'" Archer said.

"And there are still dense clouds of dust and gas out there that we can use to hide ourselves," Reed said.

O'Neill's voice suddenly returned, slightly distorted by the high volume setting of Archer's communicator. *"Captain, I've figured out what's going wrong with the docking procedure."*

Archer could feel his chest lurch as his heart took a hopeful leap. "That's great, D.O. How quickly can you fix it?"

Another pause. Then, *"I'm afraid I can't, sir. Not without at least a couple of fully equipped engineers in environmental suits, and at least half an hour."*

The joyful flight of Archer's heart suddenly felt more like a meteor's fiery plunge on its way to cratering. At that precise moment, he made eye contact with Hayes, who restrained whatever fear he was experiencing behind a great bulwark of MACO stoicism.

"Explain, Lieutenant," Archer shouted into his communicator.

"Our airlock and Trahve's don't appear to be compatible, sir." She sounded embarrassed as well as frustrated. *"Without access to a transporter, the only way to establish an airtight dock between these two ships is to unroll one of our pleximer emergency tubes."*

Archer knew that he had no right to be surprised by this. After all, spacecraft built by various species, many of them never previously contacted, had docked successfully with *Enterprise*, and few crew members now regarded this fact as noteworthy in itself. However, what was really remarkable was the fact that *more* alien vessels hadn't proved incompatible with Starfleet's airlock specs.

"Tubes?" Trahve asked, his speech evidently still being translated by Reed's padd despite the noise.

"They're pressurized boarding tubes made out of a lightweight polymer plastic," Reed explained. "But setting one up would take about ten minutes more than we have."

Time seemed to dilate and distend as Archer's mind worked the problem, searching for a hitherto undiscovered angle, yet finding none. *Why do things never get this complicated in those old flat-projection sci-fi films?* he thought, suddenly experiencing an absurd desire for a comfortable seat in the crew mess, to partake in the recently lapsed *Enterprise* tradition known as movie night, a bag of fresh, hot-buttered popcorn in his lap as he watched the ancient, flickering images.

And with that fleeting, impertinent wish came another, perhaps equally absurd idea.

"Sir?" said Reed, who Archer realized was watching him with a concerned expression, as were all three of the MACOs. Trahve appeared to be very close to birthing puppies.

"Respectfully, Captain," Reed continued, placing a hand on Archer's shoulder. "Perhaps you should order Lieutenant O'Neill to get the shuttlepod to safety."

Archer nodded solemnly. Then he grinned, and this time couldn't help but enjoy the nonplussed expressions of everyone else present. "Maybe you're right, Malcolm. I guess we'll all find out in another minute or two."

Then he placed his left hand on a keypad on the wall and tried a couple of experimental commands. Within moments, the airlock's inner hatch slid obediently open.

The klaxons continued to blare unabated, and Archer shouted into his communicator. "Archer to Shuttlepod One. I want you to listen carefully. . . ."

FIFTEEN

Outside Shuttlepod Two

"TWENTY-SEVEN SECONDS," Guitierrez said, speaking directly into Mayweather's helmet over the strike team's open channel. Mayweather was thankful that she stopped counting aloud at that point, but a glance at the digital display on his dust-caked, gauntlet-mounted padd display quickly confirmed that the three dozen explosive devices Strike Team Hammerhead had planted were continuing to tick down toward their coordinated date with oblivion—while four members of the team, including Mayweather himself, remained electromagnetically glued to the Xindi isotope storage tanks.

As he stared at the tiny shuttlepod that still hung at the end of its tether just over the huge fuel tank's short horizon, Mayweather wondered for a fleeting instant what the coming explosion would feel like. Would death take him instantaneously? Or would a jagged piece of flying shrapnel tear his environmental suit first, treating him to all the blood-boiling, freeze-drying ravages of explosive decompression and vacuum asphyxia before he lost consciousness and died?

"There's got to be a way to stop the bombs from counting all the way down to detonation," Mayweather said, hoping that the increasingly intense static the Xindi security countermeasures were sending into the team's com channel wouldn't drown him out entirely.

"Not if the countdown gets down below five," Chang said.

Mayweather glanced again at his digital readout. TWENTY-TWO, TWENTY-ONE, TWENTY.

"Chang to Guitierrez. Activate the remote override."

"Already tried it twice, boss," Guitierrez replied, shouting over the steadily intensifying interference. *"—ignal's not getti—through to more than half of them."*

Dammit! Mayweather thought. If even half the bombs detonated, the violence of the explosion of the ignited fuel would surely be more than enough to kill everyone still stuck on the outside of the fuel tanks. The blasts would almost certainly destroy the shuttlepod as well, even though it was moored nearly half a kilometer away.

Chang's voice, crisp and businesslike, sounded again in Mayweather's ear. *"Chang to McCammon! I want you to get that shuttlepod clear.* Now!"

"Affirmative," McCammon responded after a very slight pause. *"Soon as I release the tether lines."*

Operating on instincts that had always served him well as a spaceborn boomer, Mayweather had begun speaking almost before he realized what he was saying. "Belay that order, Corporal McCammon, on Captain Archer's authority! Don't move that shuttlepod, and leave those tethers in place!"

Even though the Xindi security systems had magnetized all of the strike-team members—except McCammon—to the fuel-tank hulls, that shuttlepod still represented their only chance of escape. And the tether lines that ran from the shuttlepod to each of the three large tanks might turn out to be the only way everyone could be assured of getting back to the shuttlepod.

Assuming, of course, that the imminent—and unanticipated—explosion of the MACOs' entire incendiary arsenal didn't render the idea of escape utterly moot sometime in the next few seconds.

Chang's only response to Mayweather's challenge was a pungent string of curses, followed by a wordless silence that Mayweather knew was going to cost everyone on the team their lives—unless he continued to act precipitously and decisively. Blistered by the obvious anger behind Chang's latest string of epithets, Mayweather felt fleetingly glad that the MACO team leader's magnetized boots still rendered him immobile.

But he was far more concerned about the ticking clock than he was with Chang's wrath. *Prioritize your problems,* he thought, recalling the first rule of boomer survival that his father had taught him more than twenty years earlier.

He immediately set about putting that rule into practice. "Mayweather to Guitierrez. Keep sending that override signal to the bombs."

"—knowledged. Dunno what—ood it'll do, tho—"

"Shuttlepod Two, do you copy?"

Static hissed and screamed in his ear like a feral animal. *"—still here, and I've left the tether lines up. If you're wrong, you're in deep sh—"*

"We're all in it deep, Corporal. Now listen. Guitierrez's remote override signal can't pierce the interference." He glanced down at his padd's readout again. FIFTEEN. FOURTEEN. *Shit!* "Can you use the shuttlepod's transceiver to boost her gain?"

"—unno. Which buttons do I push?"

TWELVE. ELEVEN.

Unbelievable, Mayweather thought, suddenly wishing yet again that he'd listened to Chang and agreed to stay aboard the shuttlepod—not for the sake of his own safety, but because he knew what to do with the ship's instruments, unlike these arrogant, undereducated—

Easy, Travis, he told himself as he began frantically entering commands into his padd's manual interface, hoping all the while that his suit's bulky gloves hadn't introduced some critical error into his string of override code.

EIGHT. SEVEN. SIX.

Done, he thought, watching the countdown approach the point of no return with a weird sense of equanimity. *One way or another.*

FIVE.

He stared unblinking at his instrument readouts for several seconds. The number continued staring back at him, unchanged. Except for the faint grinding of the joints of his grit-camouflaged suit, the entire universe seemed to have gone abruptly silent, as though holding its breath.

"Mayweather to McCammon. You there, Corporal?"

A pause, followed by another brief blast of static. *"—inally breathing again, Ensign."*

"What did you do?" Chang said. Like McCammon, he also seemed to have just rediscovered how to operate his lips and lungs. Mayweather noted that Chang was speaking over the private channel that linked the other man's suit to his own, rather than addressing the entire strike team.

"My transmitter is close enough to the shuttlepod that I was able to take control of her com systems remotely, using my personal access codes. And that includes the onboard detonation control interface."

"Looks—Looks like it worked. Nice job."

Mayweather grinned at Chang, who remained stuck in a standing position nearby. Thanks to the failure of their helmet lamps, there was no glare to prevent him from seeing the relieved expression on the MACO team leader's face.

He was grateful, however, *not* to be the person in charge of cleaning Chang's suit after the mission.

"All part of the service," Mayweather said wryly. "By the way, I didn't mean to step on your authority just now. But under the circumstances I thought it would be better to ask for forgiveness than permission."

"We can discuss that once we're back on the shuttlepod," Chang said, much of his earlier anger evidently having evaporated. *"After we get our feet unstuck."*

Switching over to the team channel, Mayweather said, "Mayweather to McCammon. Would you do us all a huge favor?"

"—ame it, Ensign."

"Try not to touch anything else on the com console. Okay?"

"Got it, flyboy. But why?"

Chang responded, evidently needing to reassert his authority over the team. *"Because if that countdown somehow gets started up again before we figure out how to get everybody back aboard the shuttlepod, nothing will be able to stop it."*

"And that would be a Very Bad Thing," Mayweather said.

"—got my hands in my pockets already—"

As the stars wheeled by in the blackness overhead, Mayweather looked down at his heavily booted feet, which remained rooted in place against the fuel tank's slightly curving surface. The frigid metal seemed to be drawing all of his body heat away, apparently because his suit's thermal homeostasis was continuing to falter. How long would it be before their suits' life-support systems shut down entirely? And would that happen before or after their radios failed?

"Now let's see what we can do about getting back to our ride and blowing this place up from a safe distance."

"That's easy enough to say," Chang said. *"We still have to shut down whatever's got our feet bolted in place."*

"Then that's the problem we'll have to tackle first," Mayweather said, looking toward the horizon, where the shuttlepod hung suspended. The little vessel's dim, hard-to-distinguish shape conjured up old stories he'd heard during childhood about starving, parched desert travelers tantalized by mirages.

"Any ideas on how we might do that?"

Mayweather's eyes traced the delicate, almost invisible line drawn across the shuttlepod's hull by one of her tether cables.

He smiled. "As a matter of fact, I think I do."

A violent shiver ran down her spine, moving almost as quickly as the high-speed funicular railway she'd once ridden across the Andes as a little girl.

Corporal Selma Guitierrez stood at Target Baker—on the exterior of the Xindi fuel depot's largest, most centrally located fuel tank—perhaps a meter and a half from the cable that still tethered Shuttlepod Two to the tank's hull. The cable lay just out of reach.

So close, she thought, turning her helmeted head in the direction of Private Eby, who was also magnetically rooted to the tank's surface, only a little farther than she was from the cable.

"Is that squid serious about this?" Eby said over the private channel he shared with Guitierrez. *"Using the tether lines to disable this damned booby trap?"*

Guitierrez shrugged, then realized that Eby almost certainly couldn't see the gesture through her bulky, unilluminated and dust-camouflaged environmental suit. "If it doesn't, then we'll just have to come up with something else."

But she knew she was kidding herself. If Mayweather's little stunt—sending power directly from the shuttlepod's impulse-drive generators through the tethers—failed to disable the Xindi fuel depot's magnetic security countermeasures, then they were all dead, and might as well simply open their helmets up to the vacuum to hasten the end.

Even if the ensign's trick worked as advertised, it could still ignite all the fuel in the tanks, killing everybody that way—maybe even including McCammon, back aboard the boat.

She considered the second scenario the more likely one. Of course, it wouldn't be the optimal way to satisfy Corporal Chang's main mission objective—blowing up the Xindi fuel depot—but it would certainly get the job done. Nelson would understand, if he never learned the particulars about how she had died.

That would also pretty neatly solve my other *problem,* she thought. *Nelson's, too.* She considered with more than a little wistfulness the new life that was growing within her, utterly innocent of what was very likely to happen to it in the very near future.

"Brace yourselves, everybody." The static-laden voice that spoke in her helmet, shattering her reverie, belonged to Ensign Mayweather. *"I'm charging the tethers now."*

At first, nothing whatsoever happened. Then she felt a slight, intermittent vibration that she at first attributed to her imagination. The vibration gradually intensified until it became undeniable. Suddenly, blue and gold sparks leaped from the tether line in front of her. She feared for a moment that she was standing too close to the conflagration, though she knew that there was absolutely nothing she could do to change her location so long as the Xindi booby traps remained active.

Just as suddenly as they had begun, the fireworks that had begun coruscating up and down the tether cable vanished. The vibrations beneath her boots began to fade as well, their oscillations diminishing moment by moment.

Moving with the caution of a chemist conducting an experiment with some extremely volatile compound, she tried to raise her right boot.

It came free instantly, and the rest of her body rose along with it. Luckily enough, she tumbled directly into the tether line, catching hold of it with both of her gauntleted hands.

She looked back "down" to the tank's pitted, dusty surface, where Eby was angling his helmet toward her. Because of the absence of glare caused by the failure of their helmet lamps, she could see Eby's toothy, triumphant grin, dimly revealed by the pallid light of Kaletoo's distant sun.

She realized only then, with a surprising commingling of relief and disappointment, that nothing had exploded. At least, not yet.

"Do you mind not wasting time goofing off like that, Guitierrez?" Eby said, smirking. *"We still have some serious demolitions work ahead of us."*

It's gonna work. This is actually gonna work!

Mayweather felt exhilarated as he made his way along the tether line toward the shuttlepod, just ahead of Chang. As they drew ever farther from the surface of the fuel tank—and closer to the shuttlepod—he noticed that his suit's systems were beginning to recover from the effects of the Xindi security countermeasures, beginning with the lamps on his and Chang's helmets, and the internal thermal regulators.

Forward movement along the tether was simplicity itself, although Chang was clearly not comfortable with the maneuver—nor with much of anything else about microgravity, for that matter. Since the natural gravitational pull of the fuel depot was effectively as negligible as that of the shuttlepod, all they'd had to do was use their gravity boots to walk to the point on the tank to which the tether was attached, and then leap "upward" toward the shuttle, using the line as a hand-over-hand guide that only needed to be touched occasionally along the way, if at all, for minor course corrections.

The outer airlock hatch atop the shuttlepod's dorsal hull was already open as they glided toward it, and Mayweather sailed through it with the grace of an athlete trained specifically for a microgravity decathlon. He silently enjoyed the difficulty Chang seemed to be having arresting his motion before he clambered into the airlock, lurching awkwardly along the hatch cables and handholds as he followed Mayweather inside.

After the airlock had sealed and cycled—a seeming eternity—Mayweather and Chang doffed their helmets, and Mayweather led the way down the ladder through the companionway that linked the inner airlock hatch with the shuttlepod's pressurized interior. His freefall-related euphoria had already abated somewhat under the Earth-normal pull of the spacecraft's grav plating, though his inner ear found the newly unambiguous sensations of "up" and "down" viscerally reassuring. His nose burned with the cordite-and-garbage smell of the camouflage paste that he had concocted just before the EVA as he moved quickly forward.

"I need a sit rep, Corporal," Chang said to

McCammon, as he and Mayweather reached the cockpit almost simultaneously.

McCammon, still clad in his helmetless, dust-caked gray environmental suit, rose from the co-pilot's seat; he snapped to attention as he delivered the requested situation report. "Shuttlepod Two is ready to drop tethers and depart, once everyone is back aboard. Guitierrez and Eby are still at Target Baker, inspecting the demolition devices and the control mechanism."

I hope they aren't running into any problems out there, Mayweather thought. It made him nervous to think that people were still crawling around on one of the Xindi fuel tanks, which still might turn out to be defended by other, not-yet-discovered booby traps, or even by Xindi soldiers; they still had no absolute proof, after all, that this facility was entirely automated and unmanned.

"Let's check in on Baker," Chang said, propping his phase rifle against the bulkhead in order to lean over the com console and open a channel to his off-ship teammates. "Chang to Target Baker Squad. How soon can you get back here so we can blow this place?"

Static sizzled the air of the cockpit as Guitierrez responded. "*—oon, I think, Corporal. We just finished reprogramming the remote—etonation sequence, to make sure the bombs don't—uddenly go into count-down-to-detonation mode again.*"

"Well done, Guitierrez," Chang said. "I want you and Eby to double-time it back here as soon as you can."

Before something else goes wrong, Mayweather

thought, imagining that Chang was thinking the very same thing.

"Acknowledged," Guitierrez said, speaking around yet another blast of interference. *"But this place is stil—generating a lot of com—nterference. I'd like to test the remote-detonat—system from the—uttlepod before we come ba—aboard."*

Chang nodded toward McCammon. "Makes sense to me. Tie into Guitierrez's control signal."

McCammon's first attempt to patch into the remote-detonation padd Guitierrez carried failed completely. He succeeded in latching on to a carrier signal on the second attempt, but Mayweather could see that the data that was coming across the console was merely heavily garbled nonsense.

"Something inside that facility is still doing its damnedest to interfere with our com signals," Mayweather said as he took the pilot's seat and began working the com console with quick, economical motions born of long familiarity. A heavy-gravity feeling of apprehension was beginning to settle deep inside his belly as he imagined yet again the real live Xindi who might be lurking nearby, preparing to spring some new surprise on the team. He tried to put the thought out of his mind, since no Xindi ships or troops had come along to molest them as yet.

The com display screen on the console turned momentarily blizzard white, awash with static before settling down a few moments later to display Corporal Guitierrez's detonation-control interface; Mayweather knew he was seeing the very same read-out display that now appeared on Guitierrez's hand-held control padd. He could also see that she had set and locked the detonation interface into its "test" mode.

He keyed open Guitierrez's com channel. "Mayweather to Guitierrez. I'm going to try to take control of the detonation cycle from my console."

"Acknowledged," came her brisk reply, crackling and hissing through the cockpit speakers. He wondered again why there was still so much com interference, even after the depot's main defenses had apparently been disabled.

Mayweather cautiously entered the "initiate countdown" command, though he felt confident that nothing could go seriously amiss now that the system was safely locked into "test" mode. Then he waited several seconds for a response from the tightly cross-linked network of onboard computers built into each of the bombs.

Nothing happened. A second attempt yielded an identical result, or rather a complete lack of same.

"What's wrong, Ensign?" Chang said.

Mayweather shook his head. "I don't know. But I can't access the detonation controls remotely anymore. At least not from this far away."

"But we're only half a klick away from the bombs," Chang protested.

Mayweather glowered at Chang, and spread his hands in a gesture of frustrated helplessness. *You're welcome to go back down there and light the match yourself, dear roommate,* he thought. He refrained from vocalizing the thought, but only barely.

"Damned interference," Guitierrez said. *"Looks like I still have control down here."* Mayweather could see on his monitor that her control padd remained con-

nected to the shuttlepod via her suit's com system.

"Maybe putting the detonation interface back into 'live' mode will work better," McCammon ventured. At Chang's affirmative nod, he took the seat beside Mayweather's and began accessing the system.

Mayweather wasn't keen on watching anyone noodle around with a system like this in "live" mode—even if that person was a combat-scarred MACO who knew what he was doing. After all, under "live" protocols, the bombs could actually receive and act on the commands that would make them all detonate. As he watched McCammon's large, ungainly fingers begin working the console, Mayweather found himself wishing fervently that Lieutenant Reed had come along on this junket rather than the one headed up by Captain Archer.

McCammon entered several commands with no obvious results. Then Mayweather noticed that something was going terribly wrong; he just wasn't sure yet exactly what it was.

"Oh, boy," McCammon said, quickly turning white all the way from the top of his shaved head to his stubble-speckled chin. "This is not good at all."

"Don't tell me you've got the damned bombs locked into another countdown to detonation," Chang said.

"No, but it's almost that bad."

Slaving the monitor screen on the pilot's side of the console to McCammon's, Mayweather studied the very readouts that had so evidently unnerved McCammon.

He could see immediately that the bombs were in fact in no immediate danger of premature detonation. But that fact gave him scant reassurance.

Because he suddenly understood that whatever happened next was certain to be a Very Bad Thing indeed.

"Why?" Guitierrez asked, her voice tremulous with shock. She kept herself from drifting away from the Xindi fuel tank entirely only by wrapping her gloved left hand around the tether line that still connected the tank to Shuttlepod Two. Eby stood nearby, the magnetic surfaces of his boots holding him in place.

Both the timbre and the pitch of Corporal Chang's voice were badly distorted by waves of static and interference, but his meaning was unmistakable. *"The Xindi depot is still interfering with some of our com frequencies—including the one our detonator network is using. Only your transmitters are close enough to the bombs to activate the countdown sequence."*

The thirty-second *countdown sequence,* she thought as she began to realize the full import of what her team leader was telling her.

"Thirty seconds is pretty slim timing for an evac," she said with a coolness that surprised her. "If you keep the shuttlepod nearby long enough for a dust-off, there's a pretty good chance everybody will get fried in the explosion."

"Understood," Chang said. *"That's why I'm prepared to reel you both in right now and get us all out of here."*

Without setting off the explosives the team has already risked so much to set? The idea deeply offended her MACO sensibilities, though she understood that Chang was merely taking what was, in his command judgment, the most responsible course of action now available to him. After all, deciding which hill to abandon to the enemy and which one was worth dying on was a CO's prerogative.

"Corporal Chang, are you taking volunteers to stay behind?" The words had left her mouth almost before she had realized it. But considering the enormous difficulties that lay ahead in her personal life, to say nothing of Sergeant Kemper's, the snap decision she had just made seemed utterly right. And hadn't she already made peace with the idea of dying when she'd expected Mayweather's electrified tether line to kill her?

Hell, I made peace with dying the day I signed the recruiter's contract, she thought.

The private channel linking her suit with Eby's suddenly crackled to life. *"Guitierrez, have you gone completely spacehappy?"*

She chuckled as she toggled over to her squadmate's private frequency. "I suppose I have. Now, why don't you just get back to the shuttlepod?"

His response was distorted by a howl of static that whistled like an incoming mortar round. *"Because I think suicide missions are bad policy when they aren't necessary."*

Chang, who had apparently been nonplussed by Guitierrez's unexpected offer, seemed to have finally recovered his voice. *"I want you both back aboard this boat, double-time. That's an order."*

While Chang was speaking, Guitierrez reached for the phase rifle that was shipped across her back, her movements rendered aqueously slow by the bulky, grit-caked shoulder joints and the hard upper carapace of her environmental suit.

The rifle sprang into her hands like an obedient

familiar. "Go back to the shuttlepod now, Colin," she said, using the private channel. She kept the barrel of her weapon pointed squarely at the other MACO.

It was only then that she noticed that Eby had leveled his own rifle at her. *"This is the perfect solution for your little problem, isn't it?"*

Her hands began to shake, and she found she had to fight to keep her rifle level. "What are you talking about?"

"Oh, come on, Selma. Did you think I was just kidding when I asked if you were pregnant? A few of us have been seriously wondering about it. How long did you think you could keep it hidden from the rest of the company?"

She swallowed hard, her saliva having just metamorphosed into something that felt and tasted a lot like sawdust. "I only just took the test. How . . . how did you know?"

"I think McKenzie was probably the first to figure it out, based on how you've been acting for the past week or so. And this little stunt you're trying to pull now only confirms the rumors I've been hearing. Guess you'll want to start kicking some asses over that, once you get back to Enterprise*."*

If I go back to Enterprise, she thought, *I'd have to thrash this whole thing out with Major Hayes. And face either the end of my career, or the end of this pregnancy. Or probably both.*

She felt utterly lost, though she maintained her grip on her weapon, and continued aiming it straight at Eby's heavily insulated midsection.

But Eby also kept his rifle leveled at Guitierrez. *"This really is perfect for you, isn't it?"* he repeated.

"You get to be a big hero, and wiggle out of a personal problem all at the same time. Conquering champion and craven coward, all rolled into one."

Surprised by the sudden brashness of the usually reserved, almost shy private, she gripped her phase rifle so hard that her suit's gauntlets seemed to be flaying both of her hands. "Shut up, Colin. You don't understand anything."

"Show me I'm wrong, then. Please."

But she knew that would be useless. "If I follow through with Chang's original plan—and waste this place—it'd be a real blow to the Xindi."

"I suppose it would, Selma. But is it really worth getting killed over?"

"How can you even ask me that, Colin? We're both MACOs. We fight, and sometimes we die."

"But we usually don't get to pick those battles, do we? Our superiors do. We follow their orders, and go where they send us. And Chang just ordered us back to base."

She laughed mirthlessly. "Chang's modified his own superiors' orders often enough. Including today's mission, if I recall the sub-commander's original instructions correctly. I think our Fearless Leader might cut me some slack if I do the same."

"Maybe you're right. Maybe this is even the right thing to do. I just think you might be doing it for the wrong reasons."

She made a show of preparing to fire her weapon. "Go back to the shuttlepod, Colin. We both don't have to die out here."

Despite the glare of the helmet lamps, Eby's faceplate revealed an uncharacteristically thoughtful expression, though his weapon remained trained on her, and at the ready.

"Maybe you're right about that, too," he said.

Chang's excited voice suddenly issued from the team channel, interrupting the private standoff. *"Target Baker Squad, we have another huge problem. Incoming Xindi vessel, closing fast."*

A beat of stunned silence passed between Guitierrez and Eby. Then, on the private channel, Selma Guitierrez said, "You almost had me convinced, Colin. But it still looks like it's going to be either you or me."

She raised her weapon.

Shuttlepod Two

What the hell is going on down there? Mayweather thought as he tried to bring the shuttlepod's impulse drive up to full power, only to discover that his earlier efforts to disengage the depot's electromagnetic booby traps had left the engine's fuel supply greatly depleted. Whether Guitierrez and Eby would make it back to the shuttlepod in time remained to be seen.

Through the cockpit's forward window, only the star-bejeweled blackness of space was visible, since the shuttlepod was oriented so that its dorsal surface—and therefore its airlock—faced the Xindi fuel depot, from which Corporal Guitierrez and Private Eby were already supposed to be departing.

But Mayweather could see already that the black depths of space contained more than just stars and swirls of dust and debris. One of the distant, brilliant pinpoints was moving noticeably, in spite of the light-obscuring effects of the surrounding dust cloud. The vessel had displayed a typically Xindi fuel-exhaust profile once it had come out of warp, and passive scans had indicated that it was a large vessel, perhaps some sort of warship. Mayweather had no desire to stay around long enough to learn the hard way about whatever armaments it carried.

Whether or not the Xindi ship had already detected the relatively tiny, still camouflaged shuttlepod was still anybody's guess.

Chang stood in the cockpit, directly behind the pilot's and copilot's seats. "Can we build up enough speed to stay ahead of the shock wave after those tanks blow?" he asked, after Mayweather had finished explaining about the shuttlepod's depleted power supply.

It was obvious that the MACO team leader already knew that it would be useless to ask if the shuttlepod could outrun the approaching Xindi ship.

"I think we can probably keep from getting caught in the blast, as long as we time everything just right," Mayweather said. He carefully watched the engine indicators while maintaining the shuttlepod's position relative to the Xindi facility. "But it may be a bit of a bumpy ride once those tanks go."

"Then get us out of here as soon as the Target Baker team is back inside the airlock," Chang said.

Mayweather nodded. *If there's enough time.* Staring straight ahead, he watched as the Xindi vessel quickly resolved itself into what appeared to be an expanding disk, then became recognizably cylindrical. Mayweather already thought he could make out portholes and antennae and weapons ports, though he knew that his imagination might be working a double shift right now.

"Think our camouflage will hide us from the Xindi ship, Ensign?" Chang asked.

"Probably not," Mayweather said. *At the rate they're approaching, there's no way they can miss us,* he thought. *Camouflage or no camouflage.*

"Airlock shows as occupied," said McCammon, who continued running the instruments on the copilot's side of the cockpit. "Outer hatch closing."

Before either Mayweather or Chang could comment, an amber-colored alarm began flashing quickly on the sensor console to Mayweather's left. The shuttlepod was being scanned via some active means. "Make that definite—the Xindi know we're here."

The com system blared to life, reproducing a voice garbled by so much distortion—probably the result of deliberate jamming by the approaching ship—that Mayweather would have been hard-pressed to identify its owner. *"Detonation network armed. Proceeding with final countdown. Thirty. Twenty-nine. Twenty-eight . . ."*

Frowning, McCammon muted the speakers; the forward consoles continued to display the countdown's steady downward progression.

"Disengaging tethers," Mayweather said. The Xindi vessel loomed larger, on a heading directly for the shuttlepod. "Approaching vessel has slowed. Range, two klicks and closing."

They probably want to take us prisoner, Mayweather thought. *They want to interrogate us, find out how much we've learned so far about their plan to destroy Earth.*

"Let's dust off, team," said Chang.

Mayweather glanced up and sideways at the team leader, who exchanged an unusually genial grin with him; the young pilot then faced front and engaged the throttle.

Depleted though they were, the engines immediately hurled Shuttlepod Two into a long parabola that carried her quickly away from the doomed Xindi depot. No one spoke as the craft raced away.

It was evidently only then that Chang noticed the heading Mayweather had chosen.

"Ensign, did that EVA give you brain damage? You're on a collision course with that Xindi ship!"

The Xindi vessel abruptly grew immense in the forward window, its running lights showing off its frightening array of weapons. The alien warship had angular, aggressive lines, and Mayweather estimated it to be at least twice the size of *Enterprise*.

"Looks that way, doesn't it?" said the pilot. "Strap yourselves in, folks. And send word back to the airlock to grab the handholds."

Chang clambered into a seat, and both MACOs present in the crew compartment began fastening their belts and crash webbing as quickly as humanly possible. McCammon shouted a terse warning to the airlock via the com system before turning to face Mayweather, who kept his eyes both on the windows and on his flight console.

"What the hell do you think you're doing?" McCammon asked. Mayweather glanced at him, and noted that his face had taken on an almost lime-green, spacesick hue.

"I need to keep that Xindi ship heading toward the

fuel depot for as long as possible," Mayweather said, keeping his voice level. "Otherwise, she might still be around to chase us down after the fireworks start."

"Let's hope we're still around then, too," Chang said, hanging onto the arms of his seat.

Mayweather skimmed the Xindi ship's dorsal hull, passing almost close enough to trade hull paint with it before abruptly pulling up and angling away. Crossing his fingers, he opened the throttle up all the way. The impulse engines whined in angry protest, but the little ship complied, however grudgingly, with the dictates of the rudder.

Glancing down at the console's tactical display, Mayweather could see that the Xindi ship appeared to be trying to turn in order to give chase, though it couldn't make the maneuver quickly enough to alter its heading from the fuel dump.

Looking elsewhere on the console, Mayweather monitored the progress of the detonation countdown as it continued toward and past the point of no return.

FIVE.

FOUR.

THREE.

TWO.

ONE.

The three dozen synchronized explosions that followed were silent, but they made their combined arrival known instantaneously nevertheless. Retina-searing brilliance flooded the aft and side viewports, and was even visible through the forward window, even though that portion of the shuttlepod was pointed in the direction opposite that of the fuel facility's spreading conflagration. Shuttlepod Two rocked as the bow shock met her blunt stern, rattling and shaking her, but also carrying the little ship forward like a board skimming along atop a high, horizontally rolling tube of Risan ocean surf.

The tactical monitor on the console displayed an aft view of the secondary and tertiary explosions that had begun tearing through the hull of the Xindi vessel, even as what remained of the combined fuel depot and asteroid-mounted mining facility continued to consume itself in a bright nimbus of molecular fire.

Mayweather turned toward Chang, grinning. "I don't think they'll be following us home, Chang." Chang returned the grin, and McCammon made an enthusiastic war whoop that must have come close to blowing out the forward window.

"I don't know how Guitierrez managed to pull this off," Chang said a moment later, releasing himself from his crash webbing and standing behind the pilot's and copilot's seats. "Without staying behind with the fireworks display, that is."

Chang's last comment froze the base of Mayweather's spine as he realized that he, too, could not account for Guitierrez's all but miraculous long-distance detonation of all the planted bombs; the sudden appearance of the Xindi ship had distracted him, preventing him from thinking anything else through. *In order to get back aboard in time for the evac, she had to have set off the detonators nearly from the shuttlepod's range. And that's . . .*

Impossible, or at least not very likely. After all, he'd seen McCammon try and fail to arm the bombs from this very cockpit.

Mayweather exchanged a significant glance with Chang, who was obviously doing the very same math. McCammon's eyes, too, were widening with dawning awareness.

Reacting to the brief, pressure-equalizing hiss that heralded the opening of the inner airlock hatch, Mayweather turned his seat toward the shuttlepod's aft section. He watched as a lone figure clad in a gray, dust-caked environmental suit clambered awkwardly down the companionway ladder that led down into the crew cabin.

Nobody else followed.

SIXTEEN

Courier Ship Helkez Torvo

AS THE OVERLOADING propulsion system entered what Archer assumed to be its terminal stage, orange alarm lights flashed brightly enough to send patterns of spots scattering before the captain's eyes. He blinked them away, even as shrieking emergency klaxons reverberated throughout the little ship with painful intensity.

Archer did his best to ignore both.

"Everybody into the airlock! Now!" he shouted, struggling to be heard over the clamor. There was little time, and he knew he would get only one chance to implement his hasty plan—one that he hoped would work as well today as it had on the one other occasion when he'd seen it attempted.

The captain stepped over the raised rim of the airlock's inner hatchway right behind Reed, who immediately took up a position next to the locking controls mounted on the bulkhead. Archer turned, pausing just inside the chamber's open, almost two-meter-wide threshold to watch Kemper, Money, and Hayes as they hurriedly brought up the rear.

Kemper and Money were slowed down only somewhat by the man they carried between them. An obviously terrified La'an Trahve, still handcuffed, kicked at the empty air, his soft-booted feet swinging ineffectually a few centimeters above the deck. The MACOs hefted the alien pilot further upward to get him over the airlock's rim while simultaneously trying to stay out of the way of his wildly flailing legs.

"Hold still," Archer said, almost bellowing to compete with the crashing tide of sound. "Unless you enjoy being stunned at point-blank range, that is."

Trahve grabbed at the rim of the airlock, using both of his manacled hands to keep himself just outside the inner hatchway. "I'm *not* leaving my ship behind, Archer!" he cried.

"A few seconds from now, your ship won't *be* a ship anymore," Hayes shouted. He seemed utterly incredulous at Trahve's reluctance to leave this death trap behind.

But Trahve held firm. "Not if you let me vent the warp core. Or try to jettison it."

Archer could feel the deck plates vibrating ominously beneath his boots. He shook his head. "I think it's already too late for that. You have to come with us. We'll get you out of here on our shuttlepod."

Trahve's eyes were alive with fear. "This ship is my livelihood, Captain! I have to try to save it!"

"What's more important?" Reed said. "Your livelihood or your *life?*"

That seemed to get through to Trahve, at least a

little. "Good point." Addressing Archer, the alien said, "But how exactly did you plan to get us onto your craft, Captain? Teleportation?"

Archer almost smiled at that. If *Enterprise* herself were waiting out there instead of one of her shuttlepods, the starship's transporter—a relatively recent invention usually reserved for use on nonliving cargo, except during dire emergencies—could have carried everyone aboard Trahve's ship to safety. *Probably,* Archer thought.

Unfortunately, beaming away via the transporter simply wasn't an option at the moment.

"No," Archer said. "I'm afraid we're going to have to disembark via the airlock—the old-fashioned way."

Trahve's already fear-filled eyes widened further still. "But your own pilot says that my airlock isn't compatible with yours! I have only two pressure suits aboard this vessel, Captain, if you include my backup unit. This airlock will get us all just as dead as staying aboard would!"

Kemper seized Trahve's manacled wrists while Money unceremoniously pried his hands from the airlock's rim. Hayes grabbed the struggling man by the shoulders and pushed him backward toward the chamber's inner threshold while Kemper continued to hold his wrists. But when the alien pilot's feet briefly made contact with the deck, he suddenly twisted out of Kemper's grip. Bobbing and weaving to avoid the trio of surprised MACOs, Trahve dived away from the airlock and headed back toward the forward cockpit section. With a curse, Kemper immediately moved to pursue him, with Money right on his heels.

"Trahve!" Archer cried. "You'll die!"

But Trahve moved with the confidence of a man who expected to survive whatever fate held in store for him. Taking that at face value—and concerned at how little time remained for his own people to make their escape—Archer made a command decision.

"Let him go!" he shouted. Kemper and Money froze in their tracks with obvious reluctance, but they both bowed to necessity without any further prompting from either Archer or Hayes. Time was simply growing too short to waste any more of it worrying about Trahve's safety, and everyone seemed to recognize that fact.

Best he can hope for is to reach some hidden escape pod, Archer thought, moving farther inside the inner airlock, followed by the MACOs. Reed, who had been the first one inside, busily entered a series of commands into the keypad on the bulkhead. Moments later, the inner door hissed shut, cutting Trahve off from the group with finality. The alert klaxons blaring out in the corridor were immediately muted down to a tolerable level, and the brightly strobing orange alarm beacons became only partly visible through the inner hatch's small window.

Reed continued standing beside the keypad, looking apprehensive as he studied its alien markings and readouts. "I don't know about this, Captain. Perhaps we should have had D.O. toss some environmental suits into Trahve's outer airlock doors."

"Suits would be nice, Malcolm," Archer said wryly. "*If* we had the time to get into them, that is. We don't. Besides, now that we're *inside* the airlock, opening that outer hatch sort of commits us to cutting corners when it comes to environmental suits."

"What about all the gravitic particles that are

floating around out there?" Reed said, his dubious frown folding in on itself, rapidly deepening toward a scowl. "Imagine getting shot by a bullet made out of compressed neutronium, or a mini black hole."

"We'll just have to hope that all the bullets miss us this time," Archer said.

"This is crazy, Captain. You do know that, don't you?" Hayes said. Kemper and Money merely stood by, owl-eyed and silent, flanking their CO.

"Absolutely," Archer agreed.

"No argument from me," Reed said dryly.

Archer grinned. "Well, I'm glad to see the two of you finally getting along so well. Now secure your gear, gentlemen. It's about to get very windy in here."

As Reed and the MACOs made certain that all of their loose equipment was strapped down or otherwise contained, Archer placed his right hand against the inside of the outer airlock door. The curved metal hatch felt as cold as the infinite, airless space that he knew lay just on its other side, like some vampiric monster that hungered to drain every last bit of warmth and life from the bodies of everyone present. Feeling that deadly cold now, holding it in his hand, he could hardly blame Reed or the MACOs for their trepidation. What he was asking everyone to do *was* crazy. Or at least highly unorthodox.

And absolutely lethal, perhaps to all five of them, if anyone here made even the slightest mistake.

As he studied the edge of the circular, approximately one-and-a-half-meter-diameter hatch, he noticed a small detail that sent his heart into an abrupt state of freefall. *Oh, shit. We may be dead after all, no matter what crazy stunt we try.*

Archer turned toward Reed, who had paused to eye the hatch controls again. When the tactical officer looked up to meet the captain's inquiring gaze, he looked decidedly unhappy as well.

"Do you want the good news first, Captain, or the bad news?"

"I think I've already figured out the bad news, Malcolm," said Archer. "The outer hatch opens inward, not outward."

"So?" said Kemper, his MACO composure clearly beginning to crack. Sweat beaded his ruddy brow.

"As you were, Corporal," Hayes said, his words clipped.

Reed adopted a more patient, almost resigned tone. "It means that we can't get the hatch open while the airlock is pressurized. The atmosphere inside the airlock will hold it closed."

Hayes looked skeptical. "So we pull it open. All five of us working together."

"The five of us *might* be able to generate enough force using pure muscle power," Reed said. "But we don't have enough door handles for everyone to grab. Which means we won't have enough leverage."

"So let's just depressurize the airlock," Kemper said.

Reed shook his head. "That would probably take several minutes, at least. We don't have that kind of time."

"And we don't have that kind of lung capacity either," Archer said. "So what's the good news, Malcolm?"

"The outer hatch is equipped with emergency explosive bolts. I believe I can tap into the detonators and fire them from inside the airlock."

Archer heaved a sigh of relief. Maybe they couldn't open the hatch from the inside. They could, however, blow it off of the ship entirely. In fact, trying to open the hatch any way other than suddenly and explosively would place the entire team at risk of being injured or killed; the blast of escaping air could easily slam them into the partially opened aperture, to deadly effect.

"Assuming that everything in here is functioning properly," Reed continued, "I should be able to blow the hatch off all at once. The outrush of atmosphere will throw the entire outer hatch assembly completely clear of the ship."

Archer nodded. "And should give us all the momentum we'll need to get ourselves to safety." Momentum was all-important, because it translated to *speed;* Archer knew that if they were to survive this stunt, it had to be done *fast.*

"Let's hope so," Hayes said as he pulled a grapple pistol—a device used predominantly for rappelling—from his Sam Browne belt. The three MACOs immediately began securing the gun's nanofilament line to each other's belts, and then attached it to Reed's.

"What about the hatch itself, Captain?" Money asked, smoothing a hank of her dark, pulled-back hair away from her eye.

"You see a problem, Private?" Archer asked.

Money stared straight ahead, at attention. "Sir, the hatch is liable to have a great deal of velocity once we blow it off."

A stricken look crossed Reed's face. "She's right, Captain. The hatch could become a deadly projectile. If it slams into our shuttlepod . . ." He trailed off, his implication already crystal clear.

Archer smiled as he added himself to the front of the human chain, securing Hayes's line to his own belt. "I think Lieutenant O'Neill already has that eventuality covered, Malcolm. We'll be fine." *So long as we get just a little bit lucky, and stay that way for the next thirty seconds or so,* he thought.

Reed regarded him with a gallows grin. "If you say so, sir. At least we'll have the wind at our backs."

Archer returned Reed's grin, then turned to address the entire group. "Is everybody ready?"

Reed nodded, as did the MACOs. The harried quintet lined up in single file before the airlock, with Archer at the forefront, followed by Hayes, Kemper, and Money. Reed stood at the end of the procession, a position that put him within easy reach of the airlock's control keypad, which he was presently busy manipulating.

Archer suddenly felt a sensation of freefall that made his belly lurch unpleasantly. "I've just neutralized the artificial gravity in the airlock chamber," Reed explained. Archer turned toward him, and thought he saw him smiling again ever so slightly.

"A little warning might have been nice," Hayes said, looking dyspeptic, slightly green, and more than a little annoyed. Kemper's florid complexion was paling as well, already well on its way to chartreuse. *At least he doesn't have to worry about spitting up inside a sealed helmet,* Archer thought, quietly amused. *I guess there's an up side to everything, including shirtsleeve space walks.*

He checked the tether line again, and for an absurd instant he flashed back to his kindergarten days, when his entire class had been trooped through the

Zefram Cochrane Museum for the very first time; each child had held the hand of the next to form a long, semiorganized human chain.

"Sorry, Major," said Reed, now obviously tamping down a smirk at the ground-pounders' plight. "Next time."

I can't believe I actually ordered this, Archer thought, although he remained as convinced as ever that he had no better alternative. Adopting a knees-bent stance before the outer hatch, Archer pulled out his communicator and flipped it open; he felt reassured, at least somewhat, by the little device's familiar electronic chirrup.

"Archer to O'Neill. We're ready to blow the hatch now."

"O'Neill here, Captain. We're ready on our end, too, sir. The shuttlepod's dorsal surface is now oriented directly toward you. But I'd advise you to get over here as quickly as you can. That ship you're on is reading pretty hot, and this Xindi installation could decide to fire something at us any second."

"Acknowledged." Archer locked his gaze with that of Malcolm, whose hands were poised above his keypad like those of a virtuoso musician about to give an honors recital. "We're blowing the hatch five seconds from my mark."

Archer quickly closed and tucked away his communicator, hoping to prevent its becoming a potentially lethal missile.

"Mark!" Reed said, beginning the countdown. "Four."

The little ship rattled and vibrated. The hull rang like a bell, as though something huge and heavy had struck it. Was Trahve doing something up in the cockpit? Or was his ship finally succumbing to its internal stresses and beginning to rip itself to pieces?

"Three. Two," Reed continued as Archer took a couple of deep breaths.

"One."

Archer then exhaled, deeply. *Empty those lungs,* he told himself, well aware of the dangers of explosive decompression.

Facing the outer hatch, Archer heard everyone else releasing air, following their EVA training. Reed's hand slammed down on the keypad, and the hull shimmied very hard a split second later as the explosive bolts fired simultaneously with a deafening roar. In that selfsame instant, the outer hatch vanished in a haze of jagged ice crystals and twisted outbound metal shrapnel, and a miniature hurricane howled briefly to life just behind Archer's back.

He gave himself to it, and it bore him forward through the breached and gaping hatchway and out into the airless void, where the hurricane's thunderous sound pealed swiftly away into a whine before devolving into a cold silence that was utter and absolute. The top of the shuttlepod beckoned from nearby amid the surrounding infinite blackness beyond, limned by the small vessel's running lights and outward-directed floodlights. Although the craft's opened airlock entrance loomed large, it still seemed impossibly far away.

Archer clenched his eyes shut tightly, hoping his eyeballs wouldn't be flash-frozen inside his head. The line attached to his belt went reassuringly taut behind him, which meant that the entire group was probably still together, for better or worse. Lungs aflame, he felt the sensation of tumbling headlong into a bottomless abyss.

And he hoped, for the sake of everybody alive at this moment back on planet Earth, that he hadn't just made the very last mistake of his career.

Shuttlepod One

Clad in a gray MACO environmental suit, Corporal Peruzzi found the sound of her own breathing distractingly loud. Standing in the shuttlepod's narrow airlock, her magnetic boots tethering her to the temporarily deactivated grav plating, her phase rifle gripped awkwardly in her gauntleted hands, she did her best to focus past the noise and concentrate on the task at hand.

The airlock's outer hatch was open to space, while the inner hatch was sealed behind her, providing the cockpit with atmosphere and life-support.

"It's showtime, Corporal," O'Neill said, speaking over the comlink in Peruzzi's suit.

"Acknowledged," Peruzzi said. "Locked and loaded." *Ever Invincible,* she thought. *Boo-Yah!*

Then someone else spoke inside her helmet. *"Mark!"*

Hearing Lieutenant Reed's voice coming to her via relay, Peruzzi raised her rifle, pointing it upward into the open hatchway, where the alien pilot's small ship—it didn't look all that much larger than the shuttlepod from here—loomed not five meters away. The other vessel's aft hatch was prominently visible, awash in the white brilliance of the shuttlepod's exterior floodlights. The huge Xindi facility, its grapple arms hastily withdrawing from the other vessel in a convincing mechanical approximation of fear, turned very slowly in the silent, trackless space that lay just beyond both vessels.

"Four," Reed counted. *"Three. Two. One."*

A flurry of unintelligible sound filled the next second or so. Then the other ship's hatch suddenly detached itself from the hull in a silent shower of bright metal fragments and misty beads of rapidly freezing atmosphere.

At once, Peruzzi's training took possession of her entire nervous system; she sighted and fired on her target in a veritable eyeblink, moving fluidly despite the helmet and the bulky suit that encumbered her.

The rifle's beam, all but invisible in the absence of atmosphere, reached out and struck the incoming missile, whose trajectory suddenly changed. The flying hatch cover went tumbling off into the stygian void, away from both vessels.

She felt a sharp stitch of heat and pain in her left thigh, which then began growing intolerably cold. Tipping her helmeted head down, she saw that her suit was torn—no, make that sliced—right over the spot from which the pain was emanating. *Gravitic particle?* she wondered, expecting to die horribly at any moment.

She saw that the rent in her suit was venting atmosphere at a furious clip. *Shrapnel,* she thought calmly, though she was relieved that she evidently hadn't been torn apart by an encounter with some particle of exotic matter peculiar to the Delphic Expanse. She felt oddly detached from the notion of dying of garden-variety decompression in a torn pressure suit; her own stoicism, a by-product of her MACO training, surprised her.

But she knew there wasn't time to worry about either her injuries or her emotional state: she saw that five human shapes were quickly falling in formation from the wounded alien ship, heading through the vacuum straight for the shuttlepod's ventral hull, and its narrow, open airlock.

And none of those five freefalling bodies were wearing environmental suits, torn or otherwise.

Peruzzi grabbed the captain first, checking much of his velocity by magnetically planting her booted feet. Despite the boots, she was nearly torn free of the deck plates and sent tumbling when Hayes, Kemper, and Money slammed into Archer from behind. Lieutenant Reed was the last to drop inside the shuttlepod.

Peruzzi wasted no time entering the "door close" command into the small control panel built into the inside bulkhead. As the incoming personnel either reached the deck or the ladder leading "down" to it from the outer hatch, she reactivated the shuttlepod's grav plating. Though Reed and Money landed none too gracefully on the still-airless deck, Peruzzi felt grateful when the familiar sensation of weight returned to her body, enabling her to disengage her magnetic boots.

"They're all aboard, Lieutenant," she said into her suit's comm system as the shuttlepod's outer hatch began to close with agonizing slowness. She grabbed at the ladder as the pain in her thigh flared up again, probably because of the abrupt reactivation of the grav plating. She also noticed that her own voice sounded faint inside her helmet, and thought she was beginning to feel light-headed. Had all her air escaped already? *Ever Invincible,* she told herself, repeating the phrase over and over in her head in an endless loop.

"Thanks, Corporal," O'Neill replied from the cockpit. *"Now I'm getting us back on the road."*

Five very distressed-looking people, two dressed in Starfleet uniforms, three in mottled, gray-camo MACO livery, grabbed for whatever handholds they could find as the alien ship and the Xindi facility—both of which had been visible a moment earlier through the closing but still narrowly open airlock—suddenly vanished.

A moment later the hatch clanged silently shut and air began hissing rapidly into the now-sealed chamber.

Boo-Yah! Peruzzi thought.

Silence reigned.

At first Archer thought it was the final silence, the silence of death. But the excruciating pain he was experiencing argued eloquently that he was still very much alive. He felt as though his lungs had been removed from his body, stretched out on a taffy-pulling rack, and then haphazardly replaced.

But at least I can still see, Archer thought, blinking rapidly in the harsh, fragmented illumination of what he recognized as the interior of Shuttlepod One's still completely depressurized airlock, whose outer hatch was still in the process of sealing the little auxiliary vessel off from the hard vacuum that embraced her hull.

The soundlessness that dominated the narrow chamber—or was it the entire universe?—was gradually replaced by a gentle hissing. The sibilant noise grew steadily louder, progressively eclipsing the pain that throbbed in his chest, a sensation that had already begun to recede like an outgoing ocean tide.

Gravity had returned, momentarily confusing his inner ear as it took notice of the outer airlock hatch suddenly reassuming its familiar direction of "up." The deck lurched beneath his feet; no doubt the inertial dampers were struggling to catch up with a sudden, large acceleration load. He braced himself against the ladder that ran from the airlock to the companionway, narrowly avoiding toppling onto the still-sealed inner hatch that led downward into the aft portion of the pressurized crew compartment. Archer saw that Reed and the three MACOs were in much the same condition he was, each of them seeking stability by grabbing at either the ladder or other nearby handholds. An environment-suited figure that Archer finally recognized, through the glare that obscured her helmet's faceplate, as Corporal Peruzzi also stood nearby on wobbly feet.

Within a few impossibly long moments, the deck had settled down, and Archer's oxygen-starved lungs were greedily gulping down air. Reed and the MACOs were doing likewise, and Archer was grateful to note that no one appeared to have been seriously injured during their transit. He disengaged his tether line in order to move toward a nearby external viewport.

Through the small port, Archer could see the fake Xindi weapons facility rapidly dropping away into the infinite dark, Trahve's small ship still right beside it, though no longer locked in place by the station's sinister-looking armatures and grapnels. Trahve's vessel, looking almost like a toy at this range, seemed to be venting great plumes of gas from the vicinity of its engine nacelles. Archer wondered if Trahve might succeed in averting the imminent detonation of his propulsion system after all—until he saw the small escape pod that darted from the vessel's belly, confirming that even Trahve had given up the ship.

At least he survived, Archer thought, not wanting Trahve's death on his conscience, whatever crimes the man might have abetted.

A painfully bright flash of light erupted an instant later, forcing Archer to raise a hand to shield his eyes. Trahve's vessel vanished, and a quickly expanding fireball took its place. Almost immediately, the fireball's edges touched and then engulfed the periphery of the Xindi facility, and continued to grow and spread across it like a summer wildfire.

Even as the initial detonation's shock wave noticeably added velocity to the shuttlepod, rapidly carrying her even farther along her departure trajectory, the blast set off a series of successively larger, even more brilliant explosions across the length and breadth of the Xindi trap. Archer had to look away entirely, his eyes clenched shut against the glare as he steadied himself against one of the bulkhead handholds during the few moments it took the shuttlepod's inertial dampers to adjust to the additional acceleration load. Emblazoned across his retinas was the afterimage of the Xindi decoy crumpling in on itself as though its hull had been no more substantial than the thermal foil that Chef used for covering leftovers in *Enterprise*'s galley.

The Xindi decoy weapon was no more. *We won. Or at least we survived.*

But Archer knew that this victory had effectively cost him the trail to the *real* Xindi particle-beam weapon, at least for the time being.

Unless a few survivors besides Trahve managed to get into escape pods right before the end came, he thought as he quickly made his way down the ladder toward the airlock's inner hatch, which Reed and Peruzzi were already cycling. Once the pressure equalized on either side of it, the hatch would open upward and admit them down into the rear of the little craft's cockpit section; in the meantime, they would all have to wait inside the cramped airlock.

Frustrated and impatient, Archer pulled out his communicator and flipped it open. "Archer to O'Neill."

"O'Neill here, sir. Welcome aboard."

"Were you able to scan the wreckage for survivors?"

"Yes, sir. I'm tracking two escape pods, one of which came from that ship you just escaped from. That one reads as a single humanoid life-form, and the other shows several life signs."

"Several life signs . . . are they Xindi?"

"They vary a bit from what's in our database, sir, but I'd say they're close enough to be cousins—or another Xindi subspecies. I'm also picking up several warp signatures, all of them closing in on the vicinity of the explosion."

Damn! Archer thought as the inner hatch finally opened, allowing him to scramble down the companionway ladder and into the shuttlepod's main section. The others quickly followed him down.

At the bottom of the ladder, Archer moved forward and took the seat beside O'Neill's, grateful to be back inside the familiar confines of the shuttlepod after having spent so much time aboard La'an Trahve's vessel.

"Can you identify the approaching ships, D.O.?" he asked as he took in the various readouts and gauges.

O'Neill shook her head. "No, sir. But I'd bet you euros to Draylax dinars that *they're* Xindi as well."

"And they're not going to want to allow any prisoners to fall into our hands," Archer said, now wishing he'd simply stunned Trahve and dragged him along instead of allowing him to escape to the tender mercies of the Xindi.

"Can we reach either of the escape pods before the Xindi get to them?" Hayes asked, still breathing somewhat heavily from his encounter with hard vacuum.

"I think so, Major," O'Neill said coolly. "But we'd never get away from the Xindi vessels afterward, and we're not exactly the most well-armed ship in the sector." She turned toward the captain, and looked more than a little worried. "Captain, I don't believe they've detected us yet. The explosion is going to make our impulse trail difficult to detect. We can still get away without attracting their attention—if we go now, that is."

"But without any prisoners," Archer said. "Or even a goddamned *clue* where to go next to try to find the Xindi homeworld." He wanted to lash out and hit something, though he knew he couldn't afford to display such weakness in front of his subordinates.

And especially not in front of Hayes.

"Sir?" O'Neill said.

Pondering his steadily narrowing set of options, Archer looked slowly around the shuttlepod's not-very-spacious interior. He was startled by what he saw—or, rather, by what he *didn't* see.

"Where is Ensign Chandra?" he asked, turning back toward O'Neill, whose mien suddenly grew sorrowful.

No, he thought.

Archer glanced toward Corporal Peruzzi, who stood nearest the airlock. Though she had removed her helmet, she was still outfitted in a standard gray MACO environmental suit.

And she was as pale as a ghost. It also didn't escape his notice that her suit's left thigh was torn and blood-spattered.

"We were ambushed on the way back to the shuttlepod, Captain," Peruzzi said. "We took the attackers down, but Chandra didn't make it. I'm sorry, Captain. It's my fault. It's my—"

The corporal's body went limp, and she displayed the whites of her eyes as she collapsed. Reed and Kemper, who were standing nearest to her, caught her before she made it all the way down to the deck. They gently lowered her to a supine position.

"Get me the emergency medical kit!" Reed shouted, and Kemper immediately scrambled to pull it down from the upper storage compartment where it was stowed.

An *Enterprise* crew member was dead. And now maybe one of Hayes's MACOs was about to join him.

"Captain, the Xindi vessels are charging weapons, and they're on an intercept course with the nearest of the escape pods," O'Neill said, her tone urgent. "If we want to get away, we'd better do it *now.*"

A sense of near-despondency seized Archer's soul. It sometimes seemed that failure and death were becoming this mission's twin leitmotifs.

"Get us back to *Enterprise,* Lieutenant. Best speed."

"I guess not all the bullets missed us this time," Archer said. "How is she?"

The captain's voice startled Reed. He hadn't heard Archer rise from behind the flight console, let alone cross to the aft section of the shuttlepod, where Reed and Kemper had just finished bandaging the unconscious Corporal Peruzzi's leg wound.

"She's lucky, sir," Reed said, pushing aside the remnants of her gray MACO environmental suit and camo uniform pant leg, both of which he had been forced to cut away in order to stop the bleeding. "The shrapnel fragment in her leg could have severed an artery if it had gone in any deeper. I think she'll be all right, though. Still, she's lost a great deal of blood. We'll need to take her straight to Phlox once we dock with *Enterprise.* Fortunately we're only about six hours away from our rendezvous."

Archer nodded silently. Reed hoped that he was consoled at least somewhat by Peruzzi's happy prognosis, though he could see in the captain's careworn expression that Chandra's death weighed heavily on him. The ensign had been a valued member of *Enterprise*'s crew; in a community as small and as tightly knit as theirs, Ravi Chandra would be greatly missed.

We'll have to have yet another funeral, Reed thought with a weary, melancholy sigh. He was uncomfortably aware that Lieutenant O'Neill must have stored the young man's lifeless body in the cargo area just below the main deck. Given the limited space aboard the shuttlepod, however, he had to concede that she'd had little alternative, other than giving him a summary burial in space.

Looking at Archer, Reed noticed that the captain's eyes were extremely bloodshot, no doubt because his brief exposure to hard vacuum had exploded countless tiny capillaries. *Vacuum blossoms,* he thought, recalling the slang term for decompression-related injuries he had picked up during his first EVA training sessions. *I suppose we'll all be wearing dark glasses for the next week or two to cover these up.*

Reed turned his attention back to the slumbering Peruzzi. Finally satisfied that the injured MACO would rest comfortably on the aft portion of the shuttlepod's deck, Reed stood and turned toward the cockpit.

And found himself facing both Major Hayes *and* Captain Archer, who were staring intently at one another. Since Peruzzi had been injured as a consequence of the captain's emergency airlock-jump maneuver, Reed braced himself for the inevitable confrontation.

"I have to admit, Captain, your evac method was brilliant," Hayes said, the MACO leader's unexpected praise startling Reed almost as much as the major's almost crimson eyes, which looked at least as bloodshot as the captain's. "What you did had to be nonregulation, I'm sure. But it was still an outstanding tactic."

Reed noticed then that Kemper and Money, both of whom were as cerise-eyed as their CO, also nodded appreciatively.

Whatever works, Reed thought, though he was still keenly aware that the shuttlepod wasn't out of the proverbial woods yet; unless Trahve had greatly exaggerated the perils of traversing this gravitic particle cloud, the ship could still be destroyed by a single high-velocity chance encounter with some infinitesimal bit of exotic matter before reaching the relatively clear space that lay beyond the cloud's boundaries. *Where we'll only have to face the Delphic Expanse's ordinary brands of weirdness.*

"Did you pick up that maneuver from Starfleet's advanced tactical training program?" Hayes asked, his gaze darting from Archer to Reed and back again.

Archer grinned, first at Reed, then at Hayes. "Something like that, Major."

Reed had absolutely no idea what to make of that.

Hayes nodded in response, still looking impressed, then moved to the aft portion of the shuttlepod, apparently to assist Money in checking on the unconscious corporal.

Following Archer forward to the flight console where O'Neill sat, Reed cast a backward glance at the MACOs, none of whom were paying any attention to him. *Maybe Hayes and his people could teach us lowly squids a thing or two about combat tactics,* he thought. *But I think we may have just taught the sharks that they don't know everything there is to know, and that they might also benefit from learning a little humility.*

Just as we *could,* Reed added silently, thinking of

Chandra—and of how close to death everyone on this mission had come.

As Archer took the seat beside O'Neill's, Reed turned toward the captain. Speaking *sotto voce,* he said, "Captain, I've taken every scrap of advanced tactical training Starfleet has ever offered. But as far as I can recall, every one of my instructors considered going EVA without an environmental suit to be a *spectacularly* bad idea."

"Same here," O'Neill said with a wry smile.

Archer paused as though carefully composing his reply, then spoke in a conspiratorial whisper, his words obviously intended only for the ears of Reed and O'Neill. "You're both right. And I hope I won't have to make another exit like that any time soon. Let me make a confession—I didn't really pick that tactic up from anyone at Starfleet."

"Then where did you get it, sir?" O'Neill asked. "If you don't mind my asking, that is."

"Truthfully? I came across it late last year, months before the MACO company came aboard *Enterprise,*" the captain said. "So it's no surprise that Hayes isn't familiar with the maneuver. After all, we haven't had a movie night on *Enterprise* since before we entered the Expanse."

Reed shook his head in confusion. "Movie night, sir?"

"That's right. I cribbed the emergency airlock flush from a twentieth-century science-fiction film we showed in the crew mess last December."

Reed quickly rummaged through his crowded but able memory for minutiae. Which old-style flat film had been showing in the crew mess all those months ago?

"Are you talking about that two-hundred-year-old First Space Age story that had an exploration ship's computer go insane and murder the crew?" O'Neill said with a thoughtful frown. "The one where the astronaut gets trapped outside his ship, then has to storm the airlock without his helmet to get back inside?"

"The same." Archer nodded, displaying a grin that Reed had seen only very rarely over the past couple of months.

Reed laughed out loud when he understood the lieutenant's reference, drawing Hayes's curious attention. It felt good to laugh, however inappropriate it might seem. But for the moment, he didn't care; he hadn't laughed nearly enough lately.

The movie he recalled from the night in question was *2001: A Space Odyssey.*

"I think it's high time we reinstituted movie night, Captain," Reed said, deadpanning. "Purely for its tactical training value, of course."

"Of course," Archer said, equally deadpan, though his eyes twinkled with restrained mischief.

Reed decided that only after such pastimes once again became a priority aboard *Enterprise* would he be satisfied that the Xindi threat had finally been brought to an end.

SEVENTEEN

Friday, September14, 2153,
Xindi Council Inner Sanctum

FOLLOWING A SEEMINGLY interminable journey from the debris field that was all that remained of the destroyed kemacite refining facility, Degra's shuttle finally touched down in the principal spaceport of the Xindi homeworld's capital city, just in time for the latest emergency session of the Xindi Council.

Not long afterward, he stepped inside the dimly illuminated Inner Sanctum, and did so with no small amount of trepidation. Degra knew, after all, that neither he nor his fellow Xindi humanoid aide Mallora had much in the way of good news to impart to the other members of the Council. And Degra could see plainly, even before he looked upon the dour faces and met the hard stares of the representatives of the other three Xindi land species who had already taken their seats around the great round Council table, that he was to be taken to task. As he and Mallora seated themselves beside the Xindi marsupials and near the wall-sized seawater tank that housed the Council's two placidly swimming Xindi aquatics, Degra knew that some, most notably the reptilians and the insectoids who sat directly across the table from the humanoids and the marsupials, might even become fairly demonstrative in voicing their displeasure over recent events.

Commander Guruk Dolim, representing the Xindi reptilians, wasted little time rising to Degra's expectations. "Your risky scheme has completely failed to halt the human incursion, Degra!" roared the military leader as he brought one of his mailed fists down heavily upon the duraplast tabletop. He rose to his feet as he spoke, his eyes blazing with fury, his gaze focusing like a weapons tube upon Degra; even his scales seemed to move, shimmering and darkening from aquamarine to deep camouflage green, reflecting his roiling emotions—and a cerebral cortex that wasn't far removed from the brain stem, a racial characteristic of the reptilians.

"We have been more than patient in indulging your passive response to the Terran threat," Guruk continued. "And yet their starship continues probing even *more* deeply into our territory than they had ventured previously. Not even the hazards of the Orassin distortion fields have deterred their progress!"

Shresht silenced his angrily chittering aide before fixing his eerie, multi-ocular gaze upon Degra as well. Speaking frenetically in the clicking, popping language of the insectoid people, he said, *"I must agree! You have gambled with the safety of our homeworld, Degra—and you have lost!"*

Degra could not bring himself to disagree entirely with Shresht's harsh assessment, however emotionally overwrought it might be. He had, in fact, taken an extraordinarily large gamble, though the odds at the time had seemed to be in Degra's favor. Yet somehow, in defiance of those odds, Archer and his human crew had won the wager he had placed against them, just as they had defied Degra's expectations a short time earlier by escaping from the trellium-mining slave camp on Tulaw. Degra had indeed lost a serious gamble. And now the time had come for him to brief the Council candidly about the costs of that failure.

After a brief pause to gather his thoughts, Degra addressed the group, which had lapsed into an expectant silence. "It is true that the destruction of the Kaletoo Sector kemacite mining and refinery station represents something of a setback in the timetable for the completion of the Weapon."

The insectoids began stridulating their stalk-like limbs and exoskeletal plates, producing shrieks of outrage. Guruk, his neck scales standing almost on end in outrage, opened his mouth to add some additional vitriol to the rising din.

"It is unquestionably a setback," Narsanyala Jannar said, speaking in a voice loud enough to be heard over the din, yet in tones controlled and modulated enough to shame the insectoids and reptilians into recovering at least some of their composure.

The great fur-covered Xindi marsupial moved and spoke with his people's characteristically deceptive slowness, though he scanned the group with eyes brimming with both intelligence and wisdom. "Yes, it is indeed a setback," Narsanyala continued. "But it is by no means an insuperable one."

Though he remained outwardly impassive, Degra heaved a great internal sigh of relief. Narsanyala and his people were great exemplars of patience; unless Degra did or said something to test that patience beyond its limits, they would remain on his side, allowing the engineering teams the time they required to complete and test the Weapon before the inevitable confrontation with Earth took place.

"Really?" Guruk said, his deep, gravel-studded voice dripping with sarcasm; he had clearly not been mollified in the least by Narsanyala's observation. "Added to the loss of the armored platform in the same sector, the loss of the kemacite facility could well compromise the Weapon Project entirely—thereby placing *all* of our species in jeopardy."

Narsanyala waved one of his huge hands, possibly in a casual gesture of dismissal—or perhaps to display his heavy, razor-sharp black claws as a polite reminder that Xindi marsupials were neither to be trifled with nor to be underestimated. Those talons clearly had uses other than anchoring their torpid-looking owners to trees for lengthy, inverted, leaf-chewing naps; they were more than capable of eviscerating a Xindi humanoid, and might conceivably make short work of even a leather-skinned reptilian.

Whatever rejoinder Guruk was planning to hurl Narsanyala's way was interrupted by the keening, musical voice of Qoh Kiaphet Amman'Sor, one of the two Xindi aquatics who drifted aimlessly in the Inner Sanctum's huge aquarium tank. *"The destroyed weapons-manufacturing platform was already outmoded many revolutions ago, Commander Guruk,"* Qoh said in a language that was as slow and stately as the speech of the insectoids was quick and urgent.

"Quite so," said Qam, the other aquatic. *"Since the platform was soon to be decommissioned and demolished anyway, it is hardly fair to penalize Degra for sacrificing it in an attempt to trap, interrogate, and kill as many of the human crew as possible."*

Guruk bared his many ranks of sharp, serrated teeth toward the great seawater tank in a gesture of evident exasperation. "All right. I will grant you that. But we still must deal with the loss of the kemacite facility. That loss has inflicted a serious blow upon our resource base. The Weapon requires vast amounts of fuel—much of which that very depot probably would have supplied." Leaning forward across the table, he turned his vertical pupils squarely back upon Degra. "How many additional moonturns will your engineers now require to properly deploy the Weapon, Degra—all because of *your* monumentally poor judgment?"

Degra closed his eyes momentarily, refusing to allow himself to be bated by the angry reptilian, who was no doubt enraged enough to be seeking a handy pretext for killing him, or perhaps for doing something even more dreadful. And as often happened during most of those brief intervals when he examined the inside of his eyelids, he saw the faces of Naara, his wife, and his grown children Piral and Jaina, who looked as they had during their earliest schooling intervals, frozen in time as carefree young children.

He was not going to allow any of them to come to harm, be it from the violence of the humans, from the increasing disunity and dissension that had plagued the Council of late, or even from his own arguable errors in judgment.

"As I said, the loss of the Kaletoo Sector kemacite depot is a setback. But it is *only* a setback. My engineering teams are now marshaling other resources to take the place of everything that was lost, and they have already redoubled their efforts to complete and test the Weapon. It *will* be ready to deploy against Earth—on schedule, and under budget."

"And well before the Earth ship's crew can hope to locate either the Weapon, or our home planet," Mallora added, still seated at Degra's side.

Narsanyala favored Degra and Mallora with a supportive nod. "I have seen no reason so far to doubt that."

Unsurprisingly, Shresht and his aide remained both agitated and unconvinced. *"But* we *can see a great deal of reason for doubt,"* Shresht clattered.

Drifting upside down in the tank, Qam sang a lengthy aria of puzzlement. *"Can you explain why, Shresht? Degra has never been anything other than honest and accurate in his engineering and construction estimates."*

Shresht's mouthparts worked quickly, though his friction-generated "speech" actually came from the sawing of his hindmost limbs against his lower carapace. *"I do not question Degra's honesty. Nor do I dispute that his engineers have maintained their promised building timetables in the past. But I fear that the human vessel's crew might have derived some advantage over us during their escape from Degra's so-called 'trap.' "*

Degra frowned, but Mallora beat him to asking the obvious question. "What sort of advantage?"

"There was a small insectoid crew posted aboard the weapons platform," said Shresht, his huge, iridescent, multifaceted eyes now tipped in Degra's direction. *"A small force, consisting of a few dozen warriors. But none of them have reported in since the platform's destruction."*

Degra nodded, though he found it difficult to muster any heartfelt concern for the fate of the insectoid crew. After all, the bugs were used to leading short, brutal lives, and they routinely expended those lives in vigorous defense of their portions of the Xindi homeworld, and did so without the slightest hesitation. Savagery and territoriality were hardwired into their nature; these traits made them ideal foot soldiers for the collective Xindi cause, especially during times such as these, when all five Xindi races faced the very real danger of joining the ancient Xindi avians in oblivion and extinction.

"I trust that the insectoid personnel stationed there managed to reach their escape pods before the humans destroyed the weapons-assembly platform," Degra said at length, working hard to be polite. He truly did not enjoy the company of these creatures, finding their fundamental physical alienness so viscerally disturbing.

Shresht and his aide erupted in a brief cacophony of exoskeletal friction that Degra could only interpret as a negative, or perhaps even as an aural expression of insectoid grief.

"Only a handful appear to have made it to the escape pods, since few apparently believed the humans to be capable of defeating the trap in which they had become entangled," Guruk said.

"Did the crew deploy the facility's disaster recorder?" asked Narsanyala. Because of their ultra-dense neutronium coating, these devices were capable of surviving almost anything short of a direct collision with a neutron star, or immolation within the heart of a sun.

"They did," said Guruk, nodding. "We eventually located it and successfully downloaded most of its contents. It revealed that the humans escaped in a small spacecraft with unknown capabilities. Unfortunately, we were not able to make this determination in time to track or locate the vessel in question. We must presume that the humans on board staged a rendezvous with their primary vessel, or perhaps even with some other vessel or vessels that we have yet to detect."

"Then what has become of the surviving crew?" Shresht asked.

Guruk moved his massive shoulders in a gesture that appeared to be the reptilian equivalent of a shrug. "Some of our ships rushed to the scene to finish off the small number of lingering survivors. Since we wished to avoid the possibility of suffering a sneak attack by some other previously unseen Earth vessel, we did our work from a safe distance."

Shresht and his aide once again exploded in a clamorous outpouring of intense insectoid emotion. Degra gathered from the increasingly outraged-sounding noise that Guruk's announcement was news to them, and that they found the reptilian's cold-blooded hindbrain logic as bizarre as Degra did.

Shresht rose to his chitinous feet, apparently ready to plunge his sharp exoskeletal pincers straight into the tough scales that covered Guruk's heavily muscled neck. Guruk reached for his sidearm, obviously more than ready to meet the insectoid's charge. The aides of both Shresht and Guruk rose and faced off against one another with hate-filled glares, aggressive postures, and hissing, rattling exterior body parts.

At that moment, Narsanyala surprised everyone present by issuing a bellow so stentorian that it brought to mind the end-of-the-world prophecies of Xindi-humanoid mythology.

Shresht subsided and resumed his seat, as did his aide. Guruk and his aide did the same a moment later.

Still somewhat shocked by Guruk's revelation, Degra had to learn more about the deaths of the weapons facility's insectoid personnel, despite the risk of inflaming the highly unusual insectoid-reptilian breach he had just witnessed. "Why didn't you try to rescue them?" he asked Guruk, his voice pitched scarcely above a whisper.

"Because we could not afford to risk giving the humans any opportunity to capture and interrogate them," Guruk said. "Any one of them might have betrayed the location of our homeworld."

"No Xindi insectoid would have done that," Shresht said, his frantic clickings somehow taking on an almost sullen quality. *"We all know our duty."*

"As do we reptilians," Guruk countered. "That is why I did what I did. And that is why we must go after the Earth ship now, using every resource at our disposal. We can no longer afford to simply observe their progress and lay ineffectual traps in their path."

That seemed to disarm the bellicose Shresht, at least somewhat. *"I must agree."*

Degra shook his head, his eyes fixed on Guruk. "Doing that would be an enormous mistake, Commander. A large Xindi counterforce would be far too easy for the humans to trace to its point of origin."

Narsanyala spoke again, addressing the whole Council in much milder tones than he had used only a few moments earlier. "I must agree with Degra. As long as the Terrans have sent only one ship of any consequence after us, they pose no significant danger."

"But we do not know for certain that the one large human ship we have seen so far has not been accompanied surreptitiously by others," Shresht chittered, reiterating the fear the insectoids held in common with the reptilians—a bond that was evidently stronger even than the blood of the insectoid warriors whom Guruk had sacrificed on the altar of that fear.

Qam sang again from the tank. *"No, we do not know that for certain. Therefore we aquatics agree that we must continue to err on the side of caution. Let us do nothing yet that would serve to attract undue human attention to our homeworld."* The Inner Sanctum fell silent, as the proxies for each of the Xindi world's sentient species stared at one another across what might well prove to be an unbridgeable gulf. For most of the duration of the current crisis, the danger posed by the human interlopers had brought unprecedented unity to the Xindi homeworld's five often contentious races.

But it had also recently introduced some entirely

new cross-species tensions, stresses that now threatened Xindi security every bit as much as did the humans themselves.

While Degra was sometimes uncomfortable with the fact that his own species resembled the Terrans much more closely than any other Xindi race did, he also thought that this resemblance gave him some insight into human motivations that members of the other Xindi species lacked.

One of those insights was this: Xindi humanoids were fairly homogeneous politically, ideologically, and philosophically. And because of the at least superficial resemblances between his species and the Terran humans, Degra had to assume that Archer and his crew had achieved a degree of unity of purpose similar to that which his own species had attained—a unanimity that now had to be spread equally among five completely disparate species if *any* of the Xindi races were to stand any chance at all of long-term survival.

A sense of deep emptiness and dark despair enfolded Degra's soul as he quietly considered these weighty matters. Was such a degree of unity even possible, especially among races as fractious as those of the Xindi homeworld? Was there even the slightest chance that the humans might be riven by internal conflicts resembling those that continually threatened to distract the Council from the urgent, essential business of slaying the enemy?

Guruk's long, hissing exhalation pulled Degra abruptly back from his reverie. "Very well. We will agree to follow your and Narsanyala's recommendation and maintain a low military profile—for now."

"As will we," Shresht said. *"Unless the human threat escalates significantly before Degra's Weapon Project is ready to deploy."*

After the formal vote that followed, Degra felt enormously relieved that all parties had voiced their assent, however grudgingly, to a motion against making any risky alterations to the Xindi homeworld's current military posture. Immediately following the tally, the reptilians and insectoids rose as one and exited the chamber, followed by Narsanyala, whose continued faith in Degra's ability to keep the Weapon Project on track was arguably all that was keeping the Council from splitting asunder and turning on itself.

Walking out into the wide, stately corridor with Mallora at his side, Degra rallied his flagging spirits with the hope that the Xindi's unity of purpose would ultimately prove at least equal to that of the humans.

For at least the several moonturns that remained until the Weapon could embark on its fifty-six-light-cycle journey to Earth, all Xindi races would stand united. They had no other viable choice.

But what's going to happen afterward is anybody's guess, Degra thought as he headed for the courtyard, eager to feel the wan light of the Xindi sun against his face.

EIGHTEEN

Friday, September 14, 2153,
Enterprise NX-01

EVER SINCE HIS MOTHER had died during his childhood, Jonathan Archer had hated funerals. But even before he entered Starfleet's command track, he had known that such affairs were unavoidable. He knew that was so no matter how much sweat and blood he might invest in safeguarding the crew in his charge—people he had come to regard over the past two years as a sort of de facto family, a feeling that had only intensified since *Enterprise*'s long, isolated, and open-ended sojourn in the Delphic Expanse had begun. And he had always been bitterly aware that the task of commemorating the passing of any member of his shipboard family was a duty that fell squarely on his shoulders, and on nobody else's.

Archer stood in silence in the armory located on the forward end of F deck, where more than two dozen assorted Starfleet personnel and MACO troopers stood facing him with somber, solemn faces, some red and moistened by their anguish, while others merely looked harder and more resolute than usual. Hoshi, Phlox, D.O., and Travis numbered among the former camp, while Hayes, T'Pol, Malcolm, and Trip belonged to the latter. Gazing briefly from face to face, from his own command crew to various members of the MACO complement, which included Corporal McKenzie and Sergeant Kemper, Archer noticed that *Enterprise*'s Starfleet contingent held no monopoly over the tears that were being quietly shed all around the room.

The armory had always seemed cramped to Archer, even when it accommodated only the various racks of variable-yield photonic torpedoes and the other weapons it was designed to hold. The large number of people who now stood inside the chamber were practically cheek-by-jowl as they quietly awaited whatever words of comfort or commemoration their captain was preparing to offer.

As if there's anything I can say that will make things right, he thought, knowing that nothing had really been right since the day of the Xindi attack on Earth.

In the forward section of the armory, next to the launch tubes, stood a single raised bier bounded by a ramp—a catafalque that held a torpedo casing draped with three banners: one was emblazoned with Starfleet's navy blue chevrons, while the other two bore the official seal of Earth's global federal government and the United Earth Space Probe Agency, the same white-on-sky-blue globe-and-laurel-leaf symbol that the United Nations had adopted some two centuries earlier.

Beside the torpedo stood a four-person MACO honor guard, immaculately turned out in dress uniforms, gloves, and ceremonial sidearms. The honor guard, among whom Archer recognized Corporal Peruzzi and Private Money, collectively held a ceremonial wooden staff that carried a flag bearing the red-and-blue shark logo of the Military Assault Command Operations organization. The troopers held the staff at a reverent forty-five degrees, taking care not to allow the attached banner to come within five centimeters of the deck. Like the flags that partially covered the torpedo tube, this flag also displayed the United Earth symbol.

Two deaths, but only one casket, Archer thought, feeling desolate. Although just one body would be interred today—the lost MACO had been vaporized during the assault on the Xindi fuel depot, leaving no remains—the crew, Starfleet and MACO alike, had congregated here to honor a pair of fallen comrades. Both of the dead had been loyal members of two unique and sometimes contentious services, each one the product of a distinct military tradition.

But whatever might have differed in their respective training, or in their view of the world, both had died in pursuit of a common noble cause: protecting their homeworld, and thereby affirming their shared humanity.

Only an EVA in freefall—conducted without the benefit of a helmet—could have made Archer feel even half as uncomfortable as he did right now. Doing what he could to put aside his own grief and pain, he stepped up to the makeshift podium that Malcolm had set up for the occasion, and cleared his throat. He squared his shoulders, gazed out across the crowded, grief-suffused room, and stepped off the edge of the verbal abyss.

"Nearly three centuries ago," Archer began, "on a battlefield in Gettysburg, Pennsylvania, on which the guns of war had only very recently fallen silent, a national leader named Abraham Lincoln addressed the survivors of a great conflict. His words not only helped to salve the grief that follows all military bloodshed, but also focused a young nation on the bright future that still lay ahead of it.

"As Lincoln noted on that grave occasion: 'It is for us the living, rather, to be dedicated here to the unfinished work which they who fought here have thus far so nobly advanced. It is rather for us to be here dedicated to the great task remaining before us—that from these honored dead we take increased devotion to that cause for which they gave the last full measure of devotion—that we here highly resolve that these dead shall not have died in vain . . .' "

Archer remembered very little of what he said after that, but did note that the assembled group—"squids" and "sharks" alike—seemed to have absorbed his words with respectful solemnity.

After he had finished speaking, a Starfleet honor guard—Donna O'Neill, Malcolm Reed, and Travis Mayweather, all spit and polish in their dress blues—approached the torpedo tube and stood at attention beside it. They watched with somber faces as one member of the MACO honor guard—Corporal McKenzie—reverently removed his service's banner from the staff. While McKenzie held the staff as though it were a sacred relic, the other three MACOs proceeded to fold the flag with crisp, rehearsed precision. Corporal Chang stepped forward and accepted the tight triangular swaddle of cloth from the honor guard, with whom he exchanged brisk salutes. Chang then turned and marched toward Major Hayes, who exchanged salutes with him and accepted the flag, which Archer knew would eventually be given to the family of the fallen MACO.

The Starfleet honor guard then turned as one, took up their service's flag from the torpedo-casket, and folded it with as much precision and veneration as the MACOs had shown to their own banner. Once that task was completed, O'Neill presented the flag to Archer, who held it with the same gentleness he might reserve for an infant.

Answering a silent nod from Archer, the Starfleet and MACO honor guards simultaneously approached the catafalque and began working together to fold the two Earth banners. Once they had finished their tandem work, the honor guards separated once again into two distinct squads, both of which carried its own tightly folded Earth flag. The flags were ritually passed to O'Neill, who held them straight in front of her, one in each hand, as she continued to stand at attention. Archer would entrust her with the task of sending the Earth banners to the families of both of the honored dead, along with all of their personal effects.

But D.O. could not write the letters explaining these deaths to the bereaved loved ones back on Earth. That was a responsibility that Archer knew fell squarely upon him, and on Hayes.

Their flag rituals discharged, both honor guards

stood at attention beside each other, facing Archer, their eyes facing straight ahead. Archer nodded to the two disciplined squads, then watched soberly as Trip and T'Pol moved from the front of the congregation toward the torpedo-casket. Very gently, they lowered it down one of the ramps and onto the tracks that fed into the torpedo launcher's hatchway.

Archer then gave a single terse order, and Trip and T'Pol quietly saw to it that the torpedo bay was locked and loaded after the casket had finished its slow, lugubrious glide through the hatch.

Moments later, in fulfillment of Ensign Ravi Chandra's written will and centuries of naval tradition, the firmament of the Delphic Expanse blazed gloriously, if briefly, with the light of a new star.

Once he had gotten back inside his austere personal quarters on E deck following the memorial service, Hayes had wasted no time exchanging his formal dress for more comfortable khaki fatigues. For some reason, he had always associated dress uniforms with funerals, although he'd certainly seen more death and horror dressed as he was now, in his gray MACO cammies and standard-duty boots.

Whenever he tried to deconstruct precisely why he felt most comfortable in his present garb, he felt vaguely uncomfortable with the results; he had decided years ago that it was best not to spend too much time considering such things, and combat duty and its accouterments were, in Hayes's considerable experience, among the best antidotes to such vexing thoughts.

"To absent friends," the MACO leader said, seated

on the edge of his bunk and raising his mug to the four fatigue-clad subordinates who had joined him in his billet for an informal memorial gathering. Gathered with Hayes in his dimly lit cabin were Sergeant Kemper and Corporals McKenzie, McCammon, and Chang.

"Absent friends," the rest of the group chorused as one, clinking their motley collection of drinking vessels together where they were seated amid the room's scant furnishings. Although their cups all contained the same fairly potent spirits—bourbon from one of the few New Orleans distilleries that had been in continuous operation since before Lake Pontchartrain had temporarily engulfed the Big Easy in the early twenty-first century—the mood among the assembled MACOs was anything but festive.

One of their comrades-in-arms was dead, and all of the MACO squads would be marching in the "missing man" formation for the next seven days, as tradition demanded.

Still, even though today had been largely set aside for remembrance and grieving, the mission would go on, even if it wasn't fated to be completed by all the same individuals who had initiated it. And that mission was far too vital to neglect for a moment longer than was absolutely necessary to preserve morale, esprit de corps, and the good order of the troops. *Finishing the mission,* Hayes thought. *We owe at least that much to every one of our fallen. And to everybody back on Earth who's expecting us to come through for them.* He downed another large swallow of bourbon, feeling perverse pleasure as the stuff burned its way relentlessly down, like caustic molecular acid eating through a ship's hull metal.

Not for the first time since the group had arrived at Hayes's quarters, a hush fell across the room, and the MACO commanding officer's eyes moved from one contemplative face to the next. He knew that everyone present had been intensely trained in the art of combat, and that many had seen death up close before; nevertheless, he could see that the company's most recent loss had affected each trooper profoundly. *Which is probably as it should be,* he thought, though he wasn't sure whether to thank or curse the fates that decreed that this be so.

McCammon looked haunted, and stared into his cup in uncharacteristic silence, his usually endless wellspring of stories, anecdotes, and braggadocio having dried up, at least for the moment.

Kemper, who was now every bit as taciturn as McCammon, seemed to have the weight of the world on his shoulders; Hayes couldn't blame him, knowing what he already knew of the young sergeant's personal life, whether he thought it was still a secret or not.

Chang had already surprised Hayes all day, and probably everyone in the MACO company as well, by failing to complain even once about the "hot-cotting" living arrangements circumstances had forced him to endure alongside Ensign Mayweather, who seemed to have become his personal nemesis, not to mention the living embodiment of disorder and entropy, more than two months ago.

But of all of Hayes's subordinates, possibly including those not present in the room, Corporal Fiona

McKenzie seemed to be holding up best of all. Though her face looked drawn and fatigued, she still seemed to radiate an indefatigable strength that Hayes felt certain had been keeping everyone here, himself included, from slipping even deeper into their cups.

If the members of a military unit were the stones of an arch, then the commander was the keystone, and recent events had forced Hayes to consider cultivating a spare keystone in order to keep that arch from toppling should something happen to him. Additionally, McKenzie's emotional rock-steadiness and knowledge of the strengths and weaknesses of each member of the MACO company had bolstered Hayes's growing certainty that the corporal was capable of handling significantly more responsibility than she shouldered already; he was becoming convinced that she was a better candidate for promotion onto the top of the command track than was Sergeant Kemper, whose personal peccadilloes might well have compromised his command objectivity beyond salvageability.

Chang was the first to break the protracted silence, extracting Hayes from his reverie. "Maybe I was wrong about them," he said.

The odd non sequitur confused Hayes. "Wrong about whom, Corporal?"

"The squids," Chang said, suddenly looking a bit embarrassed, as though realizing only belatedly that the liquor might have loosened his tongue a bit more than he'd intended. "I mean, the Starfleet people, sir. I used to think they were all soft. Undisciplined."

Hayes nodded. "Because they don't have MACO training."

"Yes, sir," Chang said, returning the nod.

Hayes refilled his mug, doing his best to keep from grinning. "Since your team included just one Starfleet officer, I assume that Ensign Mayweather is the reason for your change of heart."

Kemper and McCammon exchanged vaguely surprised expressions, while McKenzie chortled quietly. "That's pretty ironic, coming from you, Hideaki."

Chang shrugged and allowed a smile to begin creeping slowly across his lean, angular face. "Because he maintains almost uninhabitable quarters? Well, there is that."

"Even a stopped watch can be right twice a day, right?" McCammon said, downing a copious amount of bourbon a moment later.

Kemper chuckled over his cup. "Damned straight, Mac. You're living proof of that."

McCammon adopted a dramatic, wounded expression. "Hey!"

Hayes firmly stepped on the banter, wanting to hear what Chang had to say about interservice relations. "I read your after-action report, Mister Chang. I see that Ensign Mayweather went along on your EVA at the Xindi fuel station."

McCammon interposed himself, no doubt emboldened by drink. "Damned straight, sir. And letting him come along might have been what set off the booby traps."

Chang flushed visibly with anger, clearly not enjoying being second-guessed by one of the men he'd commanded on that mission.

Never having been a fan of useless recriminations, Hayes turned a steely eye on McCammon. "There's no way to know that, Corporal. For all we know, *you* might have been the one who tripped the trigger on the booby traps. And I think Mayweather proved that he knows his stuff when it comes to working the shuttlepod's systems, and even MACO ordnance controls. Whether he was on or off the boat at that moment might not have made any difference to the mission's outcome." *Or to its body count,* he added wordlessly.

McCammon turned beet red, and went as silent as a tomb.

Hayes turned toward Chang and said, "It looks to me like Mayweather's quick thinking may have saved the whole damned mission." Everybody who made it back from that mission in one piece literally owed the man their lives.

"I'd just as soon he doesn't get to hear any of us say that out loud, sir," Chang said, grinning. "At least until I make some new rooming arrangements. My billet's small enough as it is without having to step around his swelled head." Fraternal martial laughter erupted at that, and rippled through the room. Everyone tipped their drinking vessels again, consuming more of the burning liquid.

In the renewed silence that followed, Hayes considered how close every member of Chang's team had come to losing their lives out there in the debris cloud. Though he'd already given Chang's preliminary report a quick read, the events of the day—particularly the memorial service—hadn't permitted him to give either the corporal or the surviving members of his strike team a thorough debriefing prior to this moment. He still wasn't entirely certain whether or not Chang had been correct in deciding to attack the Xindi fuel depot once his team had discovered it, though he was prepared to reserve judgment pending the arrival of detailed reports. On the one hand, Chang's course of action had dealt the Xindi a blow which might well delay the deployment of their weapon; on the other, the engagement had cost Hayes's small company of troopers one of their number.

But regardless of the rightness or wrongness of the outcome, Chang had still arguably exceeded Sub-Commander T'Pol's orders; after all, the record showed that she had ordered the team to take whatever action was "appropriate, prudent, and logical," and Archer's dour Vulcan exec wasn't likely to use any of those three adjectives to describe Chang's lone-wolf operation. Exceeding one's mandate was a practice that Hayes also generally frowned upon, though he knew he also had to take into account the extenuating circumstance of Chang's being forced to operate under com silence. Sometimes a MACO squad leader simply couldn't afford the luxury of waiting for the due deliberation of the chain of command; there were always occasions when decisions had to be made on the fly, in response to the exigencies of a particular mission, as Ensign Mayweather had ably illustrated when he'd evidently pulled several gung-ho MACO asses out of the fire—and destroyed a Xindi warship and another major piece of Xindi equipment in the process.

Discipline and training are only the means, not the ends, Hayes reminded himself. *Still, Mayweather was right to interpret Sub-Commander T'Pol's orders strictly, even though it was his participation in violating them that kept Chang from losing the entire strike team. Maybe we sharks can learn a thing or two about survival and teamwork from swimming with these squids.*

The entry chime shattered the room's meditative silence, and Hayes thought he had a pretty good idea who must have just arrived at his doorstep.

"Come," Hayes said.

The door hissed open in response. On the threshold stood a figure dressed in an ordinary MACO duty uniform. Hayes looked up into the haunted eyes of the only other trooper aboard who had survived Chang's assault on the Xindi fuel station. She still wore her dress uniform, which had become somewhat disheveled during the hours that had passed since the memorial service.

"Corporal Guitierrez. Come in."

She stepped inside, allowing the door to close behind her. She remained standing, her arms held stiff at her sides. Hayes had seen raw recruits who didn't look half this awkward, and though he had a pretty good idea of what was bothering her, he felt some surprise at seeing her discomfiture on display so openly.

"It should have been me, Major. Not Private Eby. He shouldn't have had to die saving the team."

Hayes looked to the other four MACOs present, all of whom appeared nonplussed by Guitierrez's flat declaration. "Would the rest of you mind leaving Corporal Guitierrez and me alone for a bit?"

McKenzie stood at once, immediately taking control of the group by escorting her three dumbfounded comrades out the door, though Kemper very nearly had to be dragged into the corridor. The departing MACOs left their mismatched assortment of drinking vessels sitting atop the footlocker near Hayes's bed, arrayed like an honor guard around the respectably well-depleted bottle of New Orleans bourbon.

Hayes stood, still clutching his mug tightly. He and Guitierrez were alone in the cabin's dim light, regarding one another wordlessly for a seeming eternity.

"MACOs watch one another's backs, Corporal," he said at length.

"Then it sure looks like I didn't watch Eby's back closely enough, doesn't it? And now he's gone. He's dead, and it should have been me."

Hayes knew that the time had come for a reality check. Setting down his mug, he said, "Why would you say that? Unless I miss my guess, what you're facing is a pregnancy, not a death sentence."

All color seemed to drain away from her face, though otherwise she seemed strangely unsurprised to learn that he already knew about her condition. "I guess it's true what they said back in MACO basic, sir: 'There's not a sparrow that falls without your CO knowing about it.' "

He smiled gently. "Thanks for the vote of omniscience, Corporal. But being aware of my team members' troubles is part of my job."

"So why didn't you confront me about it earlier, sir?"

"I knew you would have confided in me sooner or later, Corporal. I think I can usually trust you to do the right thing."

She laughed at that, but it was a laugh devoid of all but the blackest humor. "I suppose I should have guessed that if Eby figured out that I was pregnant, then you would, too."

"It's a small ship, Selma. And it's an even smaller MACO company. Have a seat." He gestured toward the nearest chair.

She sighed, then shrugged and sat down so heavily that he wondered for a moment if something had gone wrong with the grav plating.

She sat in silence for another lengthy interval before speaking again. "So I guess Nelson—" She paused, briefly interrupting herself before continuing. "I guess Sergeant Kemper must know all about it now, too."

"I didn't post a memo, Selma. Why don't you talk to him? If he's the father, he deserves to know."

She nodded, then said in a very small voice, "I suppose my military career's over."

That took him aback. "Why? Is that what you want, Corporal?"

"Are you serious, Major? I'm *pregnant.* If I carry this baby to term, I'm going be out on a medical discharge, and probably a dishonorable one at that. And even if I *don't* get cashiered, I'll still probably be up on fraternization charges."

He absently stroked his chin as he considered her words; he watched her watching him as he weighed the options that were open to him.

Finally, he said, "The MACO company is built on discipline."

"I understand that, Major," she said, nodding. "And I've betrayed that discipl—"

"I haven't granted you permission to speak, Corporal," he said, interrupting her in a stern tone, then pausing to allow proper military protocol to reassert itself.

"Yes, sir. Sorry, sir." She lapsed into silence.

"Good," he said at length. "As I was saying, the MACO company is built on discipline."

She nodded again, this time without speaking a single syllable. Even in the cabin's dim light, he could see that her eyes were refulgent with unshed tears.

"But it also can't afford to stand on ceremony," he amended. "At least not under our current circumstances."

Perplexity tugged her head hard to starboard. "Sir?"

"We MACOs are the tip of the spear in the Delphic Expanse, Corporal, and we're only three dozen strong out here—less one, now. And God only knows if or when we're going to see our next troop rotation. I can't justify benching *anybody* if doing that might compromise the safety of either the mission or the team. In my judgment, drumming you out now could inflict serious damage on both."

Tears were beginning to stream down both sides of her dusky face. "Thank you, Major. I don't know how to thank you."

"You and Kemper can do that by continuing to do your duties to the best of your abilities," Hayes said. "Who knows?" He smiled. "We might even have these Xindi bastards all rolled up before you're too pregnant to shoulder a rifle."

She laughed and cried simultaneously, and Hayes

reached for a nearby shelf where he happened to keep a box of tissues, which she gratefully accepted.

After she had finished noisily blowing her nose, she said, "I knew Colin—Private Eby, I mean—back in basic. I even let him know I was interested in him once. Did you know that?"

Hayes wasn't at all surprised to hear this, but he shook his head anyway. "So much for my omniscience."

"He never gave me any encouragement, so I gave up and we lost touch after we were sent to different postings. Then, years later, we both ended up on the same Xindi hunt. And then I met Nelson—" She paused as though to gather her thoughts. "Sergeant Kemper."

"Why are you telling me this now?" Hayes asked.

"I'm not really sure," she said, her tears beginning to flow anew. "Maybe I'm still trying to figure out why Eby took the bullet that was meant for me."

"It might have had something to do with that Xindi ship that was bearing down on the shuttlepod," Hayes said, though he knew he was only stating the obvious. "The shuttlepod couldn't have outrun that ship, so aborting the attempt to blow up the fuel dump wouldn't have been a very good option."

Guitierrez nodded, blowing her nose again before replying. "Somebody had to stay behind to set off the ordnance."

"That's right, Selma. *Somebody.* But not necessarily *you.*"

"But why Eby? Why *not* me?"

"Maybe you reminded Private Eby of his sister, Moira. She was serving with the 22nd MACO Division, in the Alpha Centauri system, the last time I checked," Hayes said, already dreading the letter he would have to write tomorrow to Eby's sister and parents.

Or maybe Private Eby simply loved you enough to make sure that you and your baby both got a fair chance to survive, settle down, and have the family that he just couldn't have offered you himself.

"I guess I really don't have a good answer for you, Corporal," was all he said. "All I know is that things happen unpredictably during mission ops. No battle plan entirely survives an engagement with an enemy. And there's no 'bullet' with anybody's name engraved on it. We make our own destinies, at least as much as blind luck does."

Guitierrez nodded. "And some of us are lucky enough to find destinies that make us heroes. The unlucky ones get left behind to pick up the pieces of their lives."

She sighed and looked away, perhaps still digesting Hayes's comments, or maybe struggling with the reality of Eby's death—and her own survival. Hayes watched her very quietly.

Perhaps half a minute later, she met his gaze squarely. "Well, I still have one major problem to deal with." She reached toward the footlocker and grabbed the bourbon bottle and one of the empty drinking vessels. "And I don't have a lot of good options open to me."

Hayes rose from where he sat and gently took the bottle from Guitierrez, who put up no resistance.

He looked her straight in the eye. "Maybe you do, Selma. Maybe you don't.

"But I'll support whichever one you pick."

NINETEEN

SEATED AT THE CAPTAIN'S DINNER TABLE, Reed kept catching himself fidgeting, and continually had to force himself to keep his mind and hands focused on the shepherd's pie that Chef had placed in front of him.

He glanced across the table at his two dinner companions. Though Mayweather looked tired, he ate his French onion soup with slurping gusto, betraying no outward sign of feeling out of place.

How does he manage to stay so cool in the captain's mess? thought Reed, who rarely got summoned here, and always felt nervous on those rare occasions when he did. He found himself wondering just how many times the young pilot had already seen the inside of the room.

The third man present was the captain himself, who displayed no recognition of Reed's discomfiture as he tore into a thick porterhouse steak, another one of the versatile chef's apparently endless repertoire of culinary specialties. Every few bites, Archer would toss a chunk of meat to Porthos; the small, white-and-brown beagle was sitting attentively on the deck about a meter away from Archer's left.

Despite the life-affirming presence of Porthos, however, the captain didn't quite seem to be his normal ebullient self, doubtless in large part because of the double interment over which he'd just presided. And yet Reed knew that whatever was bothering Jonathan Archer this evening went even deeper than the grief and second-guessing that he must surely be experiencing in the aftermath of the loss of a valued crew member.

Reed knew that the captain's troubles had been simmering toward a slow boil for the past several weeks, because he had witnessed Archer's uncharacteristic flare-ups of temper on a number of recent occasions; one such incident had occurred about six weeks earlier, immediately before Archer had led that ill-starred expedition into the putrid trellium mines on Tulaw. Whenever the captain's angry outbursts occurred, Reed had understood them to be natural consequences of the unprecedented levels of both responsibility and frustration that Starfleet had heaped on the captain. After all, it was likely that no ship's commander had ever before been asked to shoulder such huge quantities of both—at least not until the current Xindi crisis had erupted.

But after Archer's landing party had spirited La'an Trahve away from Kaletoo, the captain had stepped past the boundaries of excusable rage and common decency, at least in Reed's opinion. Of course, it had been Major Hayes, not Archer, who had led the way across that sometimes fine, difficult-to-distinguish line, and this came as no surprise to Reed; as far as the lieutenant was concerned, the arrogant MACO commanding officer lacked even the most rudimentary shred of human compassion, and therefore simply didn't know any better.

However, Archer's decision to follow Hayes's lead in beating Xindi-related intelligence out of Trahve had been truly shocking—as well as ineffectual, since the information Trahve revealed had turned out to be nothing more than bait for a trap that had very nearly killed the entire team.

To Reed, the worst aspect of the entire affair had been the captain's decision to sanction a so-called "coercive interrogation." This had led to a display of savagery that Reed hadn't believed to be within his commanding officer's capabilities. And while Reed could certainly understand the captain's willingness to accept the sacrifice of his own personal ethical standards for the safety of the people of Earth—one might even characterize such an act as indicative of an unselfish disregard for one's own personal reputation, and whatever career consequences might result from damaging it—he nevertheless had a great deal of difficulty accepting the beatings he had seen both Hayes and Archer administering to Trahve.

Staring into his water glass, he experienced a fleeting memory of forcible immersion that made him shudder involuntarily; he wondered yet again whether the scars caused by such traumas would ever go away entirely.

Reed knew he could not consider his own hands to be entirely clean either. *We were all a party to torture on that mission, one way or another,* Reed thought, his face reddening in shame. *Myself included, for not doing enough to keep it from happening in the first place.*

It all led him to ask himself two inescapable, and fundamentally unanswerable, questions: What would he do the *next* time he witnessed such behavior on the part of either Major Hayes or Captain Archer? Would he go so far as to raise a weapon to prevent an act of torture?

He could only hope he never had to find the answers.

"Malcolm?" Belatedly, Reed realized that the captain had been speaking to him.

"Sir?" Reed said, ignoring Mayweather's wry grin at his absentmindedness. He struggled to concentrate instead on the captain's wearily inquisitive gaze.

"I was asking if you knew Ensign Chandra well," Archer said as he tossed another gobbet of steak to Porthos, who snatched it expertly out of the air.

Reed looked back down into his disarrayed but still largely uneaten shepherd's pie, and decided that he really wasn't very hungry. "We were really only acquaintances, Captain. We played racquetball once or twice. But I honestly can't say I knew him very well."

That admission made Reed's face blaze with chagrin yet again. One of his tactical-studies instructors from back in his wet navy days had once told him that "career" was merely another way to spell "isolation." Sure enough, those words had proved to be true enough for Reed, who now spent the lion's share of his time honing *Enterprise*'s tactical capabilities rather than forging anything more than the most superficial of friendships. Reed rarely paused even to consider such things these days, especially since the Xindi crisis had begun. Today, however, he found that he profoundly regretted this particular aspect of his life.

"I knew him a little bit," Mayweather said. "We shared some meals after alpha watch now and then. He had a pretty interesting family background. Northern India. Made me want to go to Earth to see it someday."

Archer pushed his plate forward, glanced down at it, then handed the remainder of his steak, bone and all, down to Porthos. The beagle wasted no time getting on the outside of it. Then the captain sat back in his chair and cast an unfocused stare at the bulkhead behind and above Reed's head.

"I barely knew him at all," he said in a hushed tone better suited for a priest's confessional than for the captain's personal mess. "I should have known him better. I should know *all* of them. Then, at least when I'm writing that last letter to their families—" He stopped himself, clearly about to be overcome with emotion, and just as clearly unwilling to allow that to happen, even in front of two of his most trusted officers.

Reed recognized and understood Archer's pain instantly: whatever very occasional complaints Reed might have had about his duties interfering with his social life, the captain's personal situation had to be at least an order of magnitude busier and more stressful than Reed's was. *He must be the loneliest man in the universe.*

Archer raised his glass and took a large quaff of

the light-colored beer he'd been using to wash down his dinner. Setting the half-emptied glass down in front of his plate, he turned his eyes first on Reed, then on Mayweather, and suddenly presented a decidedly businesslike demeanor.

"I've been a bit busy these last few hours with the memorial service and composing that letter to Ensign Chandra's family," Archer said. "So I haven't had time yet to conduct a thorough after-action mission debriefing with either of you, or with the other members of the shuttlepod crews."

"I'm ready now, sir," Reed said.

Mayweather nodded. "Me, too, sir. Just give the word."

Archer held up both hands in a *slow down* gesture. "All the fine details can wait until tomorrow morning, after everybody's had a good night's sleep." The captain paused, chuckling as though he'd just made an unintentional joke; Reed surmised that a good night's sleep wasn't a terribly realistic prospect for a man as weighted down with responsibility as Jonathan Archer.

"All three of us have just returned from separate integrated Starfleet-MACO operations," Archer continued. "One of those missions I know pretty intimately, since I was there." He glanced sadly at Reed, then turned to regard Mayweather. "And I gather from what you've told me so far that your team met with somewhat more success than ours did."

As long as one doesn't measure success solely in terms of lives expended, Reed thought, the glumness of the memorial service settling once again on his soul.

"Well, we did manage to blow up the Xindi fuel

depot and mining facility we discovered," Mayweather said, though he didn't sound the least bit boastful.

"Not to mention a Xindi warship," Archer said, as though trying to draw Mayweather out to accept a bit of well-earned praise.

Not yet having had the opportunity to compare post-mission notes with anyone who had partaken in the other shuttlepod mission, Reed was both surprised and impressed by what he'd just heard. "Congratulations, Ensign," he said. "Well done."

"We were very lucky," the pilot said quietly, nodding. The ensign's dour expression made it clear that he considered Private Colin Eby to have been a good deal less lucky than himself. "And I really don't think I deserve all that much back-patting—at least not for the military part of the mission. In fact, I was against tackling the depot. I even tried to talk the MACOs out of it."

"Why?" Reed wanted to know, curious.

"Because it's generally a bad idea for a junior officer to go way past the intent behind his orders, sir. Sub-Commander T'Pol wanted us to follow the Xindi fuel isotope trail to its source, reconnoiter, and return to *Enterprise* with whatever intelligence we'd gathered. I think that's the course of action she would have considered 'appropriate, prudent, and logical,' especially since our team was working without any backup."

"I take it that Corporal Chang overruled your interpretation of T'Pol's orders," Archer said.

"You might say that, sir. And I can't say I was very happy about it, either."

"And how do you feel about it in retrospect?" Archer asked.

Mayweather's face took on a thoughtful cast. "I guess there's no arguing with results, sir. Unless you happen to be Private Eby, that is, or a member of his family. If it had been up to me, I'm not sure I would have traded Eby's life for destroying that fuel depot, or that Xindi ship. Of course, Chang didn't leave very much of the mission up to me. And by the time the Xindi ship showed up, we didn't have a lot of options left."

Archer nodded grimly. "I think you're selling yourself short, Ensign. I heard that Chang's brilliant tactical improvisation might have gotten the rest of your team killed—if you hadn't come up with an impromptu solution of your own."

"Could I ask who told you that, Captain?" Mayweather asked, looking uncomfortable. "Because I *know* you didn't hear about any of that from me."

"I had a brief chat with Major Hayes just before you arrived for dinner," Archer said.

Mayweather looked as surprised as Reed felt. It wasn't that Reed lacked faith in the young helmsman's ad hoc problem-solving abilities; rather, he'd simply assumed that the arrogant MACOs would have been unable to resist the urge to take sole credit for their strike team's success, especially since they had lost one of their own on the mission.

"Maybe exceeding our orders once in a while is what it'll take to stop the Xindi from deploying their weapon," Archer said, breaking the silence that followed his revelation. He raised his glass and very quickly finished emptying it.

"Maybe, sir," Reed said. "But if you don't mind terribly, I'd like to refrain from praising the MACOs for improvising. It only encourages them."

Archer and Mayweather laughed and nodded in agreement.

Reed smiled, but didn't join in with the laughter. He wondered if the reason was that despite his inherent distrust of Major Hayes—and of the threat that the MACO company posed to Reed's continued smooth management of the tactical landscape aboard *Enterprise*—Reed found that he couldn't refute one observation that Ensign Mayweather had made about the MACOs:

There's no arguing with results.

From Ensign Travis Mayweather's Personal Correspondence File:

Dear Mom,

I know you must be relieved to be reading this. After all, my last letter dealt more with the dangers of our Xindi hunt, without really saying all that much about the tedium involved.

To be totally honest, I suppose I've had more than my fair share of both lately. Not to worry you too much more than I know you already are, I just returned to *Enterprise* from an off-ship assignment—a mission that not everybody came back from. I'll spare you the details at the moment, except to assure you that I'm fine, in perfect shape, mint condition, not a scratch (unless you count feeling a bit guilty about that, but that's going to have to be the subject of another letter). I can only hope that Captain Archer won't have to repeat this afternoon's memorial service anytime soon.

I'm pretty sure I can't count on that, though. We're still hot on the trail of mass murderers, after all, and I'm certain there's going to be combat when we finally catch up to them. This Xindi business isn't anywhere near being finished yet. And truthfully, we don't seem to be any closer now to finding the Xindi homeworld, or the weapon they're planning to use against Earth, than we were twelve weeks ago, when we first entered the Expanse. There are times when I really wish I could skip forward to the end of all of this the way you can, since I know you're going to get these letters all at once, after this Xindi business has all been settled. (I won't hold it against you if you do decide to take a sneak peek at the ending, Mom; I know you're just looking out for me, so I guess it's not really "cheating.")

But in spite of everything, I still feel as though I've contributed to a couple of major victories, even though only one of those directly involved the Xindi. Not only did I help blow up some pretty significant Xindi hardware, I also like to think that I helped tear off the blinders that have been keeping us Starfleet folk and the MACOs from being able to see that we're all on the same team.

Don't get me wrong. There's probably never going to be a love fest between me and Corporal Chang, my compulsively neat roommate (it's a little like trying to survive rooming with Paul, but I digress). But at least I no longer worry that Chang and I might actually murder each other before this mission ends.

As always, I will continue hoping for the best while preparing for the worst.

Your loving son,
Travis

EPILOGUE

Sunday, August 12, 2238,
San Francisco

SHADOWS MOVED SOMNOLENTLY beneath a leaden, overcast sky. Another raisin-sized raindrop pattered against the old man's neck, startling him back into an awareness of his surroundings.

He realized with discomfiting abruptness that young Larry Marvick was kneeling beside him at the base of the Starfleet War Memorial.

"Rainy or not, this place might start getting crowded fairly soon," Marvick said quietly, nodding toward the nearby gently sloping hillside that lay beyond the monument, where another handful of early risers, most of them evidently out-of-town civilian tourists—judging from their loose-fitting shorts and blousy shirts—were beginning to gather near the young family of four they had seen earlier. The family's pair of energetic young boys had detached from their parents, and were approaching the base of the obelisk, the older boy walking, the younger one running willy-nilly up and down the rolling hillside's gentle slope.

The old man offered Marvick a small, knowing smile. "Of course it's going to get crowded here. It's Federation Day, after all. By tonight San Francisco Bay's going to be brighter than the dome up on New Berlin. The sky's going to be full of fireworks, fog or no fog."

"But you hate crowds."

The old man scowled. "Who the hell told you that?"

"You did," Marvick said, suppressing a grin. "Maybe we ought to get moving before too many more people arrive."

"You afraid somebody might recognize me? After all these years?" *Not to mention all the surgeries,* he thought, running his hand across a wrinkled cheek that still felt unnaturally smooth and taut after the many reconstructions it had undergone.

Marvick's response was cut off by the approach of the two boys. The younger of the pair reached the monument's steps first, or rather ran right past them, accelerating back onto the neatly manicured lawn after making a close, almost grazing approach, like an old-style interplanetary spacecraft using Jupiter's gravity well to gain momentum. The boy was a dynamo, his tousled brown hair curling toward determined hazel eyes as he passed within perhaps a meter of the old man, shouting "WHOOOOSH!" as he headed out again for adventures that only he could see and hear.

"I'm a shuttle captain!" the little boy shouted, already well under way on his new outbound trajectory.

The other boy, who couldn't have been any older than nine or so, was more sedate, approaching the monument with a purposeful stride, a notepad tucked under his arm, his dark blond hair combed and tidy. After nodding politely toward Marvick and the old man, the boy placed a piece of paper against the monument's large, duranium-silver dedication plaque and began rubbing the page with the edge of an old-fashioned graphite pencil.

Smiling, the old man rose from where he had been kneeling beside his duffel, his knees cracking loudly. "What are you doing there, son?"

"Making a rubbing of the inscriptions," the boy said without looking up from his work. "For a school report."

"That's pretty industrious of you. But it's August. Isn't school out yet?"

"A lot of schoolkids are in class all year round now," Marvick said, rising to his feet as well and brushing some dust from his pants.

The old man's eyes widened in surprise. "No summer vacation? I'll be damned. Guess I stopped paying close attention to things like that a hundred or so years ago." He took a step toward the boy and gestured toward the rubbing he was making. "So which conflict are you focusing on? Romulus? Qo'noS? The Blagee? The Suliban?"

The boy paused in his work and fixed his lively hazel eyes on the old man, shaking his head. "None of those. I'm doing the history of the Starfleet War Memorial itself. Did you know it wasn't always called that?"

The old man liked the boy's open, sincere manner, and decided to play along. "I had no idea."

The boy looked pleased to have edified one of his elders. "It's true. They finished building it in 2156, and it was supposed to be just for the people who died in the Xindi sneak attack of 2153."

Seven million dead, the old man thought, nodding. A cloud of sadness passed behind his eyes, though he struggled manfully not to show it. Nevertheless, the face of his baby sister appeared in his mind's eye yet again.

"But the Romulan War started just as they were unveiling it," the boy continued. "A lot of Starfleet people were getting killed by then, and *they* needed a monument, too. So it sort of got shared between the Xindi War and the Romulan War. And with all the stuff that's happened since then."

The old man offered the boy an indulgent smile. *Let's hope your generation never has to negotiate its own share of space on this thing,* he thought.

"What's your name, son?" the old man asked.

The boy grinned, tucked his art supplies away under his left arm, and extended his right hand politely. "George. George Kirk, Junior."

The old man shook the boy's hand and started to reply, only to be interrupted by Marvick, who stepped forward to shake the boy's hand next.

"Larry Marvick," the young engineer said, taking then releasing George's hand. Nodding toward the old man, he added, "This is my, ah . . . great-uncle Carl."

Still looking out for me, the old man thought. *Even after all these years.* Not for the first time, he wondered how differently the past century might have turned out for him had Selma Guitierrez, Larry's great-grandmother, opted back in '54 not to give birth to her unexpected child—a little girl whom the old man had helped raise during the years after the Xindi crisis. If little Elena had not been born, would he have been able to rely on the Kemper, Guitierrez, and Marvick families to help guard his secrets from that first Federation Day right down to the present?

The old man now believed that child to have been the work of destiny. Like Laurence Marvick, her grandson. And that great ship now being built in the skies above San Francisco, preparing to explore the unknown and extend the Federation's olive branch of friendship across the galaxy. Without Marvick's input as an engineering designer—the indirect result of Selma Guitierrez's fateful decision more than eight decades ago—would that graceful new *Constitution*-class vessel's stated purpose have been such a noble and benign one?

"Pleased to meet you both," the boy said to both men as his little brother ran past the monument and part of the way up the hillside beyond it before looping back the way he came; as he passed, the child made more "whooshing" noises, sounds that made the old man think of centuries-old fighter jets.

"And happy Federation Day," the older boy added.

"Likewise," the old man said, smiling.

"But it's not just Federation Day today," said young George Kirk, beaming. "It's also my eighth birthday."

"Born on the Fourth of July, eh?" the old man said. "Well, happy birthday, George."

"I don't know if these gentlemen signed up for a history lecture, son," said a cheerful male voice. The old man turned and saw that it belonged to the red-headed, red-uniformed young Starfleet officer he had seen a few moments earlier accompanying his family on their walk across the gently sloping lawn toward the monument spire. He was slender but strong-looking, though he seemed impossibly young. Despite his apparent youth, he seemed remarkably self-possessed and fairly exuded optimism. The old man glanced at the man's sleeves, which bore a lieutenant's single strand of gold braid.

"He can talk your ears off, if you let him," said the attractive, extremely bright-looking brunette woman who stood beside the lieutenant. George, Jr. rolled his eyes, evidently having heard the same exchange many times before. "I'm sorry if he's bothering you."

"Not at all," the old man said, extending his hand to the boy's father, who stood nearest to him. "You must be George Kirk, Senior."

As they shook hands, Marvick interposed himself yet again, offering a handshake of his own and making introductions for both of them to Lieutenant Kirk and the woman, whom George Senior introduced as Winona Kirk, his wife and the mother of both boys.

This was the second time today that the young engineer had jumped in to cover for the old man during an unanticipated social situation. As Marvick chatted about nothing in particular with the Kirks, the old man watched the engineer's blandly pleasant expression for clues to his thoughts. *Is he just spooked by the idea of letting me speak to somebody who's wearing a Starfleet uniform?* he thought. *Or maybe he's worried that I'm finally going plain old senile. Maybe he thinks I might accidentally blurt out my real name.*

For perhaps the ten thousandth time during the seventy-seven years since he had agreed to allow history to pronounce him dead, he wondered if coming clean now would be such a bad thing after all. Would his real name, a footnote at best in Federation history, really be any more recognizable than his face was? After all, he really wasn't all that comfortable with the prospect of going to his grave known only as "Larry Marvick's ancient grand-uncle Carl."

The smaller boy's sudden entrance interrupted the old man's dour contemplations. Running in yet another great eccentric circle, Lieutenant Kirk's younger child tore right past his brother, startling him into dropping his pencil and papers with a sudden blast of mouth-generated spacecraft noise and a cry of "Outatheway, Sam!"

As the little boy barnstormed past, his surprisingly solid shoulder clipped the old man on the hip, spoiling his balance; the centenarian would almost certainly have toppled over onto the hard granite steps had Marvick not been there to catch him.

"Whoa!" Marvick shouted as he steadied the old man, who quickly regained his footing, if not his dignity.

"Looks like I nearly lived up to my old nickname just then," the old man said with a bemused chuckle as he watched the child, apparently unaware of the collision his hotdog imaginary piloting had caused, started to make another wide, elliptical loop across the lawn surrounding the monument.

"Watch it, Jimmy!" the older boy cried, his partially completed rubbing and his other drawing materials lying scattered at his feet across the moist stone.

"Who the heck is Sam?" the old man wanted to know.

"My middle name is Samuel, just like my dad," the older boy said, his furrowed brow giving him an air of seriousness far beyond his years. "Jimmy's the only one who calls me that."

Winona Kirk and her husband were rushing to the old man's side; her face was a portrait of concern, while the little boy's father exhibited durable if strained patience. "Jimmy!" shouted Lieutenant Kirk, who then turned to face the old man and Marvick. "I'm really sorry about this. That boy can be a real force of nature sometimes."

"Must be because his birthday is on March 22," observed the younger George, while recovering his fallen pencil and papers.

The date of the Xindi attack, the old man thought, briefly wondering whether that fact augured well or ill for the boy's future before dismissing the whole idea as silly.

"James Tiberius Kirk!" Winona cried. "You get back here *this instant!*"

The old man speculated momentarily on which omen was worse for the child: his notorious birth date, or having a middle name derived from a particularly bloodthirsty Roman emperor. *This kid's got to be a hell-raiser for life. It's practically written in his stars.*

He grinned at the Kirks, hoping to diffuse their vexation toward the child. "The boy didn't mean any harm. He's just a high-spirited kid. Pretty much the same as I was at about that age, or so I've been told. 'Cept I was daydreaming about building and hot-rodding shuttlecraft instead of flyin' 'em."

Though both parents were clearly pleased to see that no permanent harm had been done, the elder George Kirk nevertheless dutifully collected his errant child and frog-marched him back into the presence of the old man, to whom the little boy offered a pouting, reluctant apology before being released back into the wild blue yonder of his imagination.

Afterward, the elder Kirks bid the old man and Marvick farewell. The old man watched quietly as the Kirk family walked away, headed across the lawn in the direction of the quiet Starfleet Academy grounds. Little Jimmy Kirk was way out in front of the pack, bound yet again for parts unknown.

"You never answered my question," Marvick said as the overcast sky released several more fat raindrops onto the old man's head and shoulders. Although several other families and individuals, tourists and joggers, had appeared on the grounds surrounding the Starfleet War Memorial, the old man and Marvick were essentially alone.

"Hmmm? What question?" the old man said.

"Why you never visited the Starfleet War Memorial before now."

The old man sighed, still not at all sure how to answer, though he'd been giving the matter a great deal of thought. Squinting upward toward the tip of the stone spire that towered some six meters over his head, he tried to recall the many past occasions when he might have come here but had instead found some excuse to be elsewhere. One of those times had come seventy-seven years ago, shortly after Jonathan Archer, Nathan Samuels, Tellarite Ambassador Gral, T'Pau, Soval, and Solkar of Vulcan, and dozens of other interstellar notables had gathered in the newly renovated Candlestick auditorium to affix their signatures to the bottom of the Federation Charter. That epoch-making day remained indelibly etched upon his memory even now.

The United Federation of Planets had come into being on that day, at least on paper. And he had felt optimistically certain then that the promise of lasting interstellar amity was the only hope of redeeming the millions of lives the Xindi had extinguished with their sneak attack more than eight years earlier—both the innocent civilians whom the Xindi had vaporized unawares, and those who later had knowingly given their lives in order to put paid to the Xindi threat. *And without having to wipe out whole civilian populations, the way the Xindi did,* the old man thought.

Earth had become embroiled in other conflicts since the Xindi attack, of course, though none of these quite compared in terms of enormity. Not even the aggression of the Romulans, whose savage, five-year war against Earth had ended less than a year before the Charter signing, had cost the family of humanity so dearly. The old man had believed then, or at least had hoped, that he was no longer so embittered as he once had been about what the Xindi had done to his family and his homeworld.

But even though he had always taken pride in resisting destructive if justifiable hatreds, he had remained certain that he would never get over the death of his baby sister, even if he somehow managed to live for another century; he knew even then that he could never completely accept that Elizabeth, his Lizzie, the talented architect he had protected since she was a little girl, the promising young woman whose life had been summarily snuffed out by blind Xindi violence, was gone forever, blasted to atoms along with so many others.

The great historic city of San Francisco, which lay sprawled over the hills to the east, had seemed to hold its breath as if in anticipation of whatever unexpected fallout might come in the wake of the Federation Charter's signing. He had felt certain that this no doubt eventful future was already well on its way to arriving, whether or not the City by the Bay—or the human species, for that matter—was ready for it. Hell, the future already had arrived, the moment all those dignitaries had begun inking that piece of ceremonial parchment.

"Uncle Carl?

"Charles?

"Trip?"

It wasn't until Marvick uttered that last syllable that the old man returned to the present. Trip. He hadn't used that name in public for as long as the Federation had existed.

Charles "Trip" Tucker turned toward Marvick, whose youthful face was quickly becoming etched with lines of worry.

"Sorry, Larry. You know how we old people can get. Just woolgathering again." Trip trailed off once again into silence.

"And?" Marvick prompted gently.

"And I have absolutely no idea why I've never come here before."

Trip turned and knelt again at the base of the towering stone monument to Starfleet's war dead. With hands that had lost most of their engineer's steadiness years ago, he opened the duffel he had left on the pedestal, and slowly withdrew a large wreath festooned with flowers and leaves of every color and description.

Ignoring the involuntary tremor that seized his right hand, he slowly and gently set the wreath down at the monument's granite base.

Why haven't *I come here before now?* he asked himself. Had it been because the monument's original focus—the millions murdered by the Xindi back in '53—had been broadened right after its unveiling? Or simply because he'd been running from Lizzie's memory all these years?

Still kneeling before the memorial spire, Trip suddenly realized then that he had known the answer all along.

He had simply never expected to find his baby sister's presence here, or at any of the other monuments that had been so lovingly constructed since the time of the Xindi attack. Wherever she was now, Lizzie wouldn't be found haunting some cold, dead stone tower, however architecturally fascinating she might have found it.

None *of the dead are here. If they're here, it's because we brought them. If they're here, it's because we carry them around inside us. And we come to places like this so they can finally move on.*

And so we *can move on, too.*

Trip's gaze fell on the monument's large duranium-silver plaque, on which he saw Abraham Lincoln's name inscribed. One of Lincoln's immortal turns of phrase sprang to mind unbidden.

. . . for us, the living . . .

His vision rapidly becoming occluded by an upwelling of tears, Trip continued staring at the plaque—the same plaque from which the older Kirk boy had made his rubbing. It bore more words that he had heard Jonathan Archer utter years earlier, at the first of far too many crew memorial services he'd had to conduct during the Xindi crisis:

> The result is not doubtful. We shall not
> fail—if we stand firm, we shall not fail.
> Wise counsels may accelerate, or
> mistakes delay it, but, sooner or later,
> the victory is sure to come.
> —Abraham Lincoln,
> June 16, 1858

Although Trip knew that those words had been selected because they spoke of perseverance during a time of war, today's impending Federation Day festivities gave Lincoln's speech an additional layer of meaning—as did the new *Constitution*-class starship that Larry Marvick's team was now bringing into being far above San Francisco's cloud-bedecked skies.

Just as it had on that very first Federation Day, Earth once again stood poised on the threshold of the future. Even with the vast resources and lofty ideals of the Federation, meeting that future successfully might require of humanity just as much grit and determination as the Xindi threat had demanded of the captain and crew of NX-01. Or perhaps as much resolve and wisdom as an even earlier troubled age had required of Lincoln and his people.

Trip rose to his feet and slung the lightened duffel over his back. Raindrops pattered across his collar and back as the sky finally began to weep in earnest.

Good-bye, baby sister.

He faced Marvick, who stood blinking in the rain. "Let's go, Larry. I think it's time."

Trip took one final, lingering look back at the wreath and the rain-spattered monument. Then he turned and began walking quickly back down the hill as Marvick rushed to catch up.

The time had come at last to face whatever remained of the future.